COLD AS ICE

This Large Print Book carries the
Seal of Approval of N.A.V.H.

COLD AS ICE

ANNE STUART

WHEELER PUBLISHING
An imprint of Thomson Gale, a part of The Thomson Corporation

Detroit • New York • San Francisco • New Haven, Conn. • Waterville, Maine • London

LIBRARY OF CONGRESS CATALOGING-IN-PUBLICATION DATA

Stuart, Anne (Anne Kristine)
   Cold as ice / by Anne Stuart.
     p. cm.
     ISBN-13: 978-1-59722-503-8 (lg. print : alk. paper)
     ISBN-10: 1-59722-503-7 (lg. print : alk. paper)
     1. Large type books. I. Title.
PS3569.T785C65 2007
813'.54—dc22   2007000453

Published in 2007 by arrangement with Harlequin Books S.A.

Printed in the United States of America on permanent paper
10 9 8 7 6 5 4 3 2 1

This is for all the people, friends and family, who left me blessedly alone to write this, gave me space and freedom from demands.
And for those of you who didn't — well, you know who you are.

ACKNOWLEDGMENTS

I couldn't have done this without Jill Barnett and Barbara Samuel holding my hand and slapping me upside the head for being an idiot. I have to thank Bastien for inspiring me, blow a kiss to Clive Owen and say a special thank-you to everyone who fell in love with *Black Ice.* I'm finally getting over my hang-up about writing connected books, and having the time of my life.

1

Genevieve Spenser adjusted her four-hundred-dollar sunglasses, smoothed her sleek, perfect chignon and stepped aboard the powerboat beneath the bright Caribbean sun. It was early April, and after a long, cold, wet winter in New York City she should have been ready for the brilliant sunshine dancing off the greeny blue waters. Unfortunately she wasn't in the mood to appreciate it. For one thing, she didn't want to be there. She had a six-week sabbatical from her job as junior partner in the law firm of Roper, Hyde, Camui and Fredericks, and she'd been looking forward to something a great deal different. In two days' time she'd be in the rain forests of Costa Rica with no makeup, no contact lenses, no high heels and no expectations to live up to. She'd been so ready to shed her protective skin that this final task seemed like an enormous burden instead of the

9

simple thing it was.

The Grand Cayman Islands were on her way to Central America. Sort of. And one extra day wouldn't make any difference, Walter Fredericks had told her. Besides, what red-blooded, single, thirty-year-old female would object to spending even a short amount of time with *People* magazine's Sexiest Man of the Year, billionaire division? Harry Van Dorn was gorgeous, charming and currently between wives, and the law firm that represented the Van Dorn Foundation needed some papers signed. This was perfect for everyone. Serendipity.

Genevieve didn't exactly think so, but she kept her mouth shut. She'd learned diplomacy and tact in the last few years since Walt Fredericks had taken her under his wing.

She pulled out her pale gray Armani suit, put on the seven-hundred-dollar Manolo Blahnik shoes she hadn't even blinked at buying — the shoes that hurt her feet, made her tower over most men and matched the Armani and nothing else. When she first brought them home she'd emerged from her corporate daze long enough to look at the price tag and burst into tears. What had happened to the idealistic young woman who was determined to spend her life helping people? The rescuer, who spent her money on the oppressed, not on designer clothing?

Unfortunately she knew the answer, and she didn't want to dwell on it. In her tightly controlled life she'd learned to look forward rather than back. The shoes were beautiful and she told herself she deserved them. And she'd brought them to see Harry Van Dorn, as part of her protective armor.

They didn't make climbing down into the launch any easier, but she managed with a modicum of grace. Genevieve hated boats. She rarely got seasick, but she always felt vaguely trapped. She could see the massive white shape of the Van Dorn yacht against the brilliant horizon; it looked more like a mansion than a boat, and maybe she could simply ignore the sea surrounding them and pretend they were in a fancy restaurant. She was good at ignoring unpleasant facts — she'd learned the hard way that that was what you had to do to survive.

And her job should only take a few hours. She'd let Harry Van Dorn feed her, get him to sign the papers she'd brought with her in her slim leather briefcase, and once she'd arranged to have them couriered back to New York she'd be free. Only a matter of hours — she was silly to feel so edgy. It was

11

far too beautiful a day to have this sense of impending doom. There could be no doom under the bright Caribbean sun.

Her tranquilizers were in her tiny purse. Harry Van Dorn's crew had gotten her comfortably seated with a glass of iced tea in one hand. It was a simple enough matter to sneak one yellow pill out and take it. She'd almost planned to leave them behind in New York — she didn't expect to need tranquilizers in the rain forest, but fortunately she changed her mind at the last minute. The pill was going to take a few minutes to kick in, but she could get by on sheer determination until then.

Genevieve had been on yachts before — Roper and company specialized in handling the legal concerns for myriad charitable foundations, and money was no object. She'd gone from her job as public defender to private law practice, and she'd hoped specializing in charitable foundations was still close enough to honorable work to assuage the remnants of her liberal conscience. She'd been quickly disillusioned — the foundations set up as tax shelters by the wealthy tended to spend as much money glorifying the donors' names and providing cushy jobs for their friends as they did on the actual charity, but by then it was too late, and Genevieve was committed.

Harry Van Dorn's floating palace, SS *Seven Sins,* was on a grander scale than she'd seen so far, and she knew for a fact it was owned by the Van Dorn Trust Foundation, not Harry himself — a nice little tax write-off. She stepped aboard, her three-and-a-half-inch heels balanced perfectly beneath her, and surveyed the deck, keeping her expression impassive. With any luck Harry Van Dorn would be too busy on the putting green she could see up at the front of the ship to want to waste much time on a lawyer who was nothing more than Roper, Hyde, Camui and Fredericks's perfectly groomed messenger. Damn, she wasn't in the mood for this.

She plastered her practiced, professional smile on her Chanel-tinted lips and stepped inside the cool confines of a massive room beautifully furnished in black and white, with mirrors everywhere to make it appear even larger. She could see her reflection in at least three different directions. She'd already checked her appearance before she'd left that morning. A young woman, just past thirty, with her long blond hair neatly arranged, her pale gray suit hanging perfectly on her shoulders and disguising the fifteen pounds that she knew Roper et

13

al didn't approve of. Genevieve didn't approve of it either, but all the dieting and exercise in the world couldn't seem to budge it.

"Ms. Spenser?" It took a moment for her eyesight to adjust from the bright glare of the sun on the water to the dimmer light in the large room, and she couldn't see anyone but the indistinct shape of a man across the room. The voice held a faint, upper-class British accent, so she knew it wasn't Harry. Harry Van Dorn was from Texas, with a voice and a character to match. The man took a step toward her, coming into focus. "I'm Peter Jensen, Mr. Van Dorn's personal assistant. He'll be with you in a short while. In the meantime is there anything I can do to make you comfortable? Something to drink, perhaps? The newspaper?"

She hadn't thought of the word *unctuous* in a long time, probably not since she'd been forced to read Charles Dickens, but the word suited Peter Jensen perfectly. He was bland and self-effacing to a fault, and even the British accent, usually an attention grabber, seemed just part of the perfect personal-assistant profile. His face was nondescript, he had combed-back, very dark hair and wire-rimmed glasses; if she'd passed him on the street she wouldn't have looked twice at him. She barely did now.

"Iced tea and the *New York Times* if you have it," she said, taking a seat on the leather banquette and setting the briefcase beside her. She crossed her legs and looked at her shoes. They were worth every penny when you considered what they did for her long legs. She looked up, and Peter Jensen was looking at them, too, though she suspected it was the shoes, not the legs. He didn't seem to be the type to be interested in a woman's legs, no matter how attractive they were, and she quickly uncrossed them, tucking her feet out of the way.

"It will only take a moment, Ms. Spenser," he said. "In the meantime make yourself comfortable."

He disappeared, silent as a ghost, and Genevieve shook off the uneasy feeling. She'd sensed disapproval from Harry Van Dorn's cipher-like assistant — he'd probably taken one look at her shoes and known what she'd spent. Normally people in Jensen's position were impressed; she'd walked into a particularly snooty shop on Park Avenue in them and it seemed as if the entire staff had converged on her, knowing that a woman who spent that kind of money on shoes wouldn't hesitate to spend an equally egregious amount in their overpriced boutique.

And she had.

Genevieve steeled herself for Peter Jensen's reappearance. Instead, a uniformed steward appeared, with a tall glass of ice-cold Earl Grey and a fresh copy of the *New York Times.* There was a slender gold pen on the tray as well, and she picked it up.

"What's this for?" she inquired. Didn't they expect her to be professional enough to have brought her own pen?

"Mr. Jensen thought you might want to do the crossword puzzle. Mr. Van Dorn is taking a shower, and he might be awhile."

Now, how did that gray ghost of a man know she did crossword puzzles? In pen? It was the Saturday paper, with the hardest of the week's puzzles, and she didn't hesitate. For some irrational reason she felt as if Peter Jensen had challenged her, and she was tired and edgy and wanted to be anywhere but on Harry Van Dorn's extremely oversize, pretentious yacht. At least the puzzle would keep her mind off the water that was trapping her.

She was just finishing, when one of the doors to the salon opened and a tall figure filled the doorway. It had been a particularly trying puzzle — in the end she'd been cursing Will Weng, Margaret Farrar and Will

16

Shortz with generalized cool abandon, but she set the paper down and rose with serene dignity.

Only to have it vanish when the man stepped forward and she realized it was simply Peter Jensen again. He glanced at the folded paper, and she just knew his bland eyes would focus on the empty squares of the one word she couldn't get. "Mr. Van Dorn is ready to see you now, Ms. Spenser."

About frigging time, she thought. He moved to one side to let her precede him, and it was a momentary shock to realize how tall he was. She was a good six feet in her ridiculous heels, and he was quite a bit taller than she. He should have dwarfed the cabin and yet he barely seemed to be there.

"Enigma," he murmured as she passed him.

"I beg your pardon?" she said, rattled.

"The word you couldn't get. It's enigma."

Of course it was. She controlled her instinctive irritation; the man got on her nerves for no discernible reason. She didn't have to play this role for very much longer, she reminded herself. Get Harry Van Dorn to sign the papers, flirt a little bit if she must and then get back to the tiny airport and see if she could catch an earlier flight to

Costa Rica.

The bright sun was blinding when she stepped out on deck, and there was no more pretending she was back on the island with all the water shimmering around them. She looked up at the huge boat — not a mansion, an ocean liner — and followed Peter Jensen's precise walk halfway down the length of the ship until he stopped. She moved past him, dismissing the executive assistant from her mind as she took in the full glory of Harry Van Dorn, the world's sexiest billionaire.

"Ms. Spenser," he said, rising from his seat on the couch, his Texas accent rich and charming. "I'm so sorry to have kept you waiting! You came all this way out here just for me and I leave you cooling your heels while I'm busy with paperwork. Peter, why didn't you tell me Ms. Spenser was here?"

"I'm sorry, sir. It must have slipped my mind." Jensen's voice was neutral, expressionless, but she turned back to glance at him anyway. Why in the world wouldn't he have told Van Dorn she was there? Just to be a pissant? Or was Van Dorn simply dumping the blame on his assistant as he knew he could?

"No harm done," Van Dorn said, moving forward, taking Genevieve's hand with the most natural of gestures and bringing her back into the cabin. He was clearly a physical man, one who liked to touch when he talked to people. It was part and parcel of his charisma.

Unfortunately Genevieve didn't like to be touched.

But a client was a client, so she simply upped the wattage of her smile and let him pull her over to the white leather banquette, forgetting about the unpleasant little man who'd brought her here. Except that in fact he wasn't that little. It didn't matter — he'd already made himself scarce.

"Now, don't you mind Peter," Harry said, sitting just a bit too close to her. "He tends to be very protective of me, and he thinks every woman is after my money."

"All I'm after is your signature on a few papers, Mr. Van Dorn. I certainly wouldn't want to take up any more of your time —"

"If I don't have time for a beautiful young woman then I'm in a pretty pitiful condition," Harry said. "Peter just wants to keep my nose to the grindstone, while I believe in having fun. He doesn't have much use for women, I'm afraid. Whereas I have far too much. And you're such a pretty thing. Tell me, what sign are you?"

He'd managed to throw her completely

off guard. "Sign?"

"Astrology. I'm a man who likes my super-stitions. That's why I named the boat *Seven Sins*. Seven's my lucky number and always has been. I know that that new age crap don't mean squat, but I enjoy playing around with it. So indulge me. I'm guessing you're a Libra. Libras make the best lawyers — always judging and balancing."

In fact she was a Taurus with Scorpio ris-ing — her teenage friend Sally had had her chart done for an eighteenth birthday present, and that was one of the few details that had stuck. But she had no intention of disillusioning her wealthy client.

"How did you guess?" she said, keeping the admiration in her voice at a believable level.

Harry's laugh was warm and appealing, and Genevieve was beginning to see why people found him so charming.

People magazine hadn't lied — he was gorgeous. Deeply tanned skin, clear blue eyes with laugh lines etched deep around them, a shock of sun-streaked blond hair that made him look like Brad Pitt in his seedy mode. He radiated warmth, charm and sexuality, from his broad, boyish grin to his flirting eyes to his rangy, well-muscled body. He was handsome, charming, and any warm-blooded woman would have been interested. Right then, Genevieve couldn't have cared less.

But she had a job to do, and she knew that one of her unspoken orders was to give this very important client anything he wanted. It wouldn't be the first time she'd considered sleeping with someone for business reasons. She knew perfectly well what that made her — a pragmatist. She'd avoided it so far, but sooner or later she was going to have to be less fastidious and more practical. If it turned out that she had to sleep with Harry Van Dorn just to get some papers signed and get out of there . . . well, there were plenty of more onerous duties she'd had to perform while at Roper et al. She could perform this one if she had to.

But she knew the drill. They weren't going to get to the business she'd brought until the social amenities were covered, and with Texans that could take hours.

"You mustn't mind Peter," he repeated. "He's an Aries, with a very auspicious birth chart or I wouldn't keep him around. April twentieth, as a matter of fact. He's too damn gloomy by half, but he gets the job done."

"Has he worked for you a long time?" she asked, wondering when Harry was going to

21

take his hand off her knee. Good hands — big, tanned, perfectly manicured. There could be worse hands touching her. Like the slimy Peter Jensen's.

"Oh, it seems like forever, though in fact he's only been with me for a few months. I don't know how I managed without him — he knows more about me and my life than I do. But you know how men like that are — they get a little possessive of their bosses. Look, I don't want to spend the afternoon talking about Peter — he's about as interesting as watching grass grow. Let's talk about you, pretty lady, and what brought you here."

She started to reach for her briefcase, but he covered her hand with his big one and gave an easy laugh. "To hell with business. We have plenty of time for that. I mean, what brought you to an old-fart law firm like Roper and company? Tell me about your life, your loves and hates, and most of all tell me what you want my chef to prepare for dinner."

"Oh, I can't possibly stay. I have a plane to catch to Costa Rica."

"Oh, but you can't possibly leave," Harry mimicked her. "I'm bored, and I know your associates would want you to make me happy. I won't be happy unless I have someone to flirt with over dinner. Those oil wells aren't going to dry up overnight — nothing will happen if I don't sign the deeds of transference till later. I promise, I'll sign your papers, and I'll even see that you get to Costa Rica, though why you'd want to go to that pesthole is beyond me. But in the meantime, forget about business and tell me about you."

Genevieve let go of the briefcase, and after a moment he let go of her hand. She should have been uneasy, but he was such a simple puppy dog of a man, wanting someone to play with him, throw a ball for him, that she couldn't feel edgy. He was harmless, and she could play along for a while. As long as he didn't start humping her leg.

"Whatever your chef cares to make," she said.

"And what do you drink? Apple-tinis, right?"

Any kind of martini made her stomach turn, though she'd downed more than her share of them in order to fit in at the requisite social functions that Roper sponsored. Cosmopolitans were the worst, and everyone assumed she loved them. Her *Sex and the City* persona must have been very effective.

But he was one of the ten richest men in

the western world, and he could get anything he wanted. "Tab," she said.

She'd managed to throw him. "What's Tab?"

"A hard-to-find diet soda. And not that revolting energy drink version. Never mind, I was just kidding. Whatever you're having."

"Nonsense. Peter!" Harry barely had to raise his voice. His assistant entered the room so silently he only increased her feeling of uneasiness. "I need you to get some kind of soda pop called Tab. Apparently it's what Ms. Spenser drinks."

Jensen's colorless eyes slid over her. "Of course, sir. It might take an hour or so but I'm certain some will be available."

"That's fine, then. The original — not any new-fangled crap. Ms. Spenser is staying for dinner, of course. Tell the chef I want him to do his very best work."

"I'm afraid, sir, that the chef has left."

It was enough to wipe the charming smile off Harry's handsome face. "Don't be ridiculous. He's been with me for years! He wouldn't take off without warning."

"I'm sorry, sir. I have no idea whether his reasons were professional or personal, I simply know he's gone."

Harry shook his head. "Unbelievable! That's the fifth long-term employee of mine who's left without notice."

"Sixth, sir, if you count my predecessor," Jensen murmured.

"I want you to look into this, Jensen," Harry said in a dark voice. But then his sunny smile took over. "In the meantime, I'm sure you can find someone to take Olaf's place and rustle up something wonderful for me and my guest."

"Certainly."

"I wouldn't want to put you to any trouble in the midst of such a domestic crisis," Genevieve interrupted. "Really, you could just sign the papers and I'll take off —"

"I wouldn't hear of it," Harry said grandly. "You traveled all this way just for me — the least I can do is feed you properly. See to it, Peter."

She watched Harry's assistant disappear with a twinge of regret. There was no getting out of this. At the very least, however, she had little doubt he'd manage to scare up both Tab and a five-star chef — he had that kind of machine-like efficiency down pat. And Van Dorn was turning up his Texas charm — in a few minutes he'd no doubt be talking about his dear old pappy — and she might as well lean back and make the best of it. At the very worst she was going to be bored to death, but there were worse

25

ways to spend an evening.

Peter Jensen could move with frightening efficiency, even in the guise of the perfect executive assistant. It had taken him longer to get rid of Olaf than the others, and he was afraid he was going to have to use force, but in the end he'd done his job and the chef had decamped in a righteous snit.

Not that Peter would have minded using force. He did what he had to do, and he was very well trained. But he preferred subtlety, and brute force left bruises and bodies and too many questions. In the end Olaf had left, Hans was primed and ready to step in, and they were just about to make their well-planned move.

The girl, however, was a problem. He should have known Harry's law firm would send someone young and pretty to keep him happy. They didn't know enough about Harry's complicated appetites to realize anyone would do.

The papers she brought with her were another question — were they simply an excuse or a clue to something more important? Harry hadn't seemed the slightest bit interested, but then, Harry wouldn't.

He had to get the woman off the boat, fast, before they could put their plans into motion. They would get the go-ahead in the next few days, and he didn't want any stray civilians to get in the way and complicate things. The assignment was relatively simple — nothing he hadn't done before, and he was very good at what he did, but timing, as always, was everything.

Ms. Spenser was getting in the way, and the sooner he got rid of her, the better. He was a man who avoided collateral damage, and he wasn't about to change his ways at this point, no matter how important the mission. And while he knew only a part of Harry Van Dorn's maniacal Rule of Seven, he knew stopping Van Dorn was a very important mission indeed.

He knew what they called him behind his back. The Iceman. Both for his ice-cold control, and his particular expertise. He didn't care what they called him, as long as he got the job done.

Ms. Spenser would have to go, before it was too late. Before he was forced to kill her.

He remembered her dark eyes as they'd looked through him. He shouldn't have mentioned the crossword puzzle — that was something she might remember if someone started asking her questions once the job was finished. But no, he'd played his part well enough. She'd looked at him and hadn't seen him, and that ability to vanish was his stock-in-trade.

She'd be no threat to their mission. She was bright and pretty and clueless, and she was going to be back in her safe little world before anything bad could happen.

And she'd never know how close to death she came.

Madame Lambert looked out over the bare tree branches outside her nondescript office in a nondescript building near London's Kensington Gardens. She was slim, elegant and ruthlessly chic, with creamy, ageless skin and cool, ageless eyes. She stared at the trees, looking for some sign of life. It was April, after all, time for things to come alive again.

But it always took longer in the city, where pollution slowed the natural evolution of things. And for some reason the trees and gardens near the offices of the Spence-Pierce Financial Consultants, Ltd., tended to die. If Madame Lambert were a more fanciful person she'd think it was a sympathetic reaction to the actual work they did. Spence-Pierce was nothing more than one of a dozen covers for the covert work done by the Committee, a group so steeped in

28

secrecy that Isobel Lambert was still just learning some of the intricate details, and she'd been in charge for more than a year.

It was April, and time was running out. The Rule of Seven was in play, backed by Harry Van Dorn's brilliant brain and seemingly limitless resources, and they still didn't know nearly enough about what it was. Seven disasters, orchestrated by Harry Van Dorn, to plunge the world into chaos, chaos that would somehow be turned to Van Dorn's benefit. But the whens, the wheres, the hows were still maddeningly unclear. Not to mention who — Harry couldn't be doing this without help.

Whatever it was, it was deadly.

And it was the Committee's job to keep deadly things from happening. No matter how high the body count happened to be.

She wasn't feeling good about this, and she'd learned to trust her instincts. Peter was the best they had, a brilliant operative who'd never failed a mission.

But she had the unpleasant feeling that all that was about to change.

She shook herself, returning to the spotless walnut desk that held nothing but a Clarefontaine pad and a black pen. She kept everything in her head, for safety's sake, but sometimes she just needed to write.

She scrawled something, then glanced down at it. The Rule of Seven.

What the hell was Harry Van Dorn planning to unleash on an unsuspecting world?

And would killing him be enough to stop it?

2

Harry Van Dorn's McMansion of a yacht was large enough that Genevieve could almost forget she was surrounded by water. The smell of the sea was still there, but she loved the ocean if she wasn't on a boat, and she could easily pretend she was on some nice safe cliff overlooking the surf, rather than bobbing around in the middle of it.

Harry Van Dorn was both quirky and charming, there was no denying it, and he was focusing all that charm on her. His megawatt smile, his crinkly blue eyes, his lazy voice and rapt attention to her every word should have made her melt. Except that Genevieve didn't melt easily, even beneath the warm Caribbean sun with a billionaire doing his best to seduce her.

The Tab had appeared, of course, cold with a glass of ice as well. She knew she ought to have insisted on Pellegrino or something equally upscale — the firm would never approve of something as mundane as soda pop — but she should have been on vacation, and for now she could let little things drop. She'd even kicked off her shoes as she stretched out on the white leather chaise, wiggling her silk-covered toes in the sunlight.

She knew how to make the most self-effacing man become expansive, and Harry was hardly a wallflower. The Van Dorn Foundation had never been under her particular purview — she'd been kept busy with the relatively simple concerns of several smaller foundations — but she found his worldview fascinating. It was no wonder he collected humanitarian awards by the bucketload — he'd even been nominated for a Nobel Peace Prize, though she thought it would be a cold day in hell before he got one. The profits from his overseas production companies were cut in half because he refused to let them employ child labor, and the workers received enough of a living wage that they didn't have to send their children into factories and brothels. He still made a profit, Genevieve thought cynically, and his generous salaries were still only a fraction of what he used to pay the workers in the American factories that now lay closed and abandoned in the dying cities in the Midwest, but the humanitarian organizations ignored that part. Either ignored it, or knew that giving a billionaire an award was likely to make his charitable foundation feel even more charitable toward them.

His money came from everywhere — oil fields in the Middle East, diamond mines in Africa, investments so complicated she doubted even he understood them. All she knew was he made money faster than he could spend it, and his tastes were lavish.

But she had become used to billionaires in the past few years, and in the end there were all the same, even someone like Harry Van Dorn with his little eccentricities. She listened to him ramble on in his lazy Texas accent, telling herself she should just relax, that by tomorrow she'd be stripped of these clothes and her professional armor and be hiking through the jungles of Costa Rica, fending off mosquitoes and blisters. Compared to this plush cocoon it sounded like heaven.

She awoke with a start. Harry was still talking — apparently he'd never even noticed that she'd drifted off for a moment. She could thank her mirrored sunglasses for that — if Walt Fredericks ever knew his protégée had fallen asleep in front of a client she'd be out on her ass in a matter of hours.

33

Though there was always the good possibility that that was exactly what she wanted.

And then she realized what had woken her. Not Harry's lazy ramblings, but the feel of the boat beneath her. The unmistakable rumble of an engine, when this damn thing should be floating and silent.

"Why did they turn on the engines?" She broke through Harry's discourse on tarot cards.

"Did they? I hadn't noticed. I think they do that every now and then to check the engines. Make sure she's in good running order. Sort of like a fire drill. They don't usually do it until a few hours before we're supposed to set sail, but I have no plans to go anywhere right now. Must be some sort of maintenance thing."

She'd sat bolt upright. They'd been under the shelter of an overhanging deck when Harry had ensconced her on the chaise, but now the sun had advanced far enough that it was halfway up her legs. It was a reasonable explanation, but she wasn't buying it.

She swung her legs over the side of the leather couch, slipped on her killer shoes with barely a wince and rose. "I hadn't realized it had gotten so late — I've been so interested in your stories," she lied with the talent she'd honed over the years. "I really do need you to sign those papers — I have a plane to catch. I'm due in Costa Rica tomorrow afternoon."

"Nonsense. I wouldn't hear of you leaving," he replied. "We'll have a lovely dinner, you'll spend the night, and tomorrow I'll have my private jet take you wherever you want to go."

"I couldn't —"

"And don't think I have wicked designs on you," he said with a wink. "I do, but my mama taught me to be a gentleman where ladies are concerned. This place has seven bedrooms, each with its own bath, and there's nothing like sleeping in the rocking arms of the ocean. It'll rock your cares away."

"I don't have any particular cares at this moment," she said, lying through her teeth with utter charm. "And I couldn't ask you to go to so much trouble."

"No trouble at all." He overrode her. "I have a jet and a pilot just sitting around with nothing to do — he'd love a chance to get out for a day or so. He can even wait for you while you do your business down there and bring you back, either here or to New York."

"I'm staying for six weeks, Mr. Van Dorn."

"No one calls me Mr. Van Dorn," he protested. "That was my daddy's name. And why in hell would you spend six weeks in Costa Rica?"

"I'm going on a hiking expedition in the rain forest." She waited for his reaction.

He blinked, and for a moment she wondered just how deep his humanitarian commitment ran. "The Van Dorn Foundation has always been active in environmental issues as well. After all, this is the only earth we've got."

She wasn't about to tell him that her vacation choice of rain forest had been motivated more by the notion that she'd be unreachable than by any charitable instincts. "Indeed," she murmured. "But I really do need to be going . . ."

"Peter!" Harry barely raised his voice, but Peter Jensen was there instantly. He must have been hovering just out of sight. "I need you to get in touch with my pilot and tell him to get the jet ready. Ms. Spenser will be flying down to Costa Rica tomorrow, and I want her to be comfortable."

She opened her mouth to protest again, and then caught an odd expression lurking behind Peter Jensen's rimless glasses. It was unreadable, but definitely there, and very curious. Enigma, she thought, remembering the crossword puzzle.

"If you're certain it's no trouble," she said, keeping her pleasant demeanor firmly in place. It looked as if she was going to have to spend the night on this boat, in the middle of the damn water.

"Very good, sir," Jensen murmured tonelessly.

"And have them make up the mate's cabin for her, would you? She's going to spend the night." He turned back to Genevieve with a winning smile. "You see? All open and aboveboard. I intend to be a perfect gentleman."

For some reason Genevieve found herself glancing at the assistant. She must have imagined the sheen of contempt in his colorless eyes — a good servant never betrayed his emotions, and she suspected Jensen was a very good servant indeed. Harry could afford the best, and she'd already witnessed Jensen's machine-like efficiency.

"Very good, sir."

"You'll need to have someone fetch Ms. Spenser's bags."

"I'm afraid that's impossible, sir. I checked on them when I went to secure a new chef — it seemed prudent since I was on land. Ms. Spenser's bags were already sent on their way to Costa Rica on her scheduled flight."

Prudent. Now, there was a word you didn't hear every day, Genevieve thought. She would have been annoyed, but Jensen's "prudent" action gave her the excuse she needed.

"That was very kind of you to try, Mr. Jensen. It seems I'd better try to catch my plane after all."

"Simply doing my job, Ms. Spenser," he murmured. "I've arranged for the boat to be ready in an hour's time."

"Well, you can just unarrange it," Harry said grandly. "Ms. Spenser is spending the night. Don't tell me there aren't clothes on board to fit a pretty little thing like her, because I know different. Besides, it's April seventh, and you know seven is my lucky number. I bet your birthday's on the seventh of October, Ms. Spenser. Isn't it?"

For a moment she wondered where he'd come up with such an outlandish notion, but then she remembered she'd agreed when he asked if she was a Libra. Would he give up trying to keep her here if she said she was born on the fifteenth?

"You really are amazing," she said in a light voice, avoiding the issue altogether.

"I'm afraid all the women's clothes on

board are more likely to fit a size two or four. On your orders, sir."

Genevieve didn't know who pissed her off more, Harry Van Dorn for assuming she'd do what he wanted, or Peter Jensen for his implied suggestion that she was fat.

"I wear a size six," she said in a dulcet tone. In fact, she was an eight and sometimes even a ten, and she suspected in cheaper clothes it might even be worse than that, but she wasn't about to admit it. She just had to hope Jensen wouldn't be able to turn up some size sixes that she would have to try to squeeze into.

He didn't look skeptical — he probably knew what size she wore, even down to her shoes — but he was too well trained.

"Hell, we're informal around here," Harry said. "I'm sure you can rustle up something for her, Jensen. I wouldn't put anything past you." He turned to Genevieve. "He's an Aries, remember. Tight-assed son of a bitch, if you'll pardon my French, but he gets the job done. Whereas I'm an Aquarius — more of an ideas man. I don't usually get along with Libras, but I expect you've got one hell of a rising sign."

The only thing rising about her was her temper, but there wasn't a damn thing she could do about it. She wasn't getting out of this, she thought. Given that she worked for him, he could expect just about everything he wanted from her. So she gritted her teeth and smiled. "I'm sure I'll be fine," she said.

Peter Jensen nodded, his face as impassive as ever. She half expected him to back away like some medieval Chinese servant, but he turned and left, and she watched him go, momentarily fascinated. He looked different from the back — taller, leaner, less generic. Maybe it was the glasses and the slicked-down hair that made him appear so ordinary. Or maybe she was even more in need of a vacation than she had thought, to be having paranoid fantasies about a nondescript personal assistant.

In the end it wasn't important. She'd been efficiently roped and tied by the charming Texan — she'd let Harry Van Dorn wine and dine her and tomorrow she'd be on her way, able to leave her work and her life behind her. She wasn't going to sleep with him — she'd decided that a while ago, though she wasn't sure when. She wasn't in the mood for anything but escape and quiet.

She would survive the utter hell of falling asleep surrounded by water by taking a couple of tranquilizers to drown out the anxiety. And by this time tomorrow it would all be a distant memory.

■ ■ ■ ■

Jensen wasn't happy. Things weren't going as he'd planned, but then, things seldom did. He hadn't counted on Genevieve Spenser, or Harry Van Dorn's taking to her like a puppy with a new squeaky toy. He could turn her to his benefit, as a welcome distraction, but he still didn't have to like it. Complications were a necessary evil, but he was a man who got rid of complications. He should have arranged to get rid of Miss Spenser before she ever arrived in the islands.

He seldom wasted his time in hindsight. He would have expected a pretty bimbo, a minor inconvenience, one he could dispose of quickly. And she was very pretty, in that sleek, well-cared-for way that tended to set his teeth on edge when he allowed himself the luxury of feeling. But there was more to her than that, though she was trying to hide it. She was smarter than she wanted people to know, and angrier.

That anger was undeniably fascinating. Distracting. The women he knew hid their anger very well, channeling it into more devious endeavors. Genevieve Spenser didn't seem to have found her outlet, and he could see it simmering beneath her calm brown eyes. Blond hair and brown eyes — an interesting combination. Though her hair was probably some mousy color in its natural state.

And he was thinking far too much about her when he had a job to do. Hans was safely ensconced in the galley, a job he was well trained for, both when it came to food and knives, and Renaud was busy in the bowels of the ship, making sure everything was set to go when they got the word. The other five had been chosen by Isobel Lambert herself, and they were almost as efficient and professional as he was. They'd blended into their new jobs with effortless ease. Harry Van Dorn had no idea he was surrounded by members of the Committee.

Then again, if he was as artless as he seemed to be, he'd have no idea what the Committee was. Few people did, but he didn't quite believe in Harry's cluelessness. The kind of power and money he controlled bought a lot of privileged information.

For some reason he was getting impatient.

Harry Van Dorn should have been a simple matter. A megalomaniac billionaire with a taste for the occult and a complicated plan to disrupt the flow of commerce and the financial stability of the world, all to his own benefit.

The problem was, Harry compartmental-ized. He had people working on each branch of his plan, each branch of the Rule of Seven was self-contained, and it made discovering the details about each incipient disaster that much more difficult. One never led to another, and his army of minions seemed to have no idea that there were other armies working in concert on parallel disasters. Peter had only been on-site for four months — a relatively short time compared with his last tenure as personal assistant to Marcello Ricetti, a Sicilian arms dealer with a taste for sadism and young boys. Peter had managed to keep him away from the children during the year he'd spent with him, at a price. He'd have had to pay the same price anyway, and he hadn't thought twice about it. Even though in the end it had cost him his wife.

At least he hadn't been required to per-form more personal services for Harry Van Dorn. Peter's well-honed asexual persona was an asset — it was up to the target to make what they wanted of him, and all Harry wanted was someone to see to his every comfort. He could provide for his own sexual needs.

Which brought him around to Genevieve

Spenser again. It would probably be better if she slept with Harry. If she were alone in the mate's cabin it would be harder to keep Renaud from cutting her throat. Though in the end they might have no choice — it would be very dangerous to let her go back to her pampered life in New York and have to answer questions about the disappearance of Harry Van Dorn and his yacht. A casualty of war, Thomason would have said. But Thomason was gone, and Peter had hoped that the ruthlessness that was part and parcel of the Committee could be tempered by restraint.

But people who knew too much were always a problem. The drugs that had been developed were volatile; they could wipe out too much memory or too little. When the stakes were high enough one couldn't afford to take chances.

But maybe it wouldn't come to that. Maybe he could get her off the boat after all — she certainly seemed desperate to go. It wouldn't take long — if Van Dorn's jet was out of commission she'd have to fly out on a commercial plane, and it would be easy enough to arrange a flight for the crack of dawn, necessitating that she spend the night on the island. She'd seen him, of course, but she wouldn't remember anything about him. It was one of his many dubious talents.

He was making things needlessly complicated, all for the sake of a spoiled little rich girl. She was here, and she could stay here. He'd deal with the ramifications of that later. He'd keep her alive if he could. If not, he'd make certain it was swift and merciful. After all, being born into privilege was no great crime. Only a moral misdemeanor.

The mate's cabin was an expansive suite that belonged more in a five-star hotel than on a boat. The king-size bed took up only a quarter of the room, and a picture window overlooked the gently rocking ocean. Genevieve pulled the curtains.

She took a lengthy shower, simply for the novelty of it, pampering herself. She'd finally gotten used to those little elegances — a childhood of scrimping, of making sure appearances were kept up, had done a complete turnaround, to such a well-kept extreme that it sometimes amused her. Who would have thought the well-bred, desperately poor little Genny Spenser would end up so pampered? There'd been a certain cachet in being one of the *nouveau pauvre.* The money her robber baron ancestors had amassed was long gone, and all that was left was the expectation of privilege without the money to buy it. Not that her parents would admit to that. In public they were still the Spensers, socially above those who actually had to work for a living. Inside the house with the leaking roof, the closed-off wings, the weed-choked driveway and the empty rooms, they ate boxed macaroni and cheese resentfully prepared by her mother.

They were lucky they had a roof over their heads. Her black-sheep father was the only Spenser left in their branch of the family, but upon his death the house was already in trust to the state of Rhode Island. So he'd simply sold anything he could — all the surrounding land, every piece of furniture worth something. The art had already been divested in a previous generation, and her grandmother had survived by selling off her jewelry. There was very little left to sell by the time Genevieve's parents moved in.

No one was allowed to visit, of course, because then the secret would be out. They were always in the midst of massive renovations, her parents would say, and returned social commitments at a restaurant or club. And Genny and her sister would eat butter-and-potato-chip sandwiches for weeks to pay for it.

Now she could buy anything, eat anything, wear anything she wanted. It was no wonder

she had those wretched fifteen pounds —
there were just too many lovely things to
partake of. If her ruthlessly slim mother had
been alive she would have been horrified.

But her parents were dead, the house was
gone, and Genevieve Spenser earned a
fortune at the hands of Roper, Hyde, Camui and Fredericks. She belonged with a
man like Harry Van Dorn, her mother
would have said, though she would have
wrinkled her nose at his politically correct
factories. The only acceptable way to have
money was to inherit it, according to her
mother. Her father would simply have had
another scotch.

The shower was huge, somehow managing to be both tasteful and ostentatious, and
she let the water pound some of the tension
from her body. She'd take another tranquil-
izer before she joined Harry again, though
she'd have to watch her intake of wine. And
she'd sleep alone in that luxurious bed,
doubtless beneath Egyptian-cotton sheets
with an astronomical thread count, and
tomorrow night she'd be in a sleeping bag
on the ground. And she'd be a hell of a lot
happier.

It was getting dark when she came out of
the shower, and she could see lights from
the shoreline through the filmy curtains. She

wasn't sure they were a reassurance that land was nearby or a reminder that she wasn't on it, but she left the curtains closed anyway as she dressed in the new clothes, pulling off the tags that had been left on. Size eights. She didn't know whether to be annoyed or relieved.

She reached for her bottle of pills, and at the last minute popped two in her mouth. It had to be the ocean water that was making her paranoid, uneasy, convinced that something, somehow, was wrong. But the pills would take care of that, and after tomorrow she could throw them away. Or at least pack them until she had to return to the city and the way of life she'd chosen.

She sank down in one of the oversize chairs, closing her eyes as she waited for the Zenlike calm to envelope her. It would all be all right. It would be lovely. And then she'd be gone.

She was a pretty little thing, Harry Van Dorn thought, watching her on the closed-circuit television in his stateroom. A little too padded for her clothes, but stripped she was just right. He'd gotten tired of bone-thin models who performed tirelessly.

But then, that was normal for him. He was a creature of impulse, and he had a short attention span. He became obsessed with something, overindulged, and then lost interest. He'd gone through virgins, older women, ugly women and handsome men. He'd stayed longest with the children, but they tended to cry too much, and even when he found a good one they had an unfortunate tendency to age, and he'd never cared for anyone over eleven.

His taste for models had been a fortunate alternative — it was socially acceptable, even encouraged, and he had no trouble attracting them. He was just as much a trophy as they were, and the relationships were mutually beneficial.

The only problem was he couldn't hurt them without paying a huge price. Their bodies were their livelihood, and any kind of scarring, any broken bones or bruising would diminish their value. He'd gone a bit overboard with one, and then had to try to buy her off. She'd made the very grave mistake of refusing, and no one had thought it the slightest bit strange that an anorexic supermodel had been found starved to death in a little French château.

But that was in the past. He looked at Genevieve Spenser's creamy, beautiful skin and knew he was going to have her. His lawyers knew how to quiet things up, and if he made a mistake, went a bit too far, his ass would be covered. No, Ms. Genevieve Spenser was a downright thoughtful gift from the universe, as well as those contracts she'd brought with her. The ones that severed his connections to some of his most lucrative oil fields. The ones that were going to be blown up in just about two weeks' time.

The Rule of Seven, his lucky number. Seven disasters to throw the financial world into an uproar, the kind of uproar a smart man could benefit from. And he considered himself a smart man. The decimation of the oil fields was number three, and nothing would stop it. Nothing would stop him.

Until he had everything he wanted.

And the nice thing about that was, he always wanted more.

3

Of course it had to be tonight, Peter thought savagely, closing the communication device that was so visionary it didn't even have a name. Word had come down from Madame Lambert — the time for waiting was past, and tonight was the night. There was no wiggle room; at midnight, when the harbor patrol changed, they were taking over Harry's *Seven Sins* and disappearing. The course had been plotted long ago, and the men in the wheelhouse were some of the best. No one would be able to find them, even with the most advanced surveillance systems.

Then again, no one would be looking for them. Harry Van Dorn was known to take off when the mood struck him, and the time he spent aboard the *Seven Sins* usually involved the world's idea of romance. If he disappeared, it would first be assumed he had some sort of assignation, probably at his private island. And Peter Jensen had been on-site long enough to know how to steer nosy people in the wrong direction.

Harry did have an assignation on Little Fox Island, all right. But it wasn't with a leggy model. He had an appointment with death, and the longer Jensen was around him the more he knew it was long overdue.

But why the hell did Madame Lambert have to pick tonight? When a relative innocent had strayed into their path? He was used to dealing with anomalies, but his choices had never been quite so clear cut. He had to get her off the boat. Or she had to die.

And he had only a few hours to make that happen.

Questioning orders was frowned upon by the Committee, and Peter didn't even consider it. He did his job with single-minded determination and ignored the larger ramifications. He didn't want to be the one making the life-or-death decisions. If he had to make them, he might have trouble carrying them out, and the world couldn't afford that.

Saving the world, one murder at a time, Peter thought, putting his wire-rimmed glasses back on his face. The funny thing was, he really didn't want to kill Harry Van

Dorn. For the simple reason that he was afraid he might enjoy it, and then he'd really be lost.

It was going to be an antiseptic, long-distance hit, and he'd let Renaud do the honors. Renaud had no qualms about his work; he reveled in it a bit too much, which could always be a liability. Peter's icy control was money in the bank — the job got done with deadly efficiency and no fuckups.

There'd be no fuckups on this one either. But he had to get rid of Genevieve Spenser. Now.

She'd miscalculated. Genevieve sat in one of the elegant lounges on Harry Van Dorn's megayacht, forcing herself to eat sparingly of the food that was far too good for a pick-up chef, and drank too much wine. She should have paid attention, but even by her recently pampered standards the wine was extraordinary, and it would have been a crime to ignore it. She knew herself well enough to know when she'd had enough, but it was too late at that point, and her only choice was to manage a dignified retreat.

It hadn't been a bad evening — Harry was charming, full of flattering attention and entertaining stories that poked fun at both himself and the high and mighty. At some other time Genevieve might have felt like reciprocating that flattery — he was movie-star handsome, and she hadn't been involved with anyone in longer than she wanted to remember. The firm would approve, and she could have a night of pleasure to send her on her way to the rain forest.

The problem, of course, was that it wouldn't be particularly pleasurable. The first time she slept with a man it tended to be uncomfortable, nerve-racking, even unpleasant. Even with the wine and the tranquilizers she would only manage to relax enough to do it but not enjoy it. No, Harry Van Dorn was flirting heavily, but he didn't seem likely to push it, and she was just as happy to be able to keep a relative distance.

"I've got a busy day tomorrow," she said, rising on thankfully steady feet. "I've had a lovely evening, but I'm afraid I'm going to have to say good-night."

Harry rose, towering over her, his big Texas grin almost tempting. "Are you sure I can't talk you into an after-dinner liqueur? Maybe view my etchings?"

She laughed, as she was supposed to. "I think I'll take a rain check on the etchings," she said. "I'm so exhausted I'll probably fall asleep on my feet."

"We can't have that. I suppose I'd better call Jensen!"

The ghost appeared, seemingly out of the woodwork, and his sudden presence momentarily cleared the fog in Genevieve's brain. "Shall I see Ms. Spenser to her quarters, sir?"

Harry didn't look pleased at Jensen's rapid appearance.

"I can find my own way," she protested, just as the boat shifted beneath her, and she had to reach out and catch the back of the banquette.

"The wind has picked up a bit, and we wouldn't want you to slip or get lost. The SS *Seven Sins* is a big ship. Besides, Jensen's here to serve, aren't you?"

"Yes, sir," he murmured, his voice as colorless as his eyes.

She almost changed her mind. Stupid, of course, she chided herself, but for a brief, wine-fogged moment she felt safer with Harry Van Dorn and his straightforward attempts at seduction than the almost invisible servant with the empty eyes.

But she hadn't had *that* much to drink. She put her best smile on her face. "If you wouldn't mind, Mr. Jensen?"

"It's his job, Genevieve," Harry drawled.

She glanced up at Jensen's impassive face. She really needed this vacation — she had no reason at all to feel so uneasy in his presence. Maybe the pills she took to calm her down had backfired, making her more paranoid.

None of it mattered. She'd be gone by tomorrow, and she wouldn't have to be anyone but herself.

"This way, Ms. Spenser," he said, opening the door for her, and she squashed down her misgivings.

"Thanks again for a lovely evening," she said to Harry. It wasn't really a lie — it hadn't been that unpleasant. She just desperately wanted to be somewhere else.

"It was entirely my pleasure. Jensen will see you safely to your room and we'll meet for an early breakfast."

She knew she should make some polite response, but right then she was too tired for social amenities. She'd smiled and laughed and responded till she felt like a trained monkey, and she hadn't even gotten the papers signed. Papers he'd insisted on having brought to him. First thing tomorrow morning, she promised herself hazily. And then if he didn't let her go she'd damn well jump overboard.

She followed Jensen along the outside passageway. She could see the lights of the island, too close and yet too far away. The faint rocking of the boat was even more pronounced as the wind whipped through her carefully coiffed hair, and then they were inside again, the passageway small, dimly lit, almost claustrophobic. "Is this the way we came?" she asked, unable to disguise the faint nervousness in her voice.

"I'm taking a shortcut. You looked like you needed to get to your cabin as soon as possible. Unless . . ."

He stopped, and she barreled into him, much to her embarrassment. He wasn't a ghost at all, but warm, solid flesh. "Unless what?"

"I could arrange for a launch to take you back to the island. That way you could catch a flight out tomorrow morning and not have to bother with Mr. Van Dorn's pilot."

Her contact lenses had been in for far too long, and she was having trouble focusing. For a moment she was tempted — dry land, no more Harry Van Dorn or business of any sort. But the goddamn papers weren't signed, the reason she was sent here in the first place, and she couldn't afford to offend an important client by disappearing and refusing his hospitality and his private jet. She was on the fast track at Roper, Hyde,

Camui and Fredericks, and she wasn't ready to throw that overboard. Literally.

"I'm sure this will be fine. Besides, what sane woman would trade a ride on a private jet for a commercial flight?" she said flippantly. *Me,* she thought, *in a New York minute.*

He said nothing for a moment, and then nodded. "As you wish, Ms. Spenser," he murmured in that bland, empty voice that didn't seem quite real, and continued down the passageway.

He'd tried, Jensen thought. He could go one step further, knock her cold and have one of the men take her back to the island, but that would leave far too many questions, and he couldn't risk it. Collateral damage was a necessary evil, something he'd done his best to avoid most of his career, but if she was going to end up dead then it was due to her own greed. He should make peace with that unpleasant fact and take her back to her room.

He wondered how many of those pills she'd taken. He'd searched her purse, of course, more out of habit than any particular suspicion, only to discover that Ms. Genevieve Spenser had a fondness for tranquilizers. Maybe he could just keep her drugged the entire time, until Harry and the rest of them could disappear. But that would leave her wondering why Harry had chosen to take off to his private island and leave her behind, doped and groggy. She was too smart not to be suspicious. Discretion was as much a part of his assignment as getting it done.

He'd also gone through that slim black briefcase, photographing the details and sending them on to London. One more piece of the puzzle of the Rule of Seven. But what did oil fields in the Mid East have to do with a dam in India? What did it have to do with anything?

Apparently Madame Lambert had decided it wasn't worth waiting to find out. Which was fine with Peter, if this goddamn woman hadn't stumbled into his path.

He was taking her the long way on purpose. She was slightly out of it and hiding it very well indeed, but with his roundabout path she'd never find her way back to Harry Van Dorn, assuming she even wanted to.

The one thing that didn't make sense was her not sleeping with her host. People didn't say no to Harry Van Dorn, and she had to have. She might be a lesbian, but he doubted it, his fine-tuned instincts ruling out the possibility. More likely she was frigid. Or maybe she only liked it when she could be in control, and Harry was a topper if ever there was one.

Peter had asked London for intel on her, but they didn't seem in any particular hurry to get back to him, and he was still working in the dark. It would be easier if he knew a little more about her.

But he didn't need to waste his time thinking about how Genevieve Spenser liked or didn't like sex. He needed to figure out how to get rid of her without sacrificing discretion. Collateral damage, he reminded himself as he turned down one of the narrow service passageways.

"You might want to take off those shoes, Ms. Spenser," he said in his empty voice. "The sea's getting a bit choppy. Do you need something for seasickness?"

"I never get seasick." She stopped anyway, leaning against the side of the passageway to slip off her ridiculously expensive shoes. She was a tall woman, but the heels had added a good three inches, and she now seemed more vulnerable. He didn't like it when they were vulnerable.

"Never?" he echoed. "You strike me as someone who doesn't like boats very much, and I assumed it was a tendency toward seasickness that caused it."

Her eyes jerked up, suddenly sharp, and he could have kicked himself. Jensen might have noticed her dislike of boats, but he would have gone no further than that. He certainly would never have mentioned it.

"I don't like feeling trapped," she said in a tight voice.

"Then you must not like this passageway either," he said, another mistake. It was long and narrow, with the dim lighting Harry considered atmospheric, and if she had a problem with claustrophobia she'd be hyperventilating at any moment.

"I don't. But just because I don't like something doesn't mean I'll run from it."

He wanted to smile. She sounded like a feisty little kid instead of a corporate mannequin. "I can still arrange for that launch."

"Are you trying to get rid of me, Mr. Jensen?"

Too sharp, despite the wine and the tranquilizers. She had a soft mouth, rich brown eyes, and for a moment he wanted to be someone, anyone but who he was. He was going to make a mistake, and he was going to pay for it, but at that moment he didn't give a shit.

He didn't bother telling her he was trying to save her life. He slid his hand up her neck, and while she flinched at the first touch she gentled quickly, as his long fingers cupped her face. "I have a romantic streak," he said with a faint smile, and leaned down to kiss her.

Such a mouth. He wanted to drown in it. She was too startled and maybe just a bit too drunk to do more than lean back against the wall and let him, and he took full advantage of it, kissing her with a leisurely thoroughness that he hadn't let himself enjoy for a long time. And at the last minute he increased the pressure just below her ear, and she slumped into his arms, unconscious.

It was five in the morning, London time, and Isobel Lambert was still awake. In fact, she slept very little, a gift of both genetics and training. Things were just about to go down in the Caribbean, and while the operation was now out of her hands, she needed to be awake and alert, there in spirit if not in fact.

She never asked anyone to do anything she wouldn't do herself. And Peter Jensen was the best there was. She didn't tend to second-guess herself, and her gut-felt decision, to terminate Harry Van Dorn before he could implement some of the near-global damage he was planning, was the right one.

But there was the girl who'd gotten in the

way, and Jensen, usually cold as ice about such things, was dragging his heels. She could communicate directly with Renaud, have him take care of her, but she wasn't ready to do that. Renaud was a nasty piece of work, and she only liked to use him sparingly, with calmer heads like Jensen overseeing him. If there was any way to save the girl, Jensen would see to it without compromising the mission.

In the meantime, they had one more vital piece of Harry's plan. Oil fields in Saudi Arabia, a dam in Mysore, India. What else did he have in mind? And for God's sake, why?

Peter Jensen looked at the unconscious woman in his arms. It was a good trick, one he'd used a number of times, mostly to save lives. If he had to kill someone there was usually no reason for finesse. But if Genevieve Spenser wasn't going to show enough sense to take his advice and get her butt off the boat then he was going to see to it, and pick up the pieces later. Madame Lambert probably wouldn't be happy; she trusted him to know enough to veer from a plan when he had to, but she wouldn't like it. He might get his wrist slapped, but as long as no one would ever be able to trace anything back to him or the Committee they'd be fine.

Ms. Spenser was heavier than he'd thought, but he was strong enough, and he dumped her over his shoulder, leaving her shoes behind as he headed down toward the launch.

"What's that you've got there, Petey lad?" Renaud was leaning against a row of packing cases, a cigarette in his mouth, sharpening his knife. "Present for me?"

"Not quite. I want her off the boat before we get rid of Van Dorn. You need to take her back to the island and dump her somewhere."

Renaud put the knife away, rising. "She dead? Or do you want me to finish her off?"

"She's fine and I want her to stay that way. Just dump her somewhere that'll require a couple of days to find her and get back here. We're running late."

"Wouldn't be running late if I didn't have to take an extra ride in this choppy water," Renaud pointed out. "If you don't want her I'll have her. She's pretty enough."

"She's trouble."

"Then let me take care of her. Much neater all around."

Peter was getting tired of arguing. "I'll take her myself," he said.

"I don't think Hans would like it."

"And what does Hans have to say to anything? This is my operation."

"So it is. But we've all got orders to keep an eye on each other. What with the shake-up and all, the Committee isn't as trusting as it used to be."

Jensen wanted to laugh at the very idea of trust and the Committee in the same sentence, but he was too edgy and she was too damn heavy slung over his shoulder. "Fine," he said. "You take her to the island and I'll deal with Hans."

"Not a good idea, Petey," Renaud drawled. He'd always hated being called Petey, something Renaud already knew. "It's the witching hour. No time left for heroic gestures."

He was right. They'd planned the takeover for midnight, and it was too damn close to risk everything for the sake of a spoiled young lawyer.

He gave up fighting. "You're right," he said. "So much for being a gentleman. I'll dump her back in her room. Maybe we'll get done with Harry before she even wakes up."

"Yeah, you can believe that," Renaud said, dropping his cigarette on the teakwood deck and stubbing it out. "But we both know what's going to happen in the end. You're going to have to kill her."

He didn't bother to argue. Renaud was only stating the unpalatable truth. Genevieve Spenser was in the wrong place at the wrong time and she hadn't left when she could. She was going to have to live with the consequences.

And die by them.

It was a pleasant enough dream. She was being rocked, peacefully, like a babe in her mother's arms, except that her mother had never been much for rocking. She was surrounded by comfort, and yet she felt oddly free, peaceful, pampered.

Something was making a low, rumbling vibration, adding to her delicious sense of comfort. She wasn't about to wake up — it was too lovely lying there enjoying the physical sensations. There was a faint, nagging worry at the very back of her mind, but she decided to ignore it, sinking deeper into a blissful sleep.

She should have known it was coming. It always happened when she least expected it, and it took over before she could stop it. It was three years ago and she was back in that dingy little cubicle at Legal Aid in the tiny town of Auburn, New York, with her cluttered desk filled with too many hopeless cases, the industrial green on the walls stained with damp, the cold, rancid coffee and the telephone that rang and rang and then stopped like a death knell.

She should have known not to work late, alone, in that building. Too many very bad people knew where it was, and she'd made a lot of enemies in her short life. She was Joan of Arc, a heroine riding to the rescue of battered women, putting their abusive, murderous husbands in jail, helping to give the women a new chance at a decent life. She'd done such a good job of it that she was being handed all the cases involving domestic abuse, and in a poor area like Clinton County, New York, the workload was overwhelming.

But she kept at it, overworked, underpaid, foolishly thinking she was making a difference, and she never heard the footsteps down the deserted hallway. Never knew what was happening until she looked up and saw Marge Whitman's husband looming in the doorway.

He was an ugly man with an ugly temper, and a day after he got out of jail for breaking his wife's arm, cheekbone and shoulder, he'd been served with a restraining order. And he wasn't happy about it.

Genevieve had a button beneath her desk to call for help if she needed it. She pressed it with her knee as she reached for the phone.

"You don't have an appointment, Mr. Whitman, and I'm afraid I'm going to have to ask you to leave," she said. She was calm, always certain she could fix anything. "If you want to come in tomorrow and discuss your case —"

"The telephone don't work," he said, lumbering closer. He was a huge man, burly and heavily muscled, and he smelled like beer and sweat. And rage. "And I ain't got a case. You've been interfering between me and mine, and it's time somebody taught you a lesson."

He was right, the telephone was dead. That was when she felt her first inkling of fear, but there was still the button beneath her desk. She held it, thinking fast.

"We can talk about it during office hours, Mr. Whitman," she said, not a trace of nervousness showing through her calm demeanor. "In the meantime I'll have to ask you to leave."

He laughed. He didn't bother to close the glass door of the cubicle behind him — he knew there was no one there to help. "I think we'll talk about it right now. And I don't think talking is gonna cut it."

She tried to run, but he slammed her against the cubicle, and the heavy glass shattered beneath her body. There were times when she could almost forget it, and times when it came thundering back. The feel of his fists against her face, her body, so that when she fell she landed on the broken glass, as he kicked her, over and over again, and the broken shards dug into her skin. It seemed to go on forever; just when she thought he'd finished and was leaving her, another blow came, another kick, and she moaned, her mouth full of blood.

He leaned over her, yanking her up so that her face was just inches from his. "Hell," he said, "you ain't even worth killing." And he dropped her back on the floor.

She must have lost consciousness. When she woke up she was alone in the pitch-black building, lying in a pool of blood.

She'd had to crawl over the glass. She'd made it as far as the stairs and then collapsed, lying in a broken heap, unable to move, unable to speak. She could only cry.

She'd spent a week in the hospital. By the time she could talk, Whitman had disappeared, along with his wife and two children. People said Marge had gone willingly, and Genevieve had believed them.

After all, hadn't she received a bouquet of flowers with an almost illegible, unsigned note? "I'm so sorry." It could hardly have come from Whitman.

The police looked for him, but it was a halfhearted attempt. She wasn't dead, she wasn't even permanently injured. Her body healed with the help of medicine and physical therapy, her mind healed with the help of the best therapists, and she'd learned to be comfortable around men once more. She'd learned to defend herself and she'd left for the safer pastures of New York City, where she could live a peaceful life.

Until she woke up screaming. Remembering.

As she did right now.

4

Harry wasn't in the best of moods. He'd been ready to make his move on the luscious Ms. Spenser when Jensen had stuck his unwanted limey nose into the room and taken her away, and now he was feeling restless, bad-tempered and ready to take it out on someone. Preferably Ms. Spenser.

It would be no problem — the rooms were soundproofed, and even if she made a lot of noise no one would interfere. They'd either assume she was an enthusiastically noisy fuck, or that something was going on they didn't want to know about. Either way, no one would interfere.

He had better equipment in his massive stateroom, though, and he didn't like having to compromise. He firmly believed in indulging his whims whenever he could, and being refused even the tiniest little treat made him very cross indeed.

He was going to have to explain a few

things to Peter Jensen. He'd been an excellent servant for the four short months he'd been working for him, but then, he'd come with impeccable references. The kind of people he'd worked for in the past required someone with the utmost discretion, the ability to look the other way and the willingness to do whatever was asked of him, with no arguments or questions.

Jensen had proved remarkably efficient, and it hadn't been his fault that the young Thai girl last year had run away before he'd finished with her. He could blame that on one of the men who'd caught her in the first place, and he'd taken care of him in a fitting manner.

No, this was only a minor transgression, and once he gave Jensen a sharp reprimand he could go below and enjoy the undeniably luscious Ms. Spenser. Hell, he might even turn to fat women if he liked her curves well enough. There were some interesting variations on force feeding . . .

He heard a noise, and he looked up. The engines were running again, making an odd noise, and Harry had a sudden, unpleasant premonition. His horoscope said today had a potential for disaster, but whenever he didn't like his forecast he skipped to his rising sign for something more pleasant.

He rose, wandering over to the window to look out at the shoreline, when he realized the goddamn ship was moving. He let out a scream of rage, slammed open the door and headed out on deck, only to run smack into Peter Jensen.

"You son of a bitch —" Harry managed to say, before blinding pain exploded in his head. And as he sank into darkness his body climaxed in pure, murderous rage.

The boat was moving. It wasn't Genevieve's paranoid imagination, it wasn't a remnant from her nightmare. The goddamn boat was moving.

She scrambled out of bed. She was still wearing the silk slip of a dress she'd worn last night, with her bra and pantyhose in place, if a bit rumpled. She hadn't been that out of it, had she? She'd had a little too much to drink on top of a three-pill day, but still, she shouldn't be having blackouts.

She sank down on the floor beside the platform bed, dropping her head in her hands. She couldn't remember anything, not since she left Harry Van Dorn's side and headed for her room. She'd left with the gray ghost, hadn't she? But she couldn't remember anything about the walk to her cabin, whether he'd turned down her bed or kissed her good-night.

Holy shit. She'd been facetious, trying to reconstruct her last conscious moments, but the memory, no longer elusive, came flooding back. The son of a bitch had kissed her.

At least, she thought he had. Or maybe it was just part of her dreams, an earlier, less nightmarish part. Though if it involved kissing someone like Jensen then she'd almost prefer the nightmares. She'd learned how to fight back with them.

She rose on unsteady feet. At least she hadn't slept in her shoes. She walked in what she hoped was the direction of the window, feeling her way, and when she reached the heavy curtains she tugged, trying to open them.

They stayed put, obviously on some kind of heavy-duty curtain rod, but she could push the fabric out of the way enough to have her worst fears confirmed. It was midday, when she should have already landed in Costa Rica, and they were out at sea.

Harry's multi-million-dollar yacht ran smoothly and quietly through the waters, but there was no mistaking the feel of the engine beneath her, the sound of the water as the boat cut through the swells. She let the curtain drop again, swearing under her breath. If this was Harry Van Dorn's idea of a joke then she wasn't amused.

Maybe he was taking her to Costa Rica via the yacht; across the open water it wouldn't be that far, and she hadn't actually come right out and told him she hated being on a boat. Maybe it was his twisted idea of flirtation — he was so used to women falling at his feet that he assumed anyone would be thrilled by his attention.

Genevieve was definitely not thrilled. She had every intention of tracking him down and giving him an ultimatum. She hadn't seen a helicopter landing pad on this floating mansion but she was willing to bet he had one, and she was going to give him an hour to provide her with a flight out of here.

If he set Jensen to it then it would be there in half an hour. He couldn't have kissed her, could he? The man seemed totally asexual, and besides, what an absurd thing to do. She already knew how badly she needed this vacation — this paranoid delusion only proved it.

She took long enough to shower and change back into her business clothes. She'd slept in her contacts — always a mistake — and she felt rumpled and gritty and vulnerable. It took her less than fifteen minutes to put on her business persona once more; she'd become an expert at constructing

Genevieve Spenser, Esquire, in record time, even without makeup and fresh underwear and shoes. Her reflection in the mirror wasn't reassuring. She didn't look as polished and inviolate as she usually did. It didn't matter. Her justifiable anger would make up for any lingering vulnerability.

Except that the door was locked from the outside. At first she couldn't believe it — it must have been some kind of mistake. But no matter how hard she tugged and twisted the polished brass doorknob, the door wouldn't move.

She lost it then. She began pounding on the door, kicking it, yelling at the top of her lungs. "Unlock this door, you son of a bitch, and let me out of here! How dare you do this — it's kidnapping, and just because my firm represents your goddamn foundation doesn't mean I won't sue the daylights out of you, you slimy weasel." She kept pounding, kicking, yelling, until a sudden slam against the locked door momentarily silenced her.

"Be quiet!"

It was a voice she hadn't heard before, someone with a heavy accent, possibly French.

"Then unlock the goddamn door and let me out of here," she snapped.

"You have a choice, lady. You can sit down and shut up and wait until we're ready to deal with you, or you can keep making noise and force me to come in and cut your throat. The boss said to leave you alone, but he's a practical man and knows when you have to cut your losses, whether he likes it or not. I promise you I would have no problem killing you."

Genevieve froze. She wanted to laugh at the melodramatic absurdity of that disembodied voice, except that it wasn't absurd. She believed that flat, unemotional tone.

"What's going on? Why are we in the middle of the ocean and why have you locked me in here?" she asked in a deceptively calm voice.

"You'll find out when the boss says you need to. In the meantime be quiet and don't remind me that you're causing trouble. Not if you want to have any chance of making it back to your expensive lifestyle."

She should have kept her mouth shut, but right now she was having a hard time being docile. "Who's the boss?"

"No one you want to fuck with, lady."

"Is it Harry?"

The sound of retreating footsteps was her only answer. She was half tempted to call out after him, but wisdom kept her mouth shut. In her short foray into pro bono law she'd met enough sociopaths and career criminals to recognize the sound of one. The man who'd stood on the other side of the door would have no qualms about killing her. And he said his mysterious boss was even worse. Not Harry. Harry was just a harmless good ol' boy and the logical target of whatever was going on. It had to be someone else.

She tossed her jacket on the bed and proceeded to prowl around the room. She'd managed to figure out how to work the power-operated curtains, and she could open the window itself a scant ten inches. She might be able to get through it sideways, except that there was nowhere to go. It looked straight over the water, with no railing or deck beneath it, and she didn't fancy dangling off the side of a fast-moving yacht while she tried to make her way to another level.

What the hell was going on? The man had said his boss was ready to cut his losses, and it was clear she was one of those losses. The obvious center of whatever was going on had to be Harry Van Dorn and his billions of dollars. Was he being held hostage? If so, she'd be an obvious negotiator. Maybe that was why the unnamed boss had decided to keep her alive.

And where was Jensen in all this? Probably already dead — he would have been expendable. Unless he was part of whatever was going on. Though someone less like a terrorist or extortionist she couldn't imagine.

She had a Swiss Army knife in her makeup bag. No pockets in her silk suit, but she could tuck the weapon in her bra just in case. Most of all, she had to stay calm. She'd learned that, and a great many other things in the months following the attack. Just to ensure it, she found her pill bottle and swallowed two of the yellow pills. Not enough to impair her, but enough to make sure she didn't overreact. Thank God she had them.

She grabbed her briefcase, but the contracts she'd brought with her were gone, taken sometime during the night. It was the least of her worries. She pulled out a legal pad of paper with its elegant tooled-leather binding and started making lists, always a way of calming herself. There were any number of possibilities right now. Harry Van Dorn could be playing an absurd practical joke. A comforting idea but unlikely. He was more likely to be the target of whatever was going on. Kidnapping? He'd be worth an unbelievable amount of money. Or was it a political act by some disgruntled militants? What did they want with Harry? Money? Publicity? His death?

God, she hoped not. He was harmless enough, despite his faintly annoying flirtatiousness and his crackpot superstitions. He must have an army of bodyguards — anyone with real wealth did — though the only person she'd seen much of had been Jensen, and he would have been useless in a dangerous situation.

There were countless other possibilities, and her response would be dictated by which one it was. In the meantime she could reasonably assume that she was being held hostage along with Harry Van Dorn.

She looked out the window. She'd always been a strong swimmer, and she could float for hours, the one advantage of those unwanted fifteen pounds, but she had no idea how far from land they were. If they'd been at sea since she passed out last night, they could be hundreds of miles away from Grand Cayman Island.

If it was a question of life or death, she could go overboard and take her chances in the water, but at this point she needed to stay calm and not make any unnecessary assumptions.

She barely had time to scramble to her feet when she heard someone at the door. She could feel the knife tucked safely between her breasts, and she had her full, corporate-lawyer armor on, minus the shoes. The scruffy-looking individual who stood there with a semiautomatic did not look impressed.

"The boss is ready for you," he said. She recognized his voice from the other side of the door, and gave an instant, silent prayer that she'd shown enough sense to shut up. Whoever he was, he wasn't the type to make idle threats.

"And where's Mr. Van Dorn?" she demanded in a cool voice, reaching for her briefcase.

"You can leave that there," he said. "And if you need to know anything about Harry Van Dorn then someone will tell you. In the meantime shut up and come with me. And don't cause any trouble. The boss doesn't want us to be cleaning up bloodstains."

"Why bother to clean them?" She was always too mouthy when she was nervous, and the pills weren't having the desired effect. "If you're into kidnapping and extortion, then I don't think you'd care about what condition you left the boat in."

The small man blinked, a quick, dangerous movement, like a rattler about to strike, and Genevieve wondered whether she needed to dive for cover, but then the man simply laughed. "Someone will pay good money for it."

"It's a little ostentatious, don't you think? Whoever buys it can't expect to get away with it."

"I appreciate your concern, lady, but there are places that can strip a boat and change its appearance as quickly as they can with stolen cars. And most of the people who own a ship like this don't care too much about legal niceties. Now shut up and move."

Genevieve shut up and moved. He gestured with the gun, and she preceded him into the narrow passageway. She half expected to see bodies and blood, but it looked the same — spotless, deserted, normal. She kept moving, looking back every now and then to make sure her companion was with her. The gun was trained at the center of her spine, and a tiny shiver washed over her. A gun like that could do a lot of damage to a spinal cord.

It was colder out on the open water, and the stiff breeze tugged at her neatly coiffed hair. She should have had it cut — she'd intended to wear it in braids while she was in Costa Rica, but it was looking as if it was going to be a long time before she saw that place.

"Keep moving," the man behind her snarled. "Up that staircase."

She started up, wishing she'd found her missing shoes. They would have done more damage, but she'd simply have to make do without them. He was following close behind her, and she waited until the right moment, when she was at the very top of the metal staircase, and then she kicked backward, hard.

Her bare foot connected with his face and he tumbled down the steps, cursing. She didn't wait to see whether the fall had done any permanent damage — she took off. The deck was deserted, with blinding sunlight all around, and there was no place to hide. She grabbed the first doorway, only to be confronted by a utility closet, but she didn't hesitate, cramming herself inside and pulling it shut just moments before the sound of heavy footsteps made it onto the deck.

It was pitch-black inside the tiny cubicle, and it smelled like gasoline and cleaning supplies. She was covered with a cold sweat, and her heart was racing, but apart from that she could pride herself on an almost surreal calm. She'd studied hard and well on just what to do if someone ever came after her again. The circumstances hadn't been quite what she'd practiced, but close enough, and she'd definitely managed to hurt the man with the gun. The question was, if he found her, how would he pay her back?

One thing was crystal clear in the claustrophobic confines of the closet. She didn't want to die. And she wasn't going to go without a fight.

"Lost something, Renaud?" The voice came from almost directly outside her hiding place, and the cold feeling in the pit of her stomach turned to ice. She hadn't heard anyone approach, and she'd been listening intently. She didn't recognize the voice either — it was low, cool, expressionless.

"That bitch." Renaud's voice was muffled.

"Got the drop on you, did she? Maybe you should go clean up — you're bleeding all over the deck."

"I've got a score to settle with that little —"

"You don't have any scores to settle, you have a job to do. I'll take care of Ms. Spenser."

"She's got to be a plant."

"Because she managed to get away from you? I doubt it — I think you just underestimated her. Madame Lambert just came through with the best possible intel — she's simply a high-priced lawyer who stumbled into something unpleasant. Too bad for her, but no particular problem for us. Harry was just as likely to have someone with him when the mission went down."

"She's the one who's going down," Renaud snarled.

"You'll do what I tell you to do and nothing more." The voice was cold, cold as ice, and Genevieve could feel the goose bumps form on her arms. She didn't want to meet the owner of that emotionless voice — the cold water of the open sea would be warmer than the man who was dangerously close to her hiding place.

"Whatever you say, boss," Renaud muttered, clearly unhappy.

"After you get cleaned up why don't you go to her room and get rid of her stuff. We don't want any loose ends, do we?"

"What about her?"

"It's a boat, Renaud. There aren't many places to hide in the middle of the water. I'll take care of her when the time comes."

Genevieve held her breath, half expecting an argument, but Renaud had been thoroughly cowed. "Just promise me you'll make it hurt," he said.

"I'll do what I need to do to accomplish the mission, Renaud. No more, no less."

She listened as Renaud's footsteps retreated down the deck, then the belated clatter on the metal staircase. There was no other sound, but then, she hadn't heard the mysterious boss approach. It stood to reason she wouldn't hear him when he left either.

She wasn't about to take any chances. He couldn't stand there forever — if she counted to five hundred in French then she could probably risk opening the door to make a run for it.

Where she would run to was still a question. Over the side seemed the safest possibility, if she could find a life vest and a flare gun. A self-inflating raft would be even better — she could wait until the boat was out of sight before she inflated it. But if worse came to worst she'd simply go over the side as is, taking her chance with the cold water rather than the deadly cold voice of the unseen man. She had no idea whether there were sharks out there. She only knew about the human ones on board.

She counted to five hundred twice, her rusty French slowing her down. She considered trying it in Latin, but it had been too long since her high-school classes with Mrs.

Wiesen, and besides, the chances of anyone still being outside the utility closet were almost nil. If they knew she was there they would have simply opened the door.

She moved her hands blindly over the door, looking for the inside latch. Her eyes should have become accustomed to the darkness, but the door was sealed shut. If she stayed in that airless, lightless hole much longer she'd probably pass out from the chemical fumes.

She made no sound as she ran her hands down the inside of the door, her fingers finally reaching the catch. She breathed a tiny sigh of relief — she'd known a moment's panic that there might be no inside latch. After all, how many people expected to be opening a tiny closet from the inside?

The door opened with an almost inaudible click, and she pushed it open, closing her eyes against the suddenly blinding glare of the midday sun as it bounced off the waters. She squinted, then opened her eyes fully. To look straight into the impassive eyes of a man she'd never seen before.

A million emotions raced through her — instant panic, then hope as her eyes focused on the man leaning against the railing, looking at her. He was tall, dressed in loose white clothing, with long dark hair and very blue eyes, and his expression was nothing more than politely curious. She'd never seen him before in her life.

"I wondered how long you were going to stay in there, Ms. Spenser," he said in a voice that was both Peter Jensen's and a stranger's. "As you heard me tell our bloodthirsty friend Renaud, there aren't that many places to hide on a boat."

She didn't hesitate. Her only chance was taking him by surprise, and she dived for the side of the boat. She was halfway over the railing before he caught her with insultingly minimal effort, pulling her back onto the deck, against him. His body was warm, hard against her back, which somehow seemed wrong, she thought dizzily. He should feel like a block of ice, not a living, breathing human.

"Sorry, Ms. Spenser," he murmured in her ear, a soft, soothing voice. "But we can't have you complicating our very careful plans, now, can we?"

She would have said something if she could. But the stinging sensation at the side of her neck was spreading through her body, and she wondered if this was how she was going to die. If so, she wasn't going to go without a fight. She kicked back against him, but her legs felt like rubber bands as they began to collapse beneath her, and she could hear his faint laugh in her ear.

"Feisty creature, aren't you, Ms. Spenser? Just relax, and it won't hurt a bit."

Her elbow didn't work either, as she tried to jab him in the stomach. Nothing worked at all, and she let herself sink down, knowing that this was the last thing she'd remember before she died. And then she knew nothing at all.

5

Ms. Genevieve Spenser was rapidly becoming a pain in the ass, Peter thought. He ought to finish what she started, toss her unconscious body over the side of the boat and let the fish have her. In the end he doubted it would matter. As long as they found identifiable traces of Harry Van Dorn's body in the rubble of his island home the authorities would be satisfied. They wouldn't go to that much trouble trying to ascertain if his pretty little lawyer was there too.

Unless, of course, they suspected foul play. He highly doubted that — he was an expert at his job, and he seldom made mistakes. Harry Van Dorn had done a magnificent job of convincing the world what a decent, charming, humanitarian fellow he was, and most people outside of a select few would have no idea just how overdue retribution was. It was Peter's job to see to it, and if

Harry's death was supposed to look like an accident then it would. And those were his orders.

He shifted the dead weight in his arms. It would be far easier to dump her over the side than figure out what to do with her. Things had gone too far — the unpalatable fact was that she was going to have to end up dead anyway. Why complicate matters by putting it off?

Having her found on the island would be neater, and when it came to his job he tended to be fastidious. The thought would have astonished his mother. He'd never been the orderly type, and chaos had suited him very well for many years.

But his job required precision, attention to the smallest detail, a cool detachment that nothing could permeate. Ms. Spenser was undoubtedly going to die, whether he liked it or not, but now wasn't the right time.

He could have left her on the deck and had Renaud haul her into the cabin where he could keep an eye on her, but he never delegated work he could do himself. Besides, Renaud had his limitations, and he liked to hurt women. There was nothing he could do about Ms. Spenser's upcoming fate, but there was no reason why she should have to suffer. After all, he was a civilized man, he mocked himself.

He hauled her limp body over his shoulder. She wasn't that bad, not compared to some of the dead weight he'd carried in his thirty-eight years. Odd, but when someone was simply unconscious they weighed less than when they were dead. It made no sense, but it was true.

Or maybe it was the weight of his conscience when he had to dispose of someone. Except that he had no conscience — it had been surgically removed along with his soul years ago.

Still, maybe he retained a trace of sentimentality. Otherwise he wouldn't hesitate with the interfering Ms. Spenser, and he wouldn't feel the random regret about her future or lack thereof. He wasn't used to regret at all.

He dumped her down on the huge bed in the main cabin, next to Harry Van Dorn's unconscious body. She had long, pretty legs, and it was hard to forget the distracting taste of her mouth. He still hadn't figured out why he'd kissed her. An aberration, a momentary indulgence . . . he wouldn't let himself do it again.

He stared down at her for a long moment. He'd killed women before, it was inevitable in his line of work. At times the female of the species could be a lot deadlier than the male. But he'd never been forced to kill someone who'd simply gotten in the way. And he didn't want to start now, no matter how goddamn important it was.

Of course, one could argue that the world would always be a better place with one less lawyer. But looking down at Genevieve Spenser's unconscious, undeniably luscious body, he wasn't completely sure he could make himself believe it.

Genevieve came awake very slowly, letting the strange sensations wash over her. She was conscious of an odd sense of relief, quickly washed away by an unshakeable sense of entrapment. She was lying in a bed next to someone — she could hear his steady breathing, feel the weight of his body next to hers — and her panic increased. The room was shadowed, the only light at the far end, and she blinked, trying to focus, trying to get her brain to work.

She was lying next to Harry Van Dorn, and her immediate reaction was fury. Until she noticed he wasn't sleeping, he was drugged. And her hands, ankles and mouth were wrapped in duct tape.

She struggled to sit up, making a muffled

noise behind her makeshift gag. There was someone at the far end of the cavernous room, reading, but she couldn't see him clearly, and he didn't look up when she struggled to a sitting position, didn't pay attention to the noises she was trying to make.

She reached her bound hands up to try to tear away the gag, but the tape ran around the back of her neck, and her fingers couldn't gain purchase on the slippery stuff. She made another angry sound, and the man in the shadows looked up for a moment, clearly noting that she was awake, and then went back to his book.

It had been a very difficult few days, to put it mildly, and Genevieve had no intention of simply lying back down and being ignored. She swung her legs over to the side of the bed, but it was higher up than she'd thought, and she went sprawling onto the floor.

The hands that pulled her up were strong and impersonal. She'd already figured out who it would be before she saw him, and she glared into Peter Jensen's cool eyes, putting as much emotion and fury into her expression as the duct tape would allow.

His faint smile didn't help her temper. "It must be hell to be a lawyer and not be able to talk," he said mildly. Her ankles were bound so close together that she could barely stand, and it was only with his help that she remained upright. She yanked herself away, and he let her go, not moving as she collapsed at his feet. If her mouth was free she would have bit his ankles, she thought in a red haze of fury, trying to get to her feet again.

He pulled her up once more. "Don't be tiresome, Ms. Spenser," he said. "Behave yourself and this will all be a lot easier on you."

She wasn't in the mood to believe him. For a moment she thought he was going to put her back on the bed, but instead he half dragged her across the room to where he'd been sitting and dropped her down on the small sofa. She reached up and clawed at the gag again, and he made a long-suffering noise. "You won't like it if I take it off," he said. "It's going to hurt."

She kept pulling. So he pushed her bound hands down, into her lap, reached for the duct tape and yanked.

She thought her scream would have filled the cabin and even woken her drugged client, but the only sound that came out was a choked gasp as the duct tape was ripped from her face, taking a few strands of loose hair with it.

He tossed it in her lap. "Sorry," he said, sitting across from her and picking up his book.

"Sorry?" she echoed in a hoarse voice. "Sorry for what? For kidnapping me, for drugging me, for wrapping me in duct tape, you son of a bitch!"

"I have another roll of tape and I'm not afraid to use it," he said lightly. "Behave yourself, Ms. Spenser."

"You think this is *funny?*" Her voice was getting stronger now. "You have a pretty sick sense of humor."

His faint smile wasn't reassuring. "So I've been told. I'll leave the gag off if you sit there and be quiet. I have work to do."

"You're an idiot."

That got his attention, though it failed to ruffle him. In the dim light his eyes looked very dark, almost empty, but she'd managed to catch his attention, and he put the book down. "I am?"

Her brain was going very fast. "I know you didn't expect to have me on board when you carried out your nasty little scheme — you tried hard enough to get rid of me. But now that I'm here, don't you think you ought to make use of me?"

He leaned back against the chair, watching her. "And how would I do that? Are you offering to join our merry band?"

"Don't be ridiculous. Any fool can see what your plan is."

"Enlighten me."

"You've kidnapped one of the world's richest men. Clearly you did it for the money — you don't have the look of a wild-eyed terrorist. Therefore you need to negotiate the terms of the ransom, and I'm your woman."

"Are you, indeed?" he murmured. "And why don't you think I'm a wild-eyed terrorist bent on some bloody political crusade?"

"You dress too well."

He laughed. It seemed to surprise him as much as it surprised her. He sounded as if he didn't laugh very often, which was no surprise. She wouldn't have expected extortionists to be a humorous bunch.

"So whose side are you going to be on, Ms. Spenser? Mine or Harry's?"

"You want money, I want Harry safe. I imagine I can find a solution that will work for both of you. Now, why don't you take the rest of this duct tape off me and we can negotiate. You already know I'm no physical threat to you."

"Oh, I wouldn't say that," he drawled, but he rose anyway, reaching in his pocket and pulling out a small knife. He leaned down to cut through the tape around her ankles, and she brought her bound hands down hard on the top of his head.

Or at least she tried to. He caught her wrists in one hand while he slit the tape at her ankles, not even bothering to look up. He ripped the tape off her ankles and then his cold blue eyes met hers. "It's a waste of time, Ms. Spenser," he said, "and it will only annoy me. It's a boat — there's no place to go but over the side, and I've heard there are sharks in this area."

"I think I'd be safer with them," she muttered. He cut the tape at her wrists, and she realized he was using the Swiss Army knife she'd tucked in her bra. She wasn't going to think about how he'd found it, she was going to concentrate on how his grip on her wrists hurt, and decided if anyone was going to be shark bait it was going to be Peter Jensen.

"Is Jensen really your name?" she asked when he sat down again, closing the knife and tucking it back into his pocket.

"Does it matter? I've used any number of names. Jensen, Davidson, Wilson, Madsen."

"In other words your mother didn't know who your father was."

The moment the words were out of her mouth she could have bit her tongue. She almost picked up the gag that lay in her lap and slapped it back over her mouth. The man sitting across from her was probably only one step removed from a sociopath, and to call his mother a whore was beyond foolish.

His expression gave nothing away. "You're not a very good lawyer, are you, Ms. Spenser? A good lawyer knows when to keep her mouth shut."

She said nothing, and after a moment the tension in the room relaxed slightly. "In fact, I know exactly who my father was, unfortunately. You wouldn't have liked him . . . he had a very bad temper. Would you like some tea?"

She blinked. "What?"

"Would you like some tea? The particular drug I gave you tends to make your mouth feel like cotton, and being gagged doesn't help. Since we're about to enter negotiations, I want to be sure your mouth is in working order." She could positively feel his glance on her lips, and she ran a nervous tongue over them, making her feel even more conspicuous. He *had* kissed her, hadn't he?

"I'd be happier with a drink."

"Not a good idea. On top of the drugs I gave you and your little yellow pills, you might find yourself way too vulnerable. They aren't good for you, you know."

She shouldn't have been surprised that he knew about her tranquilizers — it was just one more violation. "Life is stressful," she said. "And that was before I got kidnapped and molested."

"Don't sound so hopeful. No one's molested you. Yet."

"This isn't funny," she snapped. "If being abducted and drugged isn't being molested I don't know what is."

"Oh. I thought you were referring to something a bit more sexual."

She blushed.

It was the oddest sensation. She wasn't used to blushing, and his drawled comment was casual, not suggestive, and yet she could feel the warmth staining her cheeks. She had pale skin, and she'd just been pumped full of God knows how many drugs, and it must be a reaction, she thought nervously, and he wouldn't even notice . . .

"Ms. Spenser, are you blushing?"

"A lawyer doesn't blush, Mr. Jensen," she said severely. "Now, why don't you tell me what it is you want, and I'm certain we can come to an agreement."

He said nothing. He rose and crossed the room, pushing open a hidden cupboard that exposed a small refrigerator. When he returned he put the icy can of Tab in her hand, and she almost kissed the sweating fuchsia sides. He'd already popped it open, a good thing, because her hands were shaking as she lifted it to her mouth.

"Aren't you going to worry that I'm drugging you again?" He sat back down.

"I don't care," she said, drinking half the can in one gulp, letting the cold liquid slide down her throat. She closed her eyes and let out a blissful sigh. She would have welcomed anything cold and wet, but this was almost enough to make her not want to kill him. Almost.

She opened her eyes again, to see him watching her. "So what do you want?" she asked again.

He hesitated, and he didn't seem like a man who would ever hesitate. "I'm afraid there's nothing you can offer me, Ms. Spenser. I have a job to do."

"And what is that?"

"My orders are to kill Harry Van Dorn," he said, his voice flat. "And anyone else who gets in the way."

She was tough, he had to grant her that. Only the quick blink of her eyes betrayed any kind of reaction to his bald statement.

She believed him, though. She was too smart not to.

"Why?"

"I don't know the particulars, and I prefer it that way. I'm very good at what I do, and part of the reason is that I never ask why. I figure if I'm sent to take care of someone then he must have done something to deserve it."

"Who sends you? Who gave you these orders?" she demanded.

"It wouldn't mean anything if I told you. Believe it or not, we're the good guys."

"The good guys?" she scoffed. "And you're going to kill a harmless dilettante like Harry Van Dorn in cold blood?"

"I assure you he's not quite as harmless as he seems," Peter said.

"And what about me?"

"What about you?"

"You said you were told to kill Harry Van Dorn and anyone who got in the way. Does that include me?"

He should have lied. People were better off if they didn't know they were going to die. They got panicky, did unexpected things and made his job that much harder. "Would you believe me if I told you no?"

She shook her head. "Then trust me, you aren't one of the good guys. I've never done anything remotely worth getting killed over. And I don't particularly want to die."

"Few people do."

"So how am I supposed to change your mind?"

He considered it for a moment, as he'd been considering it for the last several hours. "I don't think you can. For what it's worth, I promise it won't hurt. You won't even know what's happening."

"I don't think so." She set the empty Tab can down beside her and met his gaze quite calmly. "If you're going to murder me you're going to have to work hard to do it, and I have no intention of letting go easily. I'm going to kick and scream and fight all the way."

"It's a losing battle, Ms. Spenser." He was amazed at how calm he sounded. As if silencing unfortunate witnesses and accomplices was a normal part of his duties as one of the best-trained operatives in the Committee. He was the best marksman, brilliant with a knife and in hand-to-hand combat, and he never showed or felt emotion. The Iceman, as always, both in temperament and his specialty in putting unwanted evil on ice.

But Ms. Spenser wasn't evil. This was the first time he'd ever made the mistake of letting someone unwitting get caught in the careful trap he'd set, and he was going to have to live with the consequences. They were in the middle of one of the most complicated operations in his memory — Harry Van Dorn was up to something and all the resources and manpower of the Committee had been unable to uncover anything more than a few hints. Harry was a control freak — this wouldn't go further without him overseeing it. They needed Harry on ice, permanently, with no interference, so they could find out what the hell the Rule of Seven was, and how they could stop it.

He couldn't afford to let her go . . . she had already seen too much, knew too much. She was a smart woman — give her time and she could put together far too much information on the Committee. She'd jeopardize the lives of the men and women who risked everything. It was an equation with only one solution, whether he liked it or not.

"I specialize in losing battles," she said. "I'm not going to die, and neither is Harry. You, I'm not so sure about." She rose, stretching with all the intensity of a lazy cat, and smiled at him with utter sweetness. "In the meantime I think I'll take a shower and change into something more comfortable, and then we can continue our negotiations."

He didn't move. The door to the cabin was locked, and she wouldn't be able to get very far. "We have nothing to negotiate, Ms. Spenser," he reminded her.

"I disagree. There's a great deal of money at stake here, and if you're deluded enough to think Harry's some kind of evil monster, then your information is wrong. I have excellent instincts when it comes to people, and Harry Van Dorn might be a horny, superstitious, spoiled baby, but he's miles removed from anything evil. You wouldn't be killing one innocent bystander, you'd be killing two, and I don't think you want that. Not when the alternative is so much money your mysterious employers would never be able to find you."

"They'd find me," he said. "And everyone on this boat knows the mission. I'm sorry, but even if I wanted to let you go I couldn't. Renaud or one of the others would see to things, and they tend to be a bit more . . . brutal."

He saw the nervous shift in her eyes and felt a pang of something. It couldn't be regret or guilt, he didn't allow himself either of those emotions, no matter what the circumstances.

"If you say so," she said airily. "That doesn't mean I won't try. Tell me, is this door locked or can I come and go as I please?"

"It's locked."

"Then please unlock it," she said, more a demand than a request. "I'd like to go back to my room and change my clothes."

He knew what she was going to try, probably even before she did. It would have worked under normal circumstances, but she had no idea who she was dealing with, and that her body was telegraphing her plans loud and clear.

Best to get it over with, he thought, rising. "I don't think so," he said. And caught her as she tried to jump him, turning her easily, twisting her arm behind her back. A second later she was down on the floor, his knee in the center of her chest, and she was staring up at him with mute shock.

Madame Lambert set her encrypted PDA down on the table beside her untouched glass of wine. She prided herself on being able to make the hard decisions and do them in public — she was enjoying a solitary dinner at a quiet little restaurant not far from the office, and she had no trouble sending and receiving the information she needed.

No, she wasn't enjoying her solitary meal, she amended, picking up the glass of very fine wine and taking a sip. Right now she wasn't enjoying much of anything. She had just sent orders to Peter Jensen that he would have to kill the young woman who'd gotten in the way. And it made her sick inside.

Peter would do it, of course, no questions asked. And he'd do it in as humane a fashion as possible. But each death, no matter how justified, left a psychic wound that never healed over. The death of an innocent would be far worse. She'd known Peter too long to be happy about that.

But they were running out of time, and Harry Van Dorn would never give up a thing, no matter what they did to him. The only chance of derailing things was for him to die.

That was the problem with sociopaths like Harry, Isobel Lambert thought, taking another sip of wine. Torture was useless when the victim enjoyed pain, and even someone with Peter's expertise wouldn't be able to break him. Besides, once again there was the price to be paid for committing such acts. A clean execution was one thing.

Torture was another, and there was a limit to what the human psyche could take. She was afraid Peter Jensen was reaching his limit.

Killing the girl might put him over the top. But she had no choice.

And neither did he.

6

Genevieve couldn't catch her breath. Even on that padded, carpeted floor, he'd thrown her so hard the wind had been knocked from her, and his knee on her chest didn't help. She gasped, and then the air came back, and with it her anger.

She moved fast enough, catching his ankle and attempting to dislodge him, but he was stronger, harder than anyone she'd ever practiced with. And this wasn't practice.

He reached down, pulled her hands away and yanked her upright. He was uncomfortably taller than she was when her feet were bare, but she didn't hesitate, bringing her knee up, hard.

She didn't connect — he'd already spun her around, her arms behind her back and her face up against the wall. "You've got moves," he murmured in her ear, "but they're pretty damn pathetic. Never try to knee someone in the balls if there's any chance you won't get away. It pisses the hell out of men and they tend to get danger-ously grumpy."

She said nothing, feverishly thinking where she could try next. Behind the knee was always vulnerable, and there were vari-ous blows that she'd been warned could be lethal, blows she shouldn't hesitate trying.

And then he stepped back and she was no longer plastered against the paneled wall. He still had her wrists captive, but she wondered if she could kick backward again.

"I wouldn't try it if I were you," he said in his low, amused voice. "You telegraph every move ahead of time, and it takes no effort at all to stop you. And I warned you to stop aiming for my testicles. It annoys me."

Somehow he managed to spin her around so that she was facing him, her wrists still held tightly in one of his strong hands. She hadn't even realized he'd let go of them for a moment — she was doing a pretty pathetic job of trying to protect herself after being Master Tenchi's prize student. "I managed to hurt your friend," she said defiantly.

"So you did. But Renaud's a fool, and he underestimated you. I'm afraid he's the type to hold a grudge. I don't intend to give him a chance to pay you back, but if you annoy me enough I might change my mind."

She wanted to say something cutting, but in fact she preferred Peter Jensen to Renaud's unimaginative brutality, even if she stood a marginally better chance of getting away from the Frenchman.

Jensen wasn't even breathing hard. The eyes that she'd thought colorless were actually a very clear blue, which reminded her . . .

"Have you got any contact-lens solution?"

He stared at her, momentarily astounded. If she couldn't take him off balance with her amateur self-defense training she could at least sideswipe him with her words.

"I beg your pardon?"

"You must have been wearing tinted contacts before, which means you must have some wetting solution somewhere on this boat, and I need it. I've had my contacts in for almost forty-eight hours and they're killing me. I should have taken them out when I still had my purse, but I was more interested in getting out of here."

He didn't stay off balance for long. "Be honest, Ms. Spenser. You were more interested in your little pills," he said. "The stuff is in the head. And don't bother looking for a weapon, there's nothing in there you could use, and the window's too small for you to climb through."

111

"Is that another crack about my weight?"

His small grin was reluctant. "It's a port-hole, Ms. Spenser. No one could get through it. Why are women so ridiculous about their weight, anyway? Ten or fifteen extra pounds don't make any difference. Except when I'm having to haul your unconscious body around."

He was still holding her wrists, or she would have hit him. Of course he knew exactly how much extra weight she was carrying, as well as what size clothes she really wore. "You know the answer to that, don't you?" she said with false sweetness. "Stop knocking me out."

"Then behave yourself." He released her, and for a moment she didn't move. They stood there for a long moment. He was probably watching to see what her next move would be, but since he'd already made it clear he'd counter it before she'd even tried, she gave up. For now.

"You want to move out of the way?" she asked. "Or am I supposed to go through you?"

He stepped back, out of her way but close enough to grab her again. It was an intensely uncomfortable feeling, being trapped with someone who could guess her every move. She stalked past him, though that was hard to manage in bare feet, and slammed the bathroom door behind her.

He was right, there was nothing the slightest bit lethal in there. She ran some cold water on her face, then stuck her tongue out at her reflection. Her hair was tangled down her back, and she braided it, tying the end with dental floss, before she took her contacts out. She had no idea where her purse was, and she realized her head was aching and her hands were shaking.

She opened the bathroom door and stuck her head out. He was back where she first saw him, reading once more, as if finishing his book was the only thing that mattered. It probably was — he was the one who was completely in control of the situation.

"Hey," she said. "I need my purse. I need my glasses and my pills."

"No pills," he said. "But I'll see if Hans can find your glasses. In the meantime there's a pile of clothes on the table — find something that fits you. Armani doesn't really work for being a hostage at sea."

Naturally he knew it was Armani, the son of a bitch. She scooped up the clothes and went back into the bathroom, reaching for the lock. It didn't work, of course. She bit back a snarl as she stripped off her ruined suit. She didn't even want to think about how much it had cost her. She had more important things on her mind than the loss of her wardrobe.

She pulled on a baggy pair of khakis and a loose white T-shirt. The pants hung down around her hips, and even with her long legs they were trailing on the floor, so she rolled them up several times. She didn't bother looking at her reflection in the mirror — her eyesight was problematic without the contacts or the glasses and besides, what she looked like was of no importance in the current scheme of things. She opened the door and nearly tripped over the hem of the pants as one leg came untucked.

He looked up, but she couldn't read the expression on his face. Not that her glasses would have made any difference — he was an expert at shielding his reactions. "Your pants are too long," he said.

"News flash — I'm not as tall as Harry," she said. She sat down on the sofa where he'd initially dumped her; she hadn't given up on the notion of trying to disable him and making another run for it, but she couldn't do it if she couldn't see.

"Here," he said, tossing something at her. "Cut them off."

She caught it, by sheer luck, realizing with astonishment that he'd given her the Swiss

Army knife. She looked up at him, but it didn't need twenty-twenty to see his cool smile. "If you managed to hurt me with that little thing I'd deserve it," he said.

"You do deserve it," she muttered, leaning over and beginning to saw away at the heavy khaki at her ankle.

"I'd cut them higher if I were you. You'll have a better chance of landing a successful kick if your legs are bare. You'll be able to run faster, too."

It made sense, though why she should accept his help was a mystery. As well as why he should offer it.

She stabbed the short blade of the knife through the khaki halfway up her thigh, sawing and ripping, then followed suit with the other side. The legs were uneven, and she took another couple of inches off the first one, only to look up and find Peter watching her with great interest. She waited, expecting him to make some kind of insulting joke, but he merely nodded and returned to his book.

She folded up the knife and tucked it in her pocket, waiting to see if he remembered he'd given it to her and demand it back. "I want my tranquilizers," she said again.

" 'Fraid I can't help you there. Hans has never met a drug he didn't like, and he's already taken them."

"All of them? It would kill him!"

"Not Hans. Anyway, those pills of yours are pretty pathetic. Just mother's little helpers designed to get high-strung females through the day."

"I'm not particularly high-strung," she said. "And even you have to admit being kidnapped is stressful."

He glanced at her. "You'll survive."

"Will I? Survive, that is? I thought I was toast."

He hesitated, frowning. "I don't like collateral damage. It's inevitable if you don't do your job well, but I tend to do my job very well indeed."

"So if you're as good as you say, I won't have to die?" she asked brightly.

He didn't answer, which was somehow not encouraging. The silence lasted for a long, uncomfortable moment, and then he looked up again. "Better not let the others know you have the knife," he said calmly, dispelling her hope that he hadn't noticed. "I don't think you'd manage to do much harm with it, but you can never underestimate the element of surprise. If you hadn't made it so clear you were going to try to fight, you might have stood a better chance against me."

"You mean I could have escaped?" she demanded.

"No. I mean it wouldn't have been as insultingly easy for me to stop you. Next time, don't go for the obvious target. Even better, look at a part you're not planning on touching. If you're going to go for a man's eyes, look at his groin. If you're going to try a chop across the front of the throat then act like you're going to kick. That's one of your best targets, by the way. Landed properly, it can crush a larynx and a man can suffocate in his own blood."

"That's gross," she said automatically.

His smile was totally devoid of humor. "Death tends to be gross, Ms. Spenser. It's not neat, Hollywood-style fadeaways. It's a messy, smelly business."

"Is it? A business, I mean?"

"Sometimes."

"For you?"

"Sometimes."

He wasn't reassuring. Not that she expected him to be. "So what else?"

"I beg your pardon?"

"So polite," she murmured. "What else should I do to defend myself? Besides the chop across the neck? Maybe I just want to incapacitate someone, not make them drown in their own blood. Some of us are a bit more squeamish than others."

"Don't bother trying to sweep him with your leg. It's too common a trick, and you're not fast enough or practiced enough to get away with it. If you have a sharp object, like the pocketknife, a pencil or even a set of keys, jab them in the eyes. And don't say 'gross' again. If they can't see you they'll have a harder chance of getting you."

She didn't bother to point out that the likelihood of her having keys wasn't good if things were going to continue the way they had. "Okay," she said. "I'm still looking for something to stop them, not maim them for life."

He put his book down and looked at her for a long, thoughtful moment. "Stand up," he said. He rose, standing over her. "Come on."

She had mixed feelings about it. She didn't like him looming over her, but she wasn't too eager to stand and be that close either. She should never have even brought up the subject.

But if she didn't stand he'd pull her up — she already knew that much, so she rose, and he was close, much too close. "Turn around," he said.

That was the last thing she wanted to do. "I don't intend to turn my back on any of you if I can help it."

"You won't have a choice." He put his hard hands on her shoulders and spun her around so that she was facing the wall. She could see Harry's body on the bed, drugged and unmoving, and she wondered if he was already dead. And what in the world the poor man could have done that someone thought would merit being murdered.

A moment later she was facedown on the floor, with him down beside her, his knee in the center of her back. "Would you get off me?" she said after a moment, though her voice was muffled by the carpet.

He released her, and she rolled over on her side, away from him. He was squatting beside her, completely unruffled. "You can't afford to get distracted, worry about things that are out of your control, like Harry over there. You won't stand a chance against Renaud or Hans or any of the others."

She'd given up resenting that he always seemed to read her mind, and concentrated on what mattered. "There are others?"

"Of course there are others. An operation this complex is hardly a small-time affair."

"You must be very well funded."

"We are. And I'm not about to enlighten you on the details. I'm just trying to teach you a few tricks that might help you if Hans or Renaud decide to have a little fun with you. If you come up against one of the others then you're shit out of luck."

"I don't think my luck's been running so hot lately anyway," she said.

"You're still alive, aren't you? That in itself is a surprising piece of luck. And you probably won't have to worry about Hans — he doesn't have much use for women in the first place."

"Wouldn't that make him more likely to kill me?"

He reached out his hand and she had no choice but to let him pull her to her feet. "I doubt he would care enough to bother. You're pretty small potatoes in his scale of things."

"And what about you?" He was still holding on to her arm, the one he'd twisted behind her back, and he was absently stroking it with his thumb, just where it was most painful. She wondered whether he even knew he was doing it, and she pulled away from him, glaring at him.

"You're going to have a bruise there," he said.

"What do you want to do, kiss it and make it better?"

Silence between them. It was like another presence in the room, more intrusive than

Harry's comatose body, and for a moment she was afraid to meet his eyes. But she did anyway, though his reaction was unreadable.

It was like Pandora's box — now that the word was out there was no turning back. And it would have been a waste of time pretending — he seemed to have a wicked ability to know what she was thinking.

"You kissed me," she said abruptly. "Last night."

There was no change in his grave expression, but she was certain he was finding her amusing. The thought was infuriating. "Yes," he said. "I did."

"Why?"

"Because it was the easiest way to get close enough to render you unconscious," he said. "Shall I demonstrate?"

"No!" she shrieked, trying to back away.

He did smile then. "I didn't mean the kiss part. I mean this." Before she knew what he was doing, he'd put his hand on her neck, cool against her heated skin. He'd feel her pulse pounding, but there was no way she could disguise that fact. He was probably used to it.

"Hold still," he said as she tried to squirm away. His long fingers were caressing the nape of her neck, his thumb dancing across her throat.

"Let go of me."

"Just press your thumb against this spot." He demonstrated, and she started to black out for a moment, before he released her. "And then you don't have to worry about someone drowning in their own blood. But you have to get it just right. That's why I kissed you. It shocked you into standing still long enough for me to do it."

"And what if you're trying to knock out another man," she said, sarcastic.

There was no expression in his cool blue eyes. "Then I kiss him," he said in the calmest of voices. "Now you try it."

"I don't think so . . ." she said, trying to back away.

"I mean the move, not the kiss," he said, grabbing her hand and slapping it against his neck. "Don't be so skittish. See if you can find the right spot."

She didn't want to be touching him. His skin was cool, silky beneath her hand, and she could feel the calmer beat of his pulse, counterpoint to her own racing heart. She pressed hard with her thumb, anything to let him release her, but he shook his head, pulling her closer.

"You need to slide your hand around the back of my neck. Like a lover." His voice was soft, seductive. His hand covered hers, almost a caress, as he moved her thumb to a soft spot on the side of his throat. "You press here, but it has to be strong and steady. Which is why it works better if you're kissing someone. They're too distracted to notice what you're doing until it's too late."

"I'm not kissing you," she said sharply. Wondering if she had a chance in hell of knocking him out, and whether that was even a good idea given the other people on this boat. "That's the last thing I want."

"Now that's not true," he whispered, much too close. "But if you're happier believing that then I won't call your bluff." His hand was still covering hers, the long fingers caressing hers. And then he stepped back, and she felt deflated, limp. Lost.

"Turn your back on me."

"Not again," she protested. "We already know you can have me on the floor in a matter of seconds."

"Yes, I can. But you need to learn how to keep Renaud or Hans from doing the same thing. Because they're not likely to let you up again, and both of them are probably going to try to take you from behind. Neither has much of a sporting instinct."

"This isn't a sport!" she snapped.

"Maybe not to you. But it is to them. Turn

around, but don't think about poor old Harry lying there on the bed. Think about what's around you, what's dangerous. See if you can feel me moving in on you . . ." His voice came to an abrupt halt as she slammed her elbow into his stomach with all her strength.

He had a hard stomach — she'd probably get tendonitis from that blow. If she lived long enough. She turned to look up at him, wondering if he was going to hit her back, but he simply looked bemused. "That was better," he said.

"That's because you were distracted," she said in a smug voice. "Let's try it again —"

Back on the floor, this time on her back, with him straddling her effortlessly, holding her in place. "Don't get cocky when you score an inadvertent hit. It just makes the opponent more alert."

She looked up at him. She was having trouble catching her breath, but this time it wasn't from the force of hitting the ground. She told herself it was panic, the unpleasant sense of being trapped by someone bigger, stronger than she was. It was logical, but only partly true.

"Get off me," she said, glaring at him. "Get off me or the next time I'm anywhere near a pencil or a set of keys you're going to be blind as a bat."

That slow smile should have infuriated her. "Really?" he said. He leaned down, and the black hair that had been so carefully combed back when he was the gray ghost fell around his face, almost obscuring his expression. "I was getting the feeling you liked this. Just a little bit."

"I don't," she said, but her voice was soft, breathless, as he came closer. Maybe he was going to kiss her again, and maybe this time she could use it to her advantage, knock him off balance, slam him across the throat. Or maybe she could just lie back and let him kiss her.

His mouth hovered just over hers. "What are you thinking?" he whispered.

"I thought you could read my mind."

"Not when it really counts," he said, and he let his mouth touch hers for just a brief second. And then to her shock he rolled off her, scrambling to his feet without a backward glance, leaving her lying on the floor feeling exposed and vulnerable.

He went to the door but didn't unlock it. "What do you want, Renaud?"

She hadn't even heard him knock. She sat up, feeling bruised and foolish, but Peter didn't even glance her way.

"The launch is ready. What about the girl?

Do we take her with us or get rid of her now?"

He turned to look at her in the shadowy room, and there was no reading the expression on his face. Even if she'd had her glasses on, she doubted it would have helped. "We'll take her with us," he said.

"Makes more sense to finish her off here. Just give me ten minutes with her and I'll take care of things."

"I know how you hate to rush things," Peter drawled. "I think you can safely leave her to me. I'll do what needs to be done when the time comes."

"Whatever you say, boss." Renaud didn't sound pleased, and a stray shiver ran down Genevieve's back, remembering the small, cruel eyes. Anything would be better than Renaud.

By the time Peter moved away from the door, she'd gotten to her feet. "The launch?" she said. "Where are we going?"

"We've reached our destination. Didn't you notice we haven't been moving?"

So that explained her initial feeling of well-being when she woke up. No wonder she hadn't felt the same claustrophobic panic. "I've been distracted," she said. "Where are we?"

"Little Fox Island. Harry's private escape

from all his onerous duties as a billionaire. It's as good a place as any."

"As good a place as any for what?"

"For Harry Van Dorn to die, Ms. Spenser. I'm afraid poor old Harry's time has run out."

"And mine? Has my time run out as well?"

He didn't answer. Which was the worst answer of all.

He couldn't move. Whatever they'd used on him was damn strong; he was so doped up he couldn't even open his eyes, he could just lie on his own bed, zoned out, listening.

It wasn't a bad way to spend his time, Harry thought. He had an infinite appetite for any sort of drug, and he was enjoying the rush, perfectly at peace for the time being. Sooner or later he'd have to make an effort, find someone he could turn, but in the meantime he could just lie there and listen to the rat-bastard Jensen mess around with *his* girlfriend.

The term amused him. He liked to think of all his sexual partners, willing and unwilling, male and female, child and adult, as girlfriends. Genevieve Spenser wouldn't know what hit her.

She'd have to be disciplined, of course. She was trapped in a room with him and all she could see was Jensen. She should have been busy begging for his life, not wrestling with his enemy.

But there'd be time enough to deal with that once he bought himself an ally. They had some kind of complicated plan — he could sense that much though he was so stoned he couldn't bring himself to care. There was a reason they hadn't killed him yet, and whatever that reason was, he knew the truth.

He wasn't meant to die. He was too powerful, and his vision was too strong. The Rule of Seven was about to come into being, and no force on this earth would stop it, or him, no matter how dire things were looking.

It was all so simple, so beautiful. Seven disasters, one following the other, that would send the world into a financial uproar, the kind of chaos only a prepared man could take advantage of.

And it was so well planned that he doubted even the people who'd kidnapped him had any idea what it involved, the scope of his genius, because he'd been very careful to keep each aspect self-contained. He could buy the best, most ruthless help, and he had seven of them overseeing each of his little projects. Wipe out one, and there were still six others.

They wouldn't move until he gave the word. He doubted if any of his hired help knew he'd chosen April twentieth as the perfect date — Adolf Hitler's birthday, with the anniversaries of major American disasters such as Columbine, Waco, Oklahoma City surrounding it. They were good soldiers but they lacked imagination.

On the other hand, Peter Jensen had fooled him, something that Harry Van Dorn wasn't about to forgive. And he'd known enough to choose April twentieth as his cover's birthday. Which meant his enemies knew his timeline.

Well, he'd always liked a challenge, and even in his current situation, lying drugged and immovable on his own bed, he could already see his eventual triumph. There was no possible alternative.

He was going to see to Jensen himself, kill him slowly, gut him and watch him bleed to death. Maybe have his lawyer watch as well, since she seemed far too distracted by him.

He'd have time to enjoy himself with her before it all came together. Maybe he'd even keep her around for a while — it was easy enough to make a woman docile.

He should have known that a man born on Hitler's birthday was going to be trouble.

The coincidence had been too tempting, but it had been Harry's one mistake.

One that could easily be righted. As soon as he found someone to turn.

7

Little Fox Island could have been designed just to his specifications, Peter thought a few hours later. The main villa was on a hill on the east side of the island, with a long, sloping path leading down to a pristine beach. The island was well out of the way of the normal shipping lanes, with a dangerous riptide that discouraged all but the most foolish of tourists, and the treacherous water took care of the rest. There were sharks as well — Peter didn't know for certain but he expected Harry had had them brought in. As far as he knew, no one had managed to train sharks, but with Harry's limitless resources he'd doubtless found a way to keep them nearby to ward off unwanted visitors. It would put a damper on swimming in the ocean, but Harry had both a traditional pool and a seawater tidal pool to make up for it. And it would keep interference at a minimum.

Renaud and Hans had lugged Harry's unconscious body to the small shed by the dock and tied him up there. Not that it was necessary — the dose had been perfectly calibrated to keep Harry semicomatose until the time came. He wondered whether Harry deserved the kind of death he was about to get. He'd never know what hit him. Was it too harsh a punishment for his sins? Or was he, just maybe, getting off too lightly?

It didn't matter. He didn't waste his time second-guessing — as far as he knew no innocent person had ever been brought down by careless intel, at least by the Committee. The jobs were well researched, justified, and necessary for the greater good. Even if the details of this current mission were maddeningly vague, there was still no doubt about the catastrophic danger. The longer he stayed with Harry Van Dorn the more he'd discovered about the man's rampant evil, and he suspected he'd only seen the tip of the iceberg.

He just wasn't so sure of Ms. Genevieve Spenser.

She'd come with him docilely enough. He hadn't bothered to tie her up or blindfold her — in the end it wouldn't matter. Little Fox Island, or the greater portion of it, would be gone in an explosion — a faulty gas connection, they'd rule it. Unless he could figure out a way to get her out of there, she'd be gone as well.

She looked a little too damn good in the cutoffs. She thought she was wearing Harry's clothes, and it gave him a wry kind of pleasure to know they were actually his. She wouldn't like it. She was convinced that poor old Harry was the victim of terrorists, and she was going to keep fighting to save him. Which made her more than a pain in the ass, it made her a liability. He could tell her the truth, but keeping information on a need-to-know basis was instinctive. It didn't matter whether she thought Harry was a good guy or a bad one. The results would be the same.

They'd gotten rid of the maintenance staff a couple of days ago, and there was a damp, abandoned air to the million-dollar villa. Unavoidable, he supposed. He'd been there before, during his tenure as Harry's flawless personal assistant, and he knew everything he needed to know about the place. He hadn't taken his current companion into his calculations, but he was professional enough to be able to adjust to changing circumstances.

He'd been holding on to her arm. She didn't like it, and it wasn't necessary. If she tried to run she wouldn't get far, but for some reason he didn't want to risk Renaud or Hans catching up with her, so he'd held on. He waited until they stood alone in the middle of Harry's massive living room before releasing her, and he watched with amusement as she did exactly what he expected of her, yanking her arm away and taking several steps out of his reach. If she continued to be that predictable she'd be very little trouble at all.

"You can take the bedroom at the end of the hall," he said, nodding his head in that direction. "You might even find some new clothes, though I doubt it. Harry's guests were usually anorexic models wearing Victoria's Secret. Not that you wouldn't be delicious in sexy underwear, but I don't think that's what you have in mind right now."

"You're not going to lock me in?" she asked, clearly astonished.

He shrugged. "There's no place to run to. The yacht is already gone."

"Then how are you going to leave?"

"They'll be back, though the SS *Seven Sins* will be looking like an entirely new boat. In the meantime there's not much you can do, and I'd suggest you steer clear of Hans and Renaud. They're not nearly as charming as I am."

She made a low, growling noise at the back of her throat, but he kept his face impassive. It was no wonder he wanted to kiss her again. How many women growled at him?

"I'm hungry," she said.

"There's a kitchen. Find it."

"What about the servants? Harry must have kept a skeleton staff out here."

He could see the way her mind was working. She was looking for an ally, but in this case she was shit out of luck. "Long gone," he said. "I've seen to it we're on our own."

Genevieve looked shaken. She probably thought he'd cut their throats and fed them to the sharks, when in fact they were enjoying an unexpected holiday at their employer's expense several hundred miles away. It wouldn't be the first time they'd been sent away — there were some things Harry enjoyed that were better off without even well-paid witnesses.

Genevieve was still standing in the middle of the room, staring at him. "Aren't you hungry?" she asked.

He gave her his most charming smile, the one that his ex-wife had told him made her want to kill him. "Just a beer and a sandwich," he said.

She threw a vase at him. He'd known it was coming, of course, because he'd been goading her to it. She had no idea of the cost of the particular vase, which was probably a good thing. He ducked, of course, and it smashed into a thousand pieces on the tile floor, seventy-three hundred dollars' worth of antique French ceramic ware.

"You need more work on stealth," he observed, opening the sliding doors to the cool tropical breezes. Harry had always kept the place air-conditioned, but the house had been well designed, and the trade winds cooled the place perfectly without the artificial air.

She didn't throw anything else at him, though he was prepared. "You know what you can do with your beer and sandwich," she said in a conversational tone. "Are you going to just let me wander around this place, unwatched? Aren't you going to tie me up?"

"Only if you really want me to. You didn't strike me as that kinky, but I'm game if you are."

There were no more vases within her reach. "What's to keep me from escaping?"

He dropped down on the couch, kicked off his shoes and put his feet up on the coffee table, stretching. "Number one, Renaud and Hans are wandering about, and while I told them to keep their hands off you they're not very good at following orders. Number two, there's nowhere to go — the yacht has gone, we're hundreds of miles from the nearest island. And number three, there are sharks in the water surrounding the island. I think mines as well, though I'm not sure."

"You're kidding!" But she knew he wasn't. "So what am I supposed to do, wait until you're ready to kill me?"

"Or try to think of some way to escape," he suggested.

"You could help me."

"I could," he said, "but I won't." He wondered whether that was true. He'd never had to kill someone who just happened to get in the way. An argument could be made that Genevieve Spenser was far from guiltless, but since he didn't know specifically why the word had come down about Harry, he could hardly know if Genevieve was equally culpable.

Was she part of the Rule of Seven, whatever the hell that was? She'd brought the papers signing over the lucrative oil fields to an untraceable dummy corporation, and the Committee had already ascertained that those very oil fields were the target of a carefully planned attack in the upcoming weeks, though the actual date was unclear.

Harry's disappearance was going to put a stop to that, or at least he hoped so. Van Dorn was a control freak — if anyone was negotiating with terrorists he'd be the man, and he'd be the one holding the purse strings. Maybe the men he'd chosen for the job of destroying the oil fields were ready to die for the glory of Allah. Van Dorn knew how to exploit weakness or fanaticism. They could still need money to cover expenses and they'd want their wives and families taken care of. Without Harry's financial security there was a good chance the attack would be aborted.

But that wasn't the only thing Harry had planned. They knew that there were seven targets. They'd only identified two. They were taking it on faith that disposing of Harry would stop the other five attempts before they could come to fruition.

It all depended on how carefully Harry planned and whether he was willing to delegate, and since he and others had been in Harry's employ, watching him, there'd been little chance for him to use anyone else to implement his Rule of Seven. They'd already agreed it was useless trying to get information out of him — Harry liked pain too much to respond to torture and he kept clear of technology. No cell phone, PDA, or computer to hack into — he kept his own secrets.

Ms. Genevieve Spenser was a different matter. If she knew anything at all she'd break quite easily, and if he were thinking with his usual icy detachment he wouldn't hesitate.

But he wasn't going to touch her. He'd kill her if he had to, but he hadn't given up hoping he'd find a way out, despite the recent orders that had been handed down by Madame Lambert. Easy enough for her to decide, when she wasn't on the scene, he thought.

His priorities may have gotten a little skewed, but his instincts were still solid, and he knew Genevieve had been nothing more than an innocent courier, someone who happened to get in the way of something a lot bigger and badder than she could even begin to realize.

She was still looking at him hopefully. He considered lying to her, telling her he'd get her out safely. He'd never disobeyed a direct order in all the time he'd been with the Committee, and he wasn't about to start, but she didn't need to spend the last two days of her life being terrified.

But he didn't want to lie to her. "I can't help you," he said. "Don't waste your time on me — it won't get you anywhere. I've been playing this game a lot longer than you have, and I've seen every angle. It's going to be up to you. Just don't make stupid mistakes."

If it were up to her she'd die. There was only so much he could teach her, tell her, to give her a fighting chance. In the end it wouldn't be enough, and he knew it. But he didn't have to like it.

He would have preferred it if she'd gone looking for another priceless vase to throw. Instead, she stood very still, looking at him out of her warm brown eyes. She could probably see him clearly enough — he'd checked her glasses before he'd tossed them, and her prescription wasn't that strong. She could see him well enough to know what a worthless piece of shit he actually was, and for the first time he could see defeat in the narrow shoulders beneath his white T-shirt.

But only for a moment. She shrugged, clearly dismissing him. "Where did you say the kitchen was?" she asked in a calm voice.

He wondered whether she was going to try to take some of the kitchen knives. It wouldn't do her any more good than that tiny pocketknife — she was up against professionals. "Down the hallway to the left." He had enough sense not to renew his request for lunch. It had been mainly to goad her, keep her off balance. He was hungry; once Harry was subdued Hans hadn't felt obliged to exercise his culinary talents, and Peter hadn't eaten much at all. He tended to prefer it that way before a job — it kept him sharp. But it was going to be two more days until the job was finished, and he could hardly fast until then.

Genevieve had disappeared without a word, and he leaned back and closed his eyes. He wondered whether he needed to warn the men to keep away from her. He'd already made that abundantly clear, but he hadn't worked much with either Renaud or Hans and he wasn't entirely sure how good they were at following directions. They were only one step up from hired thugs — they weren't hobbled by any illusions that they were working for the greater good. Even he was beginning to doubt it.

Genevieve wouldn't be fool enough to try to leave the house and stray into their path. Not yet. She'd build up to it, and in the meantime he'd do everything he could to make sure she'd get through the last two days of her life unmolested.

He heard her coming back a few moments later, but he didn't bother to open his eyes. He expected her to stalk down the hallway to the room he'd assigned her, but instead he could feel her approaching him, and the trade wind brought the scent of her with it, something soft and flowery and female. He opened his eyes when she drew close, half expecting to see her brandishing a heavy knife. But no, the knife was hidden beneath the loose white T-shirt, and she was carrying a tray with a sandwich and a beer.

She set it down beside him. "You're kidding," he said, blinking.

"Any good terrorist needs to keep his strength up," she said. "Besides, I haven't given up hope of negotiating Harry's freedom."

"And your own besides?"

"Of course. In the meantime you just have to worry about whether I poisoned you."

And with that she disappeared down the hallway with her long, gorgeous legs and the lethal knife hidden underneath her clothes, and if she were ten years younger he was certain she would have stuck out her tongue at him.

Genevieve did a thorough canvass of the room, ignoring the pale, muted colors, the exquisite Renoir on the wall that might have been real, the bronze figure of a ballet dancer that might have been Degas, the sliding doors with the soft Caribbean breeze blowing through, and concentrated on what was important.

The sliding doors led to a small balcony overlooking a rocky part of the coast; if she managed to make it safely down from the balcony she'd likely break her neck on the rocks. If she survived that, there were sharks, currents and a couple of roving psychopaths. No wonder he hadn't bothered to lock her in.

She pulled the knife from beneath her shirt and tucked it between the mattress and box spring of the king-size bed that would have dwarfed any normal-size room. In this Texas-scale mansion it fit right in. At least Jensen had no idea she'd taken it — he might think she was harmless with a Swiss Army knife but he'd think twice about a lethal carving knife like this one. It was very sharp — she'd cut her finger on it when she went rummaging through the kitchen. It was as if her blood had chosen that one. She'd tucked it underneath the shirt and then went rummaging through the obscenely well-stocked refrigerator. If she was going to die, at least she was going to die well fed, she thought. And she'd never have to worry about those fifteen extra pounds again.

It was midafternoon — she could tell that much by the position of the sun — and she wondered what in hell she was going to do. The huge sandwich she'd wolfed down in the kitchen wasn't sitting very well, and in the tropical paradise everything suddenly felt rank and rotting.

She wasn't going to let her discomfort get to her — she was getting out of here in one piece, and she was taking Harry Van Dorn with her. She hadn't had much of a chance to do anything worthwhile since she'd abandoned her principles and sold her soul to Roper, Hyde, Camui and Fredericks. Maybe it was time to give something back. Harry Van Dorn wasn't going to be exterminated like some oversize tropical cockroach, on the say-so of some mysterious vigilante group. He was getting out of this alive. They both were.

She just had to figure out how.

It was getting close to midnight in London, but Isobel Lambert's day was far from over. She stared at the transmission in disbelief. Peter Jensen, the perfect operative, the Iceman in so many ways, was balking at an order. Questioning a decree from London. It was unheard of. Unimaginable.

It was healthy.

She'd been worried about him. He'd been instrumental in Bastien's desertion of their ranks, and he had to have wondered whether that was the answer for him. Bastien had been weak enough to fall in love — she sincerely doubted that Peter Jensen was even capable of such a liability.

Which worked in her favor — she couldn't afford to lose him right now, when so many lives were hanging in the balance.

But even well-oiled machines could break down, and robots could go haywire, and whether Peter wanted to believe it or not, he had a conscience, albeit one buried so deep it would be hard to find.

It seemed to be surfacing at an unfortunate moment, but Madame Lambert held the firm belief that there were no mistakes. If Peter was having doubts about his orders then he was probably right to question them.

And there was nothing she could do from five thousand miles away but trust him.

8

To her amazement Genevieve had fallen asleep. When she woke, the sun was lower on the horizon and she couldn't remember where she was.

Until she heard that infuriating voice from the doorway. "I thought you'd be busy planning your escape, not taking a nap."

She'd locked her door. She should have known it would be a futile gesture — she could barely summon up a trace of outrage. She'd fallen asleep in one of the chairs, and now she kept her gaze trained on the shimmering blue waters ahead of her, refusing to give him any attention. The house had been built on a knoll, and the view was gorgeous. Including the tactfully camouflaged stone wall and the shark-infested waters just beyond.

"I don't suppose you'd consider knocking," she said in a deceptively mild voice. "I realize it's too much to ask you to let me lock the door, but a moment of warning would be considerate."

He came into the room. He'd showered and changed and she could have kicked herself. For a short period of time he'd been relatively inattentive, and she could have made a run for it. Instead, she'd fallen asleep.

"It's a good thing you didn't try," he said. He'd read her mind again. Was she really that transparent? No, she was a decent enough poker player when called upon. Any lawyer had to be able to bluff.

Peter Jensen was just particularly good at sensing people's reactions, or he knew her better than she knew herself. She was much happier believing it was an innate talent, and not something personal.

"Why not?" She turned to give him her full attention. "Do you expect me to just roll over and play dead?"

A shame the mind reading didn't go both ways. His face was completely impassive — the notion of death hung in the air with neither of them wanting to claim it.

"The house has an experimental security system," he said after a moment. "If you try to open one of the doors or windows you'll get an electric shock. Quite a severe one, I'm afraid, and I don't think there's anyone left on the island trained in CPR."

"What about you?" Her voice was caustic. "I thought you could do anything."

"Not my area of expertise," he said. "I take lives, not save them."

There was nothing she could say to that flat statement. "So we just sit here and wait for you to demonstrate your area of expertise?" she asked.

"The security system keeps the others out as well. Count your blessings."

"Oh, I'm absolutely showered with them."

There was a faint light of amusement in his eyes. "I do like you better when you fight back," he said.

"My purpose in life is not to make you like me," she said. "Unless it means you'll let me leave. And take Harry with me."

"I'm afraid I can't let you do that."

"I don't believe that. I expect you can do anything you want."

"I'm charmed by your high opinion of me," he said. "But the fact remains that I have a job to do and I'm going to see that it's done. It's a matter of professional pride."

"Then why are we talking?" she snapped.

"The house is booby-trapped — you try to leave, and you'll get one hell of a shock. And I warned you about the waters around here. But the French doors off the living room are safe, and there are two swimming pools within the walls — one freshwater, one saltwater. Exercise might help you relax."

"I don't have a bathing suit."

"Harry had a succession of women here over the years. If you look I'm sure you'll find something that fits. Or do without one entirely."

"Oh, yes, there's nothing I'd like better than prancing around naked," she said, just managing to keep the growl out of her voice.

"Don't you think you're safe around me?"

"Oh, of course I do. You were only planning to kill me, not rape me." She pushed her hair back from her face. She was close enough that she could see his expression without her contact lenses. But as usual he gave nothing away. "Unless, of course, I could seduce you into letting me go."

For a careful man he could make a dangerous mistake. He laughed at the notion.

"You don't think I could do it?" she demanded, incensed.

"Seduce me? You could certainly do that . . . and we have two days to kill, if you'll pardon the expression. Would it make any difference? No. And the question is, would you really be able to go through with it?"

She let her eyes sweep over him in a

leisurely, insulting manner that failed to elicit any sort of reaction. "Why not?" she said. "You know perfectly well that you're passably good-looking. When you're not acting like the gray ghost."

"Passably good-looking?" Now she'd really amused him. "I think you'd hold out for something better than that."

He was flat-out gorgeous, with his long black hair curling at the back of his neck, his icy blue eyes, his long, lean body. "Beggars can't be choosers," she said blithely.

"Don't waste your time on me, Ms. Spenser. I'm an expert in all kinds of weapons, including sex. I have no emotions — I can fuck as efficiently as I can kill, and neither mean a thing to me."

"I'd never thought of sex as a weapon."

"You're either lying or you're hopelessly naive. And you don't strike me as a hopeless romantic."

Score one for her, Genevieve thought. He didn't know her that well at all. In fact, she was desperately, impractically romantic.

She leaned back in her chair, stretching her long bare legs out in front of her. "So let's sum this up," she said in her best lawyerly voice. In truth, she'd spent very little time in court, and it had never been up to her to provide the summation, but she could wing it with the best of them. "I can't leave the house because the doors and windows are electrified, but I can use the pool . . . What's to keep me from taking off once I'm outside?"

"The pool area is surrounded by an electrified fence that would kill you."

She swallowed. "All right. I manage to get past that, and then I have to deal with your sadistic cronies. I get past them and the waters are full of sharks. Which, by the way, I don't believe."

"I'd hate to see you end up as fish food," he said mildly. "My mother took me to see *Jaws* when I was a kid, and it didn't look like a pleasant way to die."

"Are there pleasant ways to die? Don't answer that — you'd probably know all too well. Anyway, I don't think you had a mother. You were hatched from an egg like the snake you are."

"Someone has to lay the eggs, Ms. Spenser," he said mildly. "But trust me, my mother had a lot in common with a viper." He turned away, dismissing her.

"That's it?" she said. "You come in here to tell me all the ways I could die and then you just walk away?"

He paused by the door. "I'm warning you of all the ways you could die prematurely.

You may as well fight it for as long as you can."

"Why? Do you get turned on when your victims struggle?"

She'd gone too far, but then she'd been trying to goad him since he'd walked through her locked door. He moved so fast she had no warning — one moment he was standing by the door, in the next he was leaning over her as she sat, his hands on the arms of the chair, trapping her, his face dangerously close to hers, a blatant invasion as his legs straddled hers.

"You don't want to know what turns me on, Ms. Spenser." How could a voice be seductive and deadly at the same time? She looked up into his undeniably beautiful face, trying not to show any reaction at all. Was he even human, or simply a block of ice in the hot tropical sun?

But she'd forgotten his genius for reading her mind. "Or maybe you think you do," he said in a soft, dangerous voice. And the softness was even more terrifying with everything else about him so hard and cold and merciless.

"No, I . . ."

He kissed her. Not the seductive caress before he rendered her unconscious, this was strange, different, angry. His mouth covered hers, and it had nothing to do with seduction. His kiss was full of anger and desperation and there was nothing she could do but let him. She clutched the arms of the chair, her fingers digging into the upholstery so that she wouldn't lift them to touch him, as some crazy part of her so desperately wanted to. She let him kiss her, shocked at the feelings that went swirling through the pit of her stomach. She could stop herself from kissing him back, but she couldn't keep her eyes from closing, and she couldn't understand the hot sting of tears behind her eyelids. Was she crying for him? For her? What the hell was wrong with her?

And then it was over. He pulled back, and he looked down at her, his eyes flecked with chips of blue ice. He wasn't even breathing hard.

She, on the other hand, couldn't catch her breath. Her heart was slamming against her chest, and she blinked, trying to banish the illogical hot tears that had stung her eyes at his cold, empty kiss. "No," he said softly. "You don't want to know." He stepped back, away from her, and it was like some kind of breath-sucking demon had departed.

And then the kiss might never have happened. "I'm going to get a few hours' sleep," he said. "You can wander around the place to your heart's content, plan all the bloody revenges and daring escapes you can think of. Whatever makes you happy."

She didn't bother to dignify that with an answer. "Go away," she said.

"Gone." And he was.

She stayed sitting in the chair for a long time. It was no longer as comfortable as it had been before — he'd invaded it, as he'd invaded every part of her life. She'd learned to meditate after the attack, as well as defend herself, but recently the pills had been taking care of everything.

The pills were gone, and she had no place to turn for that calm inside her — it had vanished. She tried breathing, she tried conscious relaxation, starting at her toes and moving upward. It didn't work, so she started with the crown of her head, trying to remember how she used to meditate, what she'd learned about chakras and the like.

She was shit out of luck. She could calm and control her limbs, but the feel of his mouth on hers came back with every deep measured breath. He'd gotten inside her, somehow, and she didn't know how to exorcise him.

How many people got to look into the face

of death? She had, twice. The first time she'd survived, just barely, and come through it a stronger person.

The odds weren't so good this time. She wasn't dealing with blind, bullying rage. This time, the danger was cold, calculating and fully as smart as she was. If she looked at the situation calmly, her chances weren't good.

That didn't mean she was going to give up. She'd be a fool not to believe Peter Jensen wouldn't do exactly as he said he would, and she'd never been a fool. Just because he had the face of an angel didn't mean his soul wasn't empty.

He'd been a gray ghost before, now he was a fallen angel. The man was a chameleon, capable of turning into anything he wanted, and he assured her those persona were lethal. And she believed him.

She pushed away from the chair, reaching out for the sliding door, then pulling her hand back at the last minute. The only safe doors were the ones leading out to the pool, he'd said.

He could have lied to her, to try to scare her. But she didn't think so. All she knew was if she stayed in his air-conditioned prison a moment longer she'd scream.

She wasn't naive enough to believe he was

attracted to her. There'd been a reason behind his kisses, cool and calculating, trying to incapacitate her, disarm her, overwhelm her. He'd succeeded the first time because she'd never seen it coming. She was marginally better prepared today, but only marginally. He was an expert at weapons, he'd said, and sex was one of them. It was no wonder that last kiss had left her shaken and confused, just the way he wanted her. Trapped and seemingly helpless.

Which reminded her of Harry. Where were they keeping him? There was no way she could take off and leave him to his fate, even if it looked as if she might have a chance to escape. But he was a big man, and if he was comatose she had no idea how she'd manage to move him.

Or where they could go. They were on a private island, and while she had her doubts about the place being surrounded by trained sharks, she wasn't sure she was ready to disprove it. She'd seen *Jaws* as well when she was younger and she'd prefer a bullet through the head, thank you very much.

But it wasn't going to come to that. She was going to get out of there. They both were. And if she had to feed Peter Jensen to the sharks, then so be it.

She found the most enveloping bathing

suit, one that was unfortunately strapless, and headed for the pool, letting the cool, clear water wash the last of the drugs out of her system, along with the slowly building panic. She could do this. She could fight back — she'd learned not to be a victim.

She swam to the shallow end of the pool and stood up, yanking the shrinking top of the bathing suit up to a more demure level.

"That's a shame," Peter Jensen's cool voice emerged from the shadows. "I was hoping gravity would win."

He was lying on the chaise, off to one side, beneath a leafy canopy that kept him out of the glare of the sun.

She stopped tugging at the bathing suit. "How long have you been there?" She didn't bother to keep the accusatory note out of her voice. "You said you were going to take a nap."

"And so I did, until you started all that thrashing about. I hadn't realized quite how energetic you could be."

She could feel his eyes on her. They were hidden by sunglasses, and there was no way she could even begin to guess what he was looking at, what he was thinking. She just had the sudden wish that she was covered from head to toe.

But she wasn't about to let him intimidate

her. She met his mirrored gaze evenly. "I needed to clear my head," she said.

"Should I be worried?"

If there was one thing she wanted to do it was wipe the amusement from his voice. "Yes," she said flatly. "You should."

He didn't make the mistake of laughing at her this time, but she knew he wanted to. Score one for the good guys, she thought. Perhaps she was beginning to get a glimmer of how his mind worked behind his cool, impassive gaze. This mind-reading thing wasn't quite as one-sided as it had been.

He expected her to run away like a scared rabbit, covering up her exposed body. But in fact, there was nothing wrong with her body — she was just curvier than she wished. Those extra fifteen pounds went straight to her hips, and the wretched truth was that clothes hung better on narrow hips and flat chests. But then she wasn't wearing clothes at the moment, just a too-small bathing suit, and even if she felt a little exposed she wasn't about to run away. It gave him an unfair advantage.

So she sat across from him, crossing her bare legs, and pushed her long wet hair behind her shoulders. "So how long do I have to live?"

She didn't take him off guard, of course.

She doubted anything could. "Feeling feisty, are we?"

"Just not particularly passive. What's your plan? I'd like some kind of timetable."

"Why? Do you need to make peace with your conscience?"

"I'd think that would be more your problem than mine," she said. "My conscience is clear. I've lived a relatively blameless life."

"I'm sorry to hear that. People tend to regret the things they don't do, rather than the things they do, and I hate to see you regretful."

"Kind of you to care," she said. "But the only thing I regret is coming to the Cayman Islands in the first place."

He looked at her for a long, thoughtful moment. "I expect that's my main regret as well," he said finally. "Harry will be dead, either way, and you could be happily stomping around the rain forest right now instead of having a conversation with a cold-blooded killer."

"And are you? A cold-blooded killer?"

"Veins like ice, Ms. Spenser."

She didn't doubt him. "Maybe it was supposed to happen this way. Maybe I'm supposed to stop you and save Harry."

He leaned back on the chaise, and she knew that even behind the mirrored sunglasses his eyes were closed with weary exasperation. "Believe what you want."

"So how much time do I have? Or are you afraid to tell me?"

His mouth curved in a slight smile, and she was sorry she'd noticed. He really did have a devastating mouth.

"I'm not afraid of anything," he said in the most gentle voice. "It would be better if I were."

"How much time?"

He sighed. "The job will be finished by tomorrow night. Does it make you feel better to learn that? Most people are better off not knowing when they're going to die."

"Then you shouldn't have told me you were going to kill me."

"I don't believe I said so in so many words."

"Your meaning was clear. Unless you've changed your mind."

"I'm afraid I don't have that luxury."

"So what are you waiting for? Why not get it over with?" That was just stupid on her part, she thought belatedly. The more time she had, the more likely she'd be able to figure out a way to escape. Though in fact, it wasn't looking likely at all.

"Sorry, but I do things on my schedule not yours."

She could have wished for even a tiny portion of his icy calm. There seemed no way she could penetrate it — not by goading him, not by ignoring him.

"Suppose I burst into tears and beg you to spare me?" She wouldn't, couldn't, she thought, but it didn't hurt to ask.

She would have hoped for some reaction from him, even a faint frown, but she got nothing more than a "Please, don't."

"Would it make it harder on you? I'm all for that."

He said nothing, and she wondered if that was the first sign she'd gotten to him. Or whether he was simply bored. Probably the latter, and she was wasting her time trying to reason with him.

"I'd like to see Harry," she said abruptly.

"Why?"

"To make sure he's still alive."

"Why? A day or two isn't going to make any difference."

"It matters." She could be cryptic, too.

Except that he could read her so well. "If Harry's dead you don't have to factor him into your escape plan. If I were you I wouldn't give Harry Van Dorn a second thought. His fate is sealed, and there's not a damn thing you can do about it. Concentrate on yourself."

"I thought my fate was sealed as well, as you put it so dramatically."

He smiled at that. "I'm a melodramatic kind of man. It's part of the job description."

A sudden stray chill danced across her exposed spine, and she wondered whether his implacable determination was finally getting to her. But he, of course, noticed and was far more pragmatic.

"You're cold," he said. "And it's getting late. Much as I hate to suggest it, you should probably change out of that fetching bathing suit while I make us something to eat. As a matter of fact, it might be better for everyone if you stayed covered up. You tend to have a lascivious effect on me."

He was mocking her again, and she wasn't in the mood for it. "Yeah, right. You're a helpless mass of frustrated desires."

"I'm never helpless."

There was something in his voice that stopped her, and she looked at him more closely. There was nothing to see. Despite the shadows, his face was rendered blank by the mirrored sunglasses and her mind reading hadn't advanced this far.

"I don't think —"

"You think too much," he interrupted. "Stop trying to annoy me and go change your clothes. Trust me, I'm impervious."

She believed him. At least for the moment. Another chill swept across her exposed skin, and she realized she was being stupid. No man in her lifetime had ever been rendered powerless by her supposed beauty, and it certainly wasn't going to happen with an emotionless, cold-blooded killer. Even if he did have the mouth of a fallen angel.

She rose with all the dignity she could muster, but the effect was slightly ruined by her need to tug the strapless neckline higher. And she knew the eyes behind the mirrored sunglasses were following her every move. She just didn't believe why.

"I just hope you know how to cook," she said. "I'm starving, and I have no intention of dying on an empty stomach."

And for once he let her have the last word, and she stalked away, refusing to look back.

"Wanna give me some more of that stuff?" Harry's voice was slurred, more than it needed to be, but it managed to scare the hell out of Renaud, who'd been sitting outside the little hut smoking a cigarette.

"What the fuck?" he demanded, scrambling to his feet. "You're supposed to be out of it."

Harry knew the power of his smile, and

he gave the squat little Frenchman full wattage, the one that made the most paranoid men in the world trust him and made presidents want to be his best friend. A little turd like Renaud was hardly immune. He must have been there on the boat — he looked vaguely familiar, but Harry seldom paid attention to the hired help.

"Hey, it takes more than that pussy drug you've been shooting into me to knock me out. It's not even that good of a rush. Got anything stronger?" They'd tied him to a chair in the little shed, and he was stiff and uncomfortable. One more insult he needed to pay back, with interest, when the time came, and the little Frenchman was only one of many.

"You're crazy, man," Renaud said, leaning against the open doorway of the shed. "They're going to kill you."

Harry grinned. "The hell you say. I'm a lot harder to kill than most people would think."

"You don't know who you're dealing with."

"That's right, I don't. Am I being held for ransom?" He already thought he knew the answer to that one. He'd only been half out of it during the time in the stateroom, but he'd managed to gather that this wasn't a financial operation but an execution.

He didn't bother to wonder why — the problem was there were far too many people and organizations who'd want to kill him, and it would take days to even remember them all. It didn't matter who right now. He just needed to get out of it. And for that he needed Renaud.

"No ransom. It's not about the money," he said.

"It's always about the money, my friend," Harry drawled. "You look like you're a Pisces to me."

"What the fuck is that?"

Idiots, Harry thought. "You must have been born in late February or early March."

"Oh, that astrology crap. Just goes to show how much you know — I was born on Christmas Day," Renaud sneered.

"How fitting," Harry said. "Then you must have Pisces rising. Either way, it means we can work together."

Renaud hooted with laughter. "Those drugs work better than you think. You're crazy."

Harry didn't like it when people called him crazy. It tended to make him a little . . . unstable, but in his current position there wasn't much he could do about it, so he overlooked the insult. For now. "You don't strike me as a man of high moral principles," he said. "Are they really paying you enough to off me? Because I can assure you, I have more."

"You don't even know who's behind this," Renaud scoffed. "These people don't make mistakes, and they don't like traitors. You couldn't pay me enough money to help you — I'd be dead in a matter of hours."

"You look like a man who's willing to take that kind of risk." He named a sum extreme enough to make Renaud's dark little eyes widen. Not that he'd ever see a penny of it, Harry thought, but it was enough to lure him.

"Shit," Renaud said. "You really are crazy."

Harry allowed himself a brief, soulful vision of exactly how he would disembowel the Frenchman, and then he smiled. "I have the money. And I want to live. Do you doubt me? I've got so much money I can protect you from your bosses. I can send you someplace they'll never find you." A grave, he thought. Damn, the Frenchman was stupid.

Harry could see that Renaud was considering it. "I'm not alone in this. There's another man taking turns watching, giving you the drugs."

"If you want to share all that money it's your choice," Harry said. "I'll leave that decision up to you. Otherwise I'm sure you won't have any trouble disposing of inconvenient obstacles."

Renaud smiled then, an ugly little grin. "You're right about that," he said. "Maybe I'm a Pisces after all."

Harry Van Dorn nodded his head. "I never doubted it for a minute, my friend."

9

Peter Jensen pushed the sunglasses up on his forehead and pinched the bridge of his nose in a futile effort to vanquish the tension that had been sitting there for what seemed like days. His usual calm practicality had abandoned him, and every time he was on the verge of achieving his normal sangfroid, Ms. Genevieve Spenser would pop up and blow it all to hell.

She was right — he should just kill her and get it over with. He could think of no way out of the current mess, and the more he struggled the tighter the bonds. He knew it would happen sooner or later — that an innocent would get caught in the crossfire. He was far from the only closer in the Committee, and everyone else took collateral damage in their stride. Why couldn't he?

He could tell himself it was a matter of professional pride. If he was good enough at his job, then only the guilty would pay the price.

But he never lied to himself, and he knew that was only part of the problem. He could live with killing an innocent, if it was for the greater good. It was a decision faced by soldiers every day.

He just didn't know if he could live without Genevieve Spenser in this sorry world.

The air was warm, and the Iceman was in danger of melting. And it scared the hell out of him.

Once she went back to her room to change out of the bathing suit she should have stayed put. It didn't matter that she was trapped by the electrified doors and feeling claustrophobic, it didn't matter that nighttime was a smarter time to try to escape — she'd have a better chance of eluding them in the dark. Even so, she still should have stayed where she was once she'd showered and changed out of the borrowed bathing suit.

But she didn't.

Thank God there were caftans in the closet, long, flowing garments that covered her from head to toe. She wanted layers and layers between her flesh and Peter Jensen's enigmatic, disturbing gaze. The underwear was a problem of Einstein proportions. There were drawers of new underwear with tags still attached. All of them designed for skinny models more interested in displaying their assets rather than supporting them. She couldn't even find anything resembling a 34-C, and the closest thing she could find made her look like a *Sports Illustrated* swimsuit model.

The panties were worse. Thongs, all of them. And she couldn't decide what made her feel more conspicuous and vulnerable — going commando or wearing the tiny bit of silk.

She finally went with the "any layer is better than nothing" defense, secure that at least the caftan covered her from her neck to her toes.

She'd forgotten that Peter seemed able to see right through her and everything about her, including an opaque layer of fabric. She just knew he could see the skimpy lingerie she'd been forced to choose.

He was in the kitchen, chopping vegetables with ominous speed and precision, but he stopped long enough to give her a thorough once-over before returning to his work.

"Too bad you couldn't find a veil to go with that nun's habit," he said. "Help yourself to a glass of wine. It's one of Harry's best — from one of his private vineyards. It's got to be tasted to be believed."

"I'm not drinking stolen property."

"Then you shouldn't be wearing stolen property," he said, unfazed. "By tomorrow night, all of this will be gone in a fiery explosion. We may as well enjoy what we can."

"I'm not in the mood to enjoy things."

"Then pour yourself a glass of wine in lieu of your precious little pills. I know you like good wine — I had to steer you toward your cabin that first night. I was afraid you were going to pass out without any help from me."

"Afraid?"

"Because then I wouldn't have had any excuse to kiss you."

She took the wine. He was right, it was almost good enough to die for. Almost. But while he was so busy with his flashing knife she should be scouting the place, looking for a way to escape.

"Don't bother, Sister," he said, not looking up from his work. "I'm a very thorough man. There's no way you're getting out of this place, unless I let you. Drink your wine and relax."

"You think I'll just give up without a fight?"

"No. But I'd rather not spend the next few hours chasing you around this place. There are no weaknesses in my defenses, Ms. Spenser." The knife flashed with deadly precision. "The sooner you accept that fact, the better. Why don't we just pretend we're two normal people, stranded on a beautiful island for a couple of days."

"I'm not into imaginary games."

"Make an effort." The knife flashed and his voice was sharp and cold.

"Or what? You'll kill me?"

He pushed his long hair back from his angular face, glancing at her out of flinty eyes. "You really are foolhardy, aren't you? Shouldn't you be trying to charm me instead of pissing me off?"

"Would it make any difference?"

"Probably not."

"Then I may as well get my kicks where I can, and annoying you seems to be one of the few pleasures left to me."

"Not necessarily." He looked up at her, and he was close enough that she thought she could read the expression in his cool blue eyes.

That was something she didn't even want to think about. "I want my purse back," she said, changing the subject. "I either need my glasses or my spare contact lenses."

"Trust me, you don't want to see what's coming."

Something snapped inside her, and she put the wineglass down, hard. Unfortunately Harry's villa came equipped with granite countertops and the glass shattered in her hand.

"I think I've lost my appetite," she said. "I'm going back to my room. Call me when it's time to die."

He ignored her flippant comment. "You're bleeding," he said.

She glanced down at her hand. The broken crystal had sliced through her skin, and blood was welling up. "Sorry — did you want to be the one to spill it?"

He ignored her jibe, setting the knife down and moving toward her. His calm approach was unnerving and she started to back away, but he caught her arm, pulling her toward him, so that the fabric of her caftan brushed up against his legs in a strangely intimate movement.

There was no pulling away from him, a reminder of how strong he really was. "You should have stitches," he said.

"Too bad there's no emergency room nearby. Guess I'll have to bleed to death, and save you the pleasure."

His small smile should have been infuriating. It was, and yet she was far from impervious. "It's not that bad, Genevieve. You'll live to bitch at me another day."

And that was about it. *One more day.* He'd never said her name before — he wrapped his voice around it in a way that was unbearably intimate.

"I prefer Ms. Spenser."

"And of course your preferences are my top priority." He pulled her from the kitchen, and she gave up trying to fight him. He'd wrapped a linen dish towel around her hand to keep the blood from dripping onto Harry's floors. The floors that would be gone soon — why did he bother?

She balked when he brought her into a huge bedroom, but he pulled her past the bed as if it didn't exist, and into a separate bathroom, half the size of her apartment. He pushed her down on the toilet seat and began to rummage through one of the many cabinets.

She regretted the loss of her wine more than the pain in her hand. She regretted that he touched her, held on to her so that she wouldn't escape, more than anything at all.

She stopped thinking about it. She looked past him, out the screened window to the Caribbean night sky with its lopsided moon.

It was a beautiful evening, the time and place for lovers, not death.

When she looked back at Peter he was almost finished bandaging her up. "Not as bad as it looked," he said. "There shouldn't be any permanent damage. The next time you slam a wineglass down on a granite countertop remember to let go of it faster."

Next time. He'd released her hand finally, and she pulled away, looking up at him.

There was an unexpectedly gentle expression in his eyes. "Stop baiting me, Genny," he said. "It doesn't do any good, and it only upsets you."

"And you're so concerned about my well-being." No one called her Genny anymore — that name belonged to someone younger, happier, more hopeful. Someone who thought she could make a difference in the world.

That girl was long gone, and there wasn't much to be hopeful about in the current situation.

"Actually, I am," he said, his voice light. "Now, come back with me and eat something, or I'll carry you back, tie you up and force-feed you."

He'd do just that, and probably enjoy it, she thought bitterly. And she wasn't about to give him that satisfaction, or any other satisfaction at all.

She rose. She was almost five foot nine in her bare feet, but he was much taller, and even in the cavernous bathroom she felt crowded, alarmingly aware of his closeness.

"You win," she said. "But then you always do, don't you?"

"Not always," he said. And his icy eyes were bleak.

He did what he had to do, Peter reminded himself, watching as the night breeze drifted in from the patio and stirred her long thick hair. He followed orders and seldom had reason to question them, even in the ruthless days of Harry Thomason's reign. Madame Lambert was a more pragmatic soul, and if the hit was ordered he could trust that it was with the best of reasons. He was well trained, a veritable artist at his job, and he could make Genevieve Spenser's eventual demise his masterwork.

Demise. Stupid word for an execution. Did you even call it that when it was a case of collateral damage? More like the fortunes of war, not execution. But Genny was no soldier, just someone in the way.

She didn't eat much, picking at the food he'd prepared. A few more weeks of this and she'd lose the fifteen pounds that curved her body so nicely. Unfortunately she didn't have a few more weeks.

He knew women's bodies well enough to know exactly what she weighed and how much she considered to be unwanted extra. She wanted to be an anorexic clotheshorse like Harry's recent taste in sexual partners. He'd be better off if she was. Maybe.

There was no question that her strong, curvy body was rapidly becoming an uncomfortable obsession. Seeing her in that poured-on bathing suit had only made things worse, and in his role as Harry's majordomo he knew exactly what kind of clothes and underwear she would have found in that room. Was she wearing some enticing bits of lace and ribbon beneath that ridiculous, nunlike caftan? Or was she wearing nothing at all?

Neither thought was particularly comforting. She was doing her best to ignore him, and he was happy enough to let her get away with it. Because her undeniably luscious body wasn't nearly as involving as her spirit.

She was a bundle of fascinating contradictions. She used her little pills to stuff down any unwanted emotion. She had very little physical fear — she'd fought Renaud and tried to take him on without a moment's hesitation. He knew she was currently without a relationship, and hadn't had one for a long time, which suggested she got her satisfaction from sublimating her desires in her career. And yet every time he touched her, kissed her, she reacted with breathless intensity.

He never should have kissed her. He'd let temptation overrun his better judgment, and he was paying the price for it now. Because he wanted to kiss her again with a need so strong it was almost a physical ache.

He wasn't going to touch her. He hadn't been reckless since he was a teenager at the tight-ass boarding school his mother had sent him to. All the Wimberley men had graced its hallowed halls, up to and including his grandfather, Dr. Wilton Wimberley, MBE. He was the one who'd seen to it that young Peter had the best education, one befitting the solid upper-middle-class values so dear to his mother.

She'd married beneath her, and a day never passed when she didn't regret it, which she made abundantly clear to her small family. He never could figure out what attracted a prissy, uptight creature like his sainted mother to a sullen bully like Richard Madsen. At least his father had found a natural outlet for his violent tendencies;

when he wasn't beating on his carping wife or his rebellious son, he could beat up criminals. He was a London policeman, with no pretensions or aspirations to anything higher, and to his mother's fury he'd turned down promotion after promotion, just to spite her.

Emily Wimberley Madsen had done her best by her only child. She'd taught him to speak in a proper posh accent, though he would slip into his father's rougher street tones just to annoy her. She'd cadged enough money from her father to send him to the best schools, never realizing that children could spot an outsider with unerring cruelty. He'd had to fight his way through school, and by the time they sent him off to Kent Hall, over his father's objections, he was a danger to anyone who crossed him.

Most of the other students picked up on that as well, and gave him a wide berth. His mother could never understand why he was never invited to the country homes of his mates — she never understood that a misfit like Peter Madsen would have no mates.

He never bothered wondering what might have happened if things had gone differently at school. Daniel Conley should have known better, but his father was a Member of Parliament with too much money, and his son had an army of sycophants who followed his orders like good little soldiers. Daniel had been a big boy — heavy boned, leaning toward fat, whereas Peter didn't reach his full height until he was out of school. At the age of seventeen he was wiry, small for his age and far more dangerous than hulking Daniel Conley would ever guess.

Daniel had outweighed him by forty pounds, and with two other boys holding him down there wasn't much Peter could do but endure the pain and humiliation of Daniel's assault.

He'd spent a week in the infirmary. No one asked any questions — Daniel's father was a major contributor to the school — and he hadn't offered any complaints. And the next time Daniel Conley tried to corner him in the third-floor washroom, he'd broken the bastard's neck.

He'd wanted to kill him, and he would have if his rage hadn't gotten in the way, making him careless. To this day Daniel Conley lived the plushest life a paraplegic could lead, supported by his father's limitless wealth.

They'd hauled Peter away, covered with the blood of Daniel and a dozen of his cronies. He had no idea where they were taking him, and by the time the blood-red haze had left him he'd grown cold and still as ice, knowing that the huge sober men were taking him someplace quiet to kill him. Upstarts didn't try to kill the privileged sons of MPs and face normal consequences. They'd bury him in some bog, and his parents would never know what had become of him.

He was right about the last part, if about nothing else. He never saw Emily and Richard Madsen again — merely a side benefit of his early recruitment to the shadowy group known simply as the Committee.

The Committee had other names. Official ones to cover any slips, names that had nothing to do with their actual work. The powers that be recognized talent when they saw it, and young Peter Madsen had shown more than promise.

He'd been trained, groomed, educated and made over. He was a crack shot, and almost as effective with a dozen other weapons. He could speak five languages fluently, he could be straight, gay, American, Scandinavian, British or German. He could kill without compunction and live under deep cover for years until it was time to strike. They'd chosen wisely when they recognized his budding potential, and he'd served them well in their bloody, supposedly noble cause.

He'd even married, briefly, a futile stab at some kind of normalcy. And because Thomason thought it would make him a better agent if there was something that mattered to him. Thomason hadn't realized that Peter was already one of the best there was, and that having a wife at home never entered his mind when he was on assignment.

He heard she remarried — a dentist maybe. She'd grown tired of being alone, and he couldn't blame her. She hadn't had enough imagination to realize he was anything other than the pharmaceutical representative he claimed to be. And he was certain she was much happier in her neat little house in Dorking. She was probably pregnant by now.

He could tell himself he missed her, but that would be a lie, and he was adept at lying to everyone but himself. He could barely remember her face.

But he missed the thought that someone was waiting for him in that tumbledown cottage in Wiltshire that sat on far too many acres. He never should have bought the place. He'd done it on a whim, because he had too much money and nothing to spend it on, because word had come down that everyone should have the cover of a stable life. He bought the house because it felt peaceful in a life devoid of peace. And he found a wife to put in it as soon as he could. It hadn't taken much — he knew how to charm women into doing exactly what he wanted with insulting ease.

Except for Genevieve Spenser, who seemed maddeningly impervious.

But the wife had never belonged in Wiltshire. And now she was gone, the house closed up, and Harry Thomason was retired. So were many of his friends — retired or dead. Of the operatives he'd started out with, Peter was the only one remaining.

Maybe he could just disappear into the wilds of America, as his old friend Bastien had. Maybe he could just walk away from it as well.

But not with a job unfinished and a thousand unanswered questions hanging in the balance. Harry's pretentious Rule of Seven hovered over them all, and what little they'd discovered was terrifying enough. If Harry's hired thugs had managed to sabotage that dam in India hundreds of thousands of people would have died. And what could possibly be his reason for instituting such carnage?

The assault on the oil fields was equally impractical — he'd chosen some of the richest deposits, ones he himself owned a major part of, though he'd planned to divest himself of his interests before the planned conflagration. Why?

What else did he have planned? And would they be as easy to circumvent once they discovered them?

In fact, each of Harry's plans was so delicately balanced that it hadn't taken much to render them harmless. He wanted the control and the thrill even more than he seemed to want a guaranteed outcome. The trick was in discovering them in the first place, and with the Indian dam it had been sheer luck. If the destruction of the oil fields went through, the death toll wouldn't be as catastrophic, but the ramifications in world financial markets would be global. Maybe that's what he had in mind. Carefully orchestrated chaos, giving Harry Van Dorn the chance to step in, well armed with information, and make a financial killing.

He already had more money than God, and thorough searches of his financial records hadn't turned up any recent losses. It hadn't taken much to find the hidden sweatshops that the humanitarian institutions had no idea existed, much less the child prostitution mills in Southeast Asia. But such things were very lucrative, and Harry didn't need more money.

But he wanted it. Peter already knew his appetites were perverse and insatiable. He just hadn't realized it included his appetite for money.

The Committee was taking a gamble, terminating Harry before they knew the full extent of his plan. They were counting on his gigantic ego — he would delegate only the barest minimum, and nothing would go down without his immediate say-so. Or so they hoped.

In the meantime, Harry would die a tragic, accidental death. And any extraneous details would be cleaned up quickly and tidily.

Extraneous details like the woman sitting across from him with calm self-assurance. Maybe she thought he couldn't go through with it. If so, then she wasn't as smart as he thought she was. He could do just about anything if he had to. Killing Genevieve Spenser was part of a bloody day's work. No more, no less.

"One would think you didn't like my cooking," he said.

"I don't have much appetite."

"And you haven't touched the wine, when

we both know how good it is."

"Neither have you."

"Do you think it's drugged? Poisoned? I assure you it's not. I'm simply not drinking because . . ."

"Because you're on a job?" she suggested mockingly. "Far be it from me to distract you from your duty. In fact, poison would probably be a fine idea — I have faith in your promise it won't hurt. And if you're simply trying to render me unconscious I don't mind that either — as you know from my tranquilizers, I have no objection to pharmaceutical aids."

"Then why aren't you drinking?"

She met his gaze, her own calm and steady. "Because I don't want to do anything foolish that would give you the excuse to touch me, thank you very much."

"You don't like being touched?"

"Not by you."

That was a lie. She knew it as well, because she turned her head, staring out into the night garden. But he wouldn't call her on it — he was neither as smug nor as cruel to push it. In truth, he had little judgment when it came to how irresistible he was. He was always playing a part, whether it was the obsequious servant who either did or did not provide sexual favors or the blandly devoted husband, whose lovemaking was as straightforward and unimaginative as he could manage. He performed just well enough to get his ex-wife to climax, figuring that a boring middle-class drug salesman could do that much, but he wouldn't let himself go past a simple, physical release. He never did, whether his partner was a shy housewife or a kinky sadist or anywhere in between. Control was everything.

He held up his hands. "No touching," he said. "Not without a specific request."

She stared at him in amazement. "Oh, please touch me," she mocked him. "I'm all atremble with desire at the thought of you strangling me. I've known perverts who think that death is the ultimate turn-on, and murdering someone midorgasm makes it all the better. Ever tried that?"

"Whose orgasm, mine or yours?" he murmured.

He'd called her bluff — there was a faint stain of color on her cheekbones. She had freckles. How could he be obsessed by a woman with freckles? No, he wasn't obsessed, just . . . distracted. "You spend a fair amount of time around perverts?" he added, since she didn't seem about to answer his first question.

"I didn't always work for a Park Avenue

law firm," she said in a steady voice. "I started out wanting to save the world, working in the public defender's office as well as the district attorney's in upstate New York."

"Now, that wouldn't even begin to keep you in Armani and Blahnik," he drawled. "Unless you come from old money."

She looked surprised.

"The old money has been gone for generations," she said. "And when I was younger I was much too idealistic to care about material things."

"You don't strike me as particularly old and jaded at the moment. Even if you were willing to whore yourself out to Harry as part of your job. You wouldn't have liked it — Harry's got some peculiar tastes you're better off not knowing about." It would have served her right if Harry had gotten his hands on her, and it was only for her sake Peter was glad he hadn't.

And that was so much bullshit. He hadn't wanted Harry to have her, even as he stood in the shadows as the gray ghost, serving her her bloody Tab.

Hell, he should have just thrown her overboard that first night, to let her sink or swim. At least she would have had a fighting chance of surviving. Whereas right now, if he followed orders, she had no chance at all.

She lifted her gaze to his. "I wasn't going to sleep with Harry," she said mildly enough. "I keep my sexual activities to times when I'm off duty."

"Are you off duty now?" The question came from nowhere, reminding him just how dangerous Genevieve Spenser could be. The only blessing was that she didn't realize it.

"If by any miracle Harry and I survive this kidnapping, then I'll be billing him an extraordinary amount of hours."

"I'm sure you will." He couldn't keep the amusement from his voice. "But the chances of Harry getting out alive are nil. But hell, if you get away, you should certainly bill his estate. I'd even pad it if I were you."

Her eyes narrowed. They were prettier without the contact lenses — a deep, warm brown.

He liked her better without makeup as well. She had beautiful, creamy skin, and the smattering of freckles across her cheeks and the bridge of her nose was ridiculously erotic.

"What about you?" she said.

He'd forgotten what they were talking about, still uncharacteristically distracted by her freckles. "I beg your pardon?"

"So polite," she said, with only a trace of bitterness. "Do you whore yourself out on the job?"

"I've already told you I use sex as a weapon. What does that tell you?" he countered.

"I would think most of the people you target were men. Doesn't that put a crimp in your style?"

He didn't want to answer her implied question. "You're sexist, Ms. Spenser. Women can be just as lethal as men."

"Have you ever killed a woman?"

Thank God she'd gotten off the other subject. "Yes," he said.

"And how was it for you?" she purred.

"A job."

"Do you fuck them before you kill them?" She was playing a dangerous game, and she wouldn't like the consequences. But they were trapped together in this billionaire's prison, and the night was growing late, and he was feeling almost as reckless as she was.

"Sometimes," he said. "If I have to."

"And the men?"

"Sometimes," he said again. "If I have to."

She was good at hiding her reaction — he had to grant her that. She'd wanted to know.

"Did you sleep with Harry Van Dorn?"

"Not his type, fortunately."

She was silent for a moment, and he had no earthly idea what she was thinking.

"I don't understand you," she said after a moment. "I don't know why I'm trying. Bisexual assassins aren't my usual acquaintances."

"I'm not bisexual. I just do what needs to be done."

"Do you come? When you're fucking on the job?"

He almost smiled. She couldn't say the word *fuck* quite as casually as she wanted to. Or maybe he just upset her with his frank answers.

"Of course," he said. "Sex is simply a programmed physical response. I can make my body do anything I want without it interfering with my emotions."

"You said you had no emotions."

"Did I? Well, that's true enough. Let's just say that using sex as a tool is no more intimate than using a fake name and learning to respond to it. It's a skill, a weapon. Something I use when the occasion calls for it."

"I don't believe it's possible," she said. Foolish girl. Didn't she know he was looking for an excuse, any excuse to put his hands on her?

"It's possible. Shall I demonstrate?" He almost wanted to laugh at her expression. Almost.

She bolted out of her chair. "I'm going to bed."

Let her go, he told himself. *Keep your bloody mouth shut and let her go.*

"Aren't you curious?" he found himself saying. "I thought you weren't going to give up without a fight. Prove me wrong. Melt my icy heart with the warmth of your tender love."

"Fuck you," she said, furious.

"That was what I was suggesting."

She should've run while she still had the chance. For a smart woman she was being astonishingly stupid. Either that, or she liked playing with fire. "You're joking," she said in a flat voice.

But they both knew he wasn't joking. He didn't know why he was doing it. He wanted her, that was a given, but he'd wanted other women and having a hard dick didn't mean he had to do anything about it.

Maybe he wanted to play with fire as well. Maybe he thought it would make things easier if he just fucked her and got it over with. Or maybe he was looking for a reason to save her.

But even if he wanted to, he couldn't. *Run*

away, he thought.

"Come here," he said.

10

Genevieve stood frozen in the middle of the room, her bare feet planted on the cool tile. The night was still and quiet around them, and somewhere out there a helpless man was bound and drugged and awaiting certain death at the hands of the man sitting so casually in the leather chair. Peter Jensen's face was all planes and angles, eerily beautiful in the twilit room, and she couldn't forget what that full, mobile mouth tasted like. Even his cold blue eyes seemed warmer, more like a still lake than an Arctic sea.

Oh, yes, he was beautiful — there was no denying that. And she'd never realized how sick she could be, to want him, to want an excuse to let him put his hands on her.

"How stupid do you think I am?" she said, barely keeping the fury from her voice.

He leaned back in the chair, his long, linen-clad legs stretched out in front of him.

He was barefoot as well, and she couldn't help but notice he had long, beautiful feet. What else was beautiful?

"We both know you're a very smart woman," he said. He began unbuttoning his loose white linen shirt, his hands tanned and graceful and deadly. "You won't miss an opportunity to gain some sort of advantage over me, either emotionally or physically, and you'd never accept the fact that it was hopeless. Since I have no emotions, that leaves the physical."

"And you've assured me that your body is simply a well-trained machine, able to function regardless of the circumstances. How would that help me?"

"Don't be so unimaginative, Genevieve. Do you really think everything I tell you is the truth? Lying is one of the three things I'm best at. And you know the other two."

She looked down at her uneaten meal. "Cooking?" she said hopefully.

"Killing. And sex."

"But if you're such a good liar, how do I know it's true?"

"You aren't going to know about the killing part until it's too late, and I'm hoping you won't even be aware of what's going on. As for the sex . . ." He stretched out his hands. "That's up to you."

"I'm going to bed. Without you." But she didn't, couldn't move.

"That's what you said before, and you're still here. I don't think that's what you want. If you can't soften my heart, you could always try to overpower me when my attention is otherwise engaged. I might even fall asleep afterward — don't men often do that?"

"Not my men," she said loftily.

He smiled. "You don't have a man, Genevieve. And you haven't in more than three years, not since you moved to New York. Do you think I don't have complete files on you? I know where you went to school, how you lost your virginity, what you eat for breakfast. I know you have a weakness for Hong Kong action movies, and French rock 'n' roll. You graduated third in your class at Harvard Law and it drove you crazy that you weren't first. I know you like it missionary style, don't want to go down on anyone, and you seldom come. And you're lactose intolerant. Come on, Ms. Spenser. I bet I can make you scream with pleasure."

She felt hot and cold at the same time. His intimate knowledge of her was horrifying and inexplicable. His resources extended past the simple procurement of a rare soda pop on a Caribbean island. If he'd already committed that much about her to memory, was there anything left to hide?

"No, you can't," she said, her voice shaky.

He rose, a mistake on his part. When he lounged in a chair he might almost look harmless, but when he rose to his full height she knew just how little she had to fight him with.

"You can always take that butcher knife you hid under your mattress and stab me midorgasm. Then you could find out for yourself how arousing it is."

"Killing you wouldn't be very arousing," she said. "Satisfying, maybe, but arousing . . . no." He knew about the knife, even where she hid it. Was there nothing he didn't know?

"If you'd rather use my bedroom I'll get another knife for you," he offered. "I'm trying my best to be helpful here."

He came up to her, and she told herself it was too late. Maybe it had been too late from the moment she saw him. He put his hands on her shoulders, sliding them behind her thick hair to meet at the back of the caftan.

"Come on, Ms. Spenser," he whispered, mocking. "I can give you the best orgasm you've ever had. Prove me wrong."

She lifted her face to kiss him because she

knew it was going to happen. This was to save her life, she told herself, closing her eyes. This was her only chance to save herself and Harry. Virgin sacrifice to the god of death.

But she was no virgin, and this was no sacrifice. She felt his hands catch the back of the caftan and rip, and she heard a shower of tiny buttons scatter over the tile floor as the fabric parted, exposing her back to the cool night air.

His hands covered her shoulders, pushing the caftan down her arms, so that she stood there, dressed only in the tiny scraps of lingerie she'd been forced to choose.

His blue eyes swept down her body, and his wicked mouth curved in a smile. "I was hoping you chose those," he murmured. "Much more fun than nothing at all."

He wasn't even breathing deeply. She reached out and put her hand against his chest, where, if he had a heart, she would feel it beating. Her own was racing. His was slow and steady, like a machine. If machines had hearts.

"Yes, I have a heart," he said, his hand covering hers and moving it inside the unbuttoned linen shirt, so that she could feel his smooth skin against her palm, her fingertips. She half expected him to feel cool to the touch, but he was warm, almost hot.

"You have a heart," she agreed.

He put his hand on her breast, and she flinched, holding still. "But yours is racing. Why, Genevieve? Are you afraid of me?"

"Shouldn't I be?"

"Yes. But that's not why your heart is racing."

"You think I'm all aflutter with desire?" she said, fighting. "I'm not that easy."

"You're child's play," he whispered against her mouth, a feather-soft touch that wasn't quite a kiss. "All I have to do is touch you and you melt."

She wondered whether she could kick him, but he'd already warned her that it tended to piss him off. Besides, she couldn't seem to summon up the energy past her initial outrage.

"You drugged me," she accused him as he kissed the side of her neck, and she could feel his teeth against her jugular. And beneath her palm, the beat of his heart was smooth and steady.

"I'm drugging you right now," he whispered. "There's more than one way to wipe out a woman's defenses." He pushed the thin ribbon strap of her bra aside to kiss her shoulder, and her own heart lurched.

"Enough," she said, stumbling back, away

from him. "I believe you. You can turn me on against my better judgment without getting excited yourself. I'm impressed. Maybe you could even give me a thousand orgasms, though I sincerely doubt it, but I'm not interested in trying. Now let me go."

But he caught her wrist, pulling her back toward him, and before she knew what he'd intended he slid her hand down the front of his linen trousers, to the shockingly hard evidence that he was far from unmoved. "Who says I'm not aroused?" he murmured. "I just know how to control my body. My cock may want you but the rest of me isn't quite as desperate."

She tried to pull her hand away, but he was too strong, his long fingers like a manacle on her wrist, holding her there, even as he pushed against her, slowly, rocking.

"Stop it," she said. "You're a sick bastard."

"I can be," he agreed. "Why don't you try to find my weak points?"

"You don't have any," she said in a strangled voice.

"You never know," he said, and kissed her, with her hand trapped between their bodies, and he grew harder still.

It wasn't the kind of kiss she'd expected — something masterful and overpowering.

Instead, it was a slow, almost curious kind of kiss, hypnotic, as he tasted her lips, her tongue, her skin. He put his other arm around her and drew her up against him, her almost nude body against the loose white linen, the caftan puddled at her feet between them. She could feel his heart against hers, the steady beat an ironic counterpoint to her own racing pulse, as he kissed her, a slow, deep, intoxicating kiss that proved what he said — he was drugging her right now, and he didn't need to use chemicals.

But she'd never been one to seek forgetfulness or release in sex. It always brought a brand-new set of problems, sometimes worse than the first, and he was right, for the last three years she'd been better off without.

Not that things could get much worse at this point. He was going to kill her — he'd made that more than clear, and there was no way out of it that she could see.

And the shameful, inescapable truth was that she was going to have sex with him. She might try to talk him out of it, talk herself out of it, but it was pretty much a foregone conclusion. She was going to make love with the man who was going to kill her. How sick was that?

But it wouldn't be making love. He would fuck her, and she would let him, just to prove a point. Not that he could make love to her and remain unmoved and uninvolved. Any man could do that.

But it would prove he wasn't as all-powerful as he thought. He used sex as a weapon, he'd said, but she was impervious. Even with a gentle, tender man who loved her, she seldom reached anything beyond a mild stirring of pleasure. She certainly wasn't about to start with her murderer, no matter how good he thought he was.

He pulled back, and she realized he was still rocking against her trapped hand, so slightly that she hadn't noticed, an imperceptible rhythm that thrummed through his body. And hers.

"You think I can't do it?" he whispered with the ghost of a laugh.

She'd forgotten he could read her so well, and her anger only fueled the cold fire in her belly.

"Can't do what? Seduce me? I don't think I have much say in the matter. You'll do what you want, with or without my co-operation. You just can't make me enjoy it."

"Yes," he said, "I can. Anyplace, anytime. We'll use your room."

She was too startled to react. The calm

decision in his voice as he took her hand, the one that he'd held pressed against him, was unnerving as he drew her through the shadowy villa. She didn't resist, stepping out of the discarded caftan and following him. In the end, what would it matter? Things had been spiraling out of control for days now, and she kept fighting back. At least this was one battle she was sure to win.

He released her when they reached her darkened room. He turned on the bathroom light, closing the door most of the way so that only a sliver illuminated the room. He stripped off his shirt and threw it over the small statue of the ballet dancer.

"I don't like cameras," he said, turning to her.

Somewhere she found her voice. "There's a camera in that thing? I guess it's not Degas after all."

"It probably is. Harry had no qualms about destroying irreplaceable works of art for his own use. There are cameras everywhere. Harry liked to know what was going on around him, and he never minded an audience himself."

"Why are you using the past tense? He's not already dead, is he?"

"Not as far as I know. I doubt Renaud would disobey my orders when it comes to something like that. Get on the bed."

He was as beautiful as she'd been afraid he was. Most Englishmen tended to be pale and skinny. Peter had tanned, golden skin and subtly defined muscles, and she already knew the feel of his warm, strong flesh.

"I can see why you use sex when other weapons fail you," she said. "You're very pretty — I would think women would have a hard time resisting you. And men," she added.

"It's not a last resort, Genevieve," he said. "Get on the bed," he repeated.

In fact, she was starting to feel a little exposed. She crossed the room to the king-size bed and slid beneath the six hundred thread-count sheets.

"No," he said, and stripped the covers off, tossing them out of reach on the floor. "Lie back."

What would he do if she tried to run? Would he come after her, hurt her? Or even worse, would he let her go?

She lay back against the pillows, and for once she was glad she couldn't see that clearly. She wished she were drunk, knocked out on pills, in some kind of place and time where panic didn't dance through her veins.

He moved to the side of the bed, reached under the mattress and pulled out the butcher knife, laying it on the mattress beside her. "Just in case you think you need it," he said. "Feel free to try."

"Is that what turns you on?" she said, unable to keep the anger from her voice.

"Don't be coy. You turn me on. And you know it."

"I could stab you."

"You could try. But I don't think you'll even remember there's a knife within reach. I don't think you'll want to do anything to stop me."

She reached out and took the knife, wrapping her fingers around the carved wooden handle. German steel — it would slice through flesh quite easily. His beautiful, golden flesh.

"Try me," she said, belligerent.

He walked over to the door, locking it, then turned to look at her from the foot of the massive bed. "I intend to."

She wasn't liking this, not one bit. She felt hot and cold all over, stretched out in lingerie that was meant to entice when that was the last thing she wanted. She forced herself to watch him as he stripped off the white linen, not looking away when she wanted to. She was uncomfortable looking at naked men, particularly aroused ones — in the past she usually tried to keep her eyes averted.

But she couldn't this time. He was beautiful — there was no denying it, and she wondered how that would affect her. The better looking the man, the more selfish his lovemaking, or so she'd discovered in her limited experience. If that held true, then Peter Jensen was going to be the worst lover she ever had.

"Very brave, Genevieve," he murmured, knowing her too well. "You'd much rather be blindfolded, wouldn't you?"

"I'm not that kinky."

"I don't know — you might be surprised."

He moved with such quick, lethal grace that she hadn't even realized he was coming, moving over her from the bottom of the bed, one hand gripping her wrist as she clutched the knife. He stretched over her, and she could feel him touching every part of her body — heated flesh against her pounding heart, his long, bare legs against her, erection at the juncture of her thighs, hard and full against her. His face hovered over hers, his mouth too close, and he looked cool and uninvolved.

"I thought you weren't afraid of the knife." She summoned up one last bit of resistance.

"It doesn't hurt to be careful," he said,

bringing her wrist up to his mouth, kissing it. She could have turned the knife, slashed at him — he barely seemed to be using any strength at all to control her. "But you're not going to stab me, Genevieve. You know what you're going to do, whether you want to or not."

Her grip tightened on the knife automatically, and his hand tightened as well, so that her fingers felt numb. She wasn't going to answer him, since she had no answers.

The bra was nothing more than bits of lace and ribbon, and he unhooked it and pulled it away, then caught the thong bikini and simply tore it, so that she was naked, exposed beneath him. "That's better," he murmured. "It levels the playing field."

She closed her eyes, terrified, and she wasn't sure why. He wasn't going to hurt her — she'd be less frightened if that was what she expected. She summoned one last ounce of fight. "Just get it over with," she said. "I'm getting bored." Her breath caught in her throat, belying her cool words, but then, she hadn't really hoped to fool him.

"Yes, ma'am," he said. And without any warning he pulled her legs apart and pushed inside her with a suddenness that left her shocked and breathless.

Neither of them moved for a moment.

"Now, why doesn't it surprise me that you're wet?" he murmured, looking down at her.

She struggled to find something, anything to say. She felt his strong hands on her legs, pulling them around his hips. She was clutching the sheet beneath her, and once he'd gotten her legs wrapped around him he prised her hands loose and placed them on his shoulders.

"I think you'd better hold on to me, Ms. Spenser. It's going to be quite a ride."

This wasn't going to work, she thought blindly. He'd barely kissed her, hadn't even touched her, he'd done nothing in terms of standard foreplay.

And yet she was wet. Aroused, in a way she'd never felt before. And he hadn't even moved.

"Don't look so stricken, sweetheart. You're supposed to like it." He pulled out, just a little, then sank back in again, a small shimmer of movement that left her gasping for breath.

"I don't want . . ." she said.

"Yes, you do."

Yes, she did. He began to move, slowly, too slowly, as if the only part of him involved was what was between his legs, between hers. She closed her eyes, trying to shut him out, but he was everywhere, on top of her, beneath her, inside her.

She told herself it didn't matter. He was just trying to make a point, trying to strip away anything she had left, but she could fight it, fight him, fight the slow, insidious buildup of response that was shimmering through her body. She caught her breath, a hoarse gasp that seemed to draw him in deeper, and she made the terrible mistake of opening her eyes.

He was bracing himself against the mattress, his hands on either side of her, and his icy blue eyes were open, staring down at her face with single-minded intensity as he kept up the steady, wicked rhythm, rocking, rocking, thick and full and deep.

"Come on, Ms. Spenser," he whispered. "Prove me wrong. You don't want to come with me inside you — you don't want me to have that satisfaction. You want to hold it back from me, don't you? Prove to me what an arrogant, conceited prick I am. You can withhold this part of yourself, can't you? You want to, don't you?"

How could he be doing this, with the slow, steady thrust of his cock inside her, his hands on the bed, not touching her, his voice teasing her with those soft, taunting words?

She couldn't answer him because she didn't know what he was asking her, why he was baiting her.

"Your nipples are hard, Ms. Spenser," he whispered, "and the room is warm. Why are your nipples hard?"

She closed her eyes again, trying to shut him out, but she slid her arms around his neck, pulling him closer, fully on top of her, body to body, not just the joining between them. He was hot, covered with a thin film of sweat, but his heartbeat was steady, unmoved.

Things were tumbling out of control. Her body was trembling and there was nothing she could do to stop it. He'd taken over, and her body no longer belonged to her. It was his, to do with what he liked. If she relaxed, that first wash of pleasure would happen, she knew it, and he'd be satisfied and leave her alone, but she couldn't do it. Couldn't let go. Couldn't, or wouldn't, give him that victory. The tension was rippling through her, and she clutched at him in desperation, her fingernails digging in, clawing at him, fighting for something just out of reach.

"Who's going to win, Ms. Spenser?" he whispered in her ear. "Your body or your mind?"

She could have answered that with no hesitation, but she'd lost her voice. He was moving faster now, and she was meeting his thrusts because she had to. His hands cupped her hips, pulling her up against him, so that he was deeper, deeper still, wet and slippery and hot and strong, and she wanted to cry out, but there was no sound, just a strangled gasp.

"I think you want to," he whispered, his voice soft and steady. "You're fighting it, but you want it. It's only a small death — nothing permanent. Give it to me, Genevieve. Give it to me now."

It shouldn't have been like that. It went through her like a bolt of lightning, an electric shock, and her body arched on the bed, her head flung back as she opened her mouth to scream.

He slapped his hand over her face to silence her, and she was gone, lost, as her body convulsed around him, an endless surge that kept moving, renewing, drowning. She couldn't breathe, and she bit down on his hand, hard, as her body dissolved into electric sparks that vanished in the night air, until there was nothing left at all.

She couldn't move. All she could do was lie there and breathe as she slowly began to drift back to this darkened bedroom, this rumpled bed, to the man on top of her, still inside her. Still hard. She blinked her eyes open, dazed.

He was looking down at her, his blue eyes cool and assessing, and he wasn't even breathing deeply. "Would you mind letting go of my hand?" he asked in the most polite of voices.

Her teeth were still clenched tight on his hand. She released him, shocked that she hadn't even realized what she was doing, shocked at the blood on his hand, the taste of his blood in her mouth.

He slid off her, lying on his side next to her, sweaty but seemingly unmoved. "I'm sorry, I didn't use a condom," he said. "I usually prefer not to leave a mess behind."

"Given the circumstances I hardly think it matters." Unfortunately it came out in a choked whisper, hardly the blasé tone she was searching for. That answered her question. She'd been so caught up in her own overpowering response that she wasn't even sure he'd bothered to finish. The wetness between her legs told her that he had.

She turned to look at him, and she put her hand on his chest, where his heart was supposed to be. Nothing but a calm, steady heartbeat. Her eyes met his, and he shrugged, and his slight smile was almost apologetic. "I warned you," he said.

"You did," she agreed, staring at him. The eyes were a window to the soul, they said, but in his case no one was home.

She managed to sit up, though she felt weak, shaky. She had to get away from him, even if it meant crawling across the floor. He'd climaxed, there was no question, but he was still hard. He hadn't let go completely, of course he hadn't. He'd proved his point magnificently — he could make her come and have only the mildest physical response.

She just didn't want him to prove it again.

"I'm going to the bathroom," she said. He couldn't very well object to that.

"You can't wash me away, Genny," he said in a soft voice, closing his eyes. "You'll never be able to, no matter how hard you try."

She didn't answer. There was nothing she could say, when she knew he was right. Had been right about everything.

She pulled the sheet from the pile of covers and wrapped it around her. Peter didn't move. He must have fallen asleep, a dubious sign that he might be human after all.

She didn't care. She was lost, drained. There was nothing left of her but a bedraggled girl in a sheet, wandering through the darkened house at the very edge of dawn, knowing that today was a good day to die.

She dropped the sheet by the edge of the pool and stepped into the water, feeling it wrap around her like a mother's arms.

And she went under, letting it close over her head.

The girl would be dead by now, Madame Lambert thought, picking at her egg sandwich, if Peter had decided to follow his orders. It had been an ugly decision, but in the end, necessary. One of those horrible choices a commander in chief had to make for the sake of the greater good. She'd never had to make one of those decisions before, and it haunted her, when little else did.

Maybe Peter never received her instructions. He hadn't responded to the last transmission, though he might have been too busy. Or maybe he got the instructions and decided to disobey them. He'd never done that before — he took orders like a machine, with no sorrow or pleasure, his soul and his conscience frozen in a block of ice.

Oh, God, she hoped so. She hoped for once Peter went with his gut rather than his orders. Isobel had no choice but to make that order. If Peter delayed, or chose not to kill the girl, there might be enough time to prove she was harmless.

Time. They were running out of time. They had another clue to the Rule of Seven — Takashi O'Brien was in place at Harry's main residence and managed to come up with a connection to a diamond mine in Africa that employed thousands of workers. Again, owned by Harry, and he'd made no effort to divest himself of it. If the planned explosion went through, the carnage would be hideous, and no one would think Harry had anything to do with it. He'd lose a bundle.

So why was he doing this, if it wasn't for money? Lust, revenge, sheer boredom? It could be all of those things. Harry was a spoiled baby who liked shiny toys and big explosions.

And Isobel had finally found out for certain when some of those noisy explosions were scheduled to take place. April twentieth. And the knowledge chilled her to the bone.

11

Peter Jensen didn't let himself sleep. That was an indulgence for the weak, something that could wait until the assignment was complete. In the meantime he could close his eyes and let the feeling of physical satisfaction drain through his body, shutting off his mind at the same time. He wasn't the kind of man to let regrets and mistakes interfere with his life. Taking Genevieve Spenser to bed was most definitely a mistake. And he didn't regret it for a moment.

She'd looked so stricken. From the admittedly hurried intel he'd received on her it was a pretty sure thing that he'd just given her the best ride of her life, and instead of purring she'd looked shattered.

He'd expected to fuck her to sleep so that he had a few hours to figure out what the hell he was going to do about her. And instead, he was the one lying in a postcoital daze, while she must be wide awake wherever she was.

She wasn't the best he'd ever had, far from it. He'd had sex with women trained for just such high-level work, he'd had affairs with women who loved sex and their own bodies and knew how to make the most of both. He'd had sex with women madly, desperately in love with him, and he'd even had sex with women who hated him. He wondered if Genevieve fit in that category. Probably.

He'd even made love, long, long ago. Helena had been a frail, doe-eyed waif with the softest mouth, and he'd gotten her out of war-torn Sarajevo and fallen in love by the time they'd reached England. She'd been a sweet, generous lover and he would have died for her. And almost did.

He was younger then, of course. And in his thirty-eight years of hard living, that was the only time he'd ever let himself be vulnerable. He still had the knife scar from when she tried to gut him. The Committee had neglected to inform him that beneath that innocent exterior was a traitor and a killer, one whose skills matched his. Almost.

Genevieve Spenser had been angry, resentful and remarkably inexperienced, if he could trust his judgment, and he usually could. He'd planned how he was going to take her, and there were no surprises — she'd responded exactly as he meant her to. No, scratch that. There was one major surprise.

His own response.

He was adept at turning off any distracting thoughts, and he did so now. He couldn't afford to be lying in bed, mooning over an uptight lawyer who was going to cease to exist for him in a few short hours.

And she'd been gone too long. His instincts came awake, full force, and he jumped out of bed, and he felt colder than he had in his entire life.

She was floating facedown in the pool, her long hair spread around her like a halo. A moment later he was in the pool with her, hauling her up, cursing as he pushed the hair out of her face.

She was limp, pale, and he was so angry he shook her, hard, as he continued to curse at her. "You idiot! You fucking stupid bitch! What the fuck do you think you're doing?"

She coughed, dumping water all over him, and her eyes blinked open. "Saving you the trouble," she said.

He shook her again, harder. He didn't care if he was hurting her, didn't care if he left bruises. His red-hot fury blinded him to everything. "Why?" he said. "So we had sex

— that's no reason to go all Ophelia on me. For Christ's sake, Genevieve, it was just a fuck."

But she still had that broken look in her eyes. The eyes that had been glaring at him, defying him for the last forty-eight hours. The eyes that were now filled with tears.

"How could you do that to me?" she whispered. "You took everything. How could you?"

He really had no choice. He pulled her into his arms, holding her tight against his body. He'd broken her completely. It had been the smartest thing he could do, what he was best at. He should feel satisfaction. Mission accomplished. And instead, he felt as if he'd lost everything as well.

She didn't fight him — she had no fight left. She let him hold her, her face buried against his chest in the waist-deep water.

"Your heart is pounding," she whispered against his shoulder after a moment. "Why?"

He didn't want to think about it. He was shaking, and the air and the water were warm. "Don't do that again," he said in a gruff voice.

"I'm not going to have the chance, am I?"

He put his hand under her chin, tilting her face up to his. He closed his eyes and rested his forehead against hers for a long moment. And then he kissed her.

It was a far worse mistake than sex. She'd knocked his defenses sideways, and he had no protection left. He kissed her deeply, fully, holding nothing back, kissed her as if he loved her. Kissed her as he'd never kissed anyone in his life.

If he were anything but what he was, he would have wanted to weep. As it was, he simply kissed her, her mouth, her cheeks, her eyelids, her neck. And she kissed him back, clinging to him as he moved out into the deeper water, bringing her with him until they were floating in the middle of the pool. She kissed him as she felt him grow hard, threaded her hands through his long wet hair and kissed him again. Kissed him as her body floated up, her legs wrapped around him, kissed him as he brought them together.

It was slow, it was sweet, and he was as focused on her mouth as he was between her legs, until everything changed, and he could feel her need building, spiraling. He pushed her back against the side of the pool, holding her there, and then it was fast and hard, and this time when she came he let her scream, not caring who heard, drinking in the sound, as her body convulsed around his in an endless spasm. He held her there, letting her climax, waiting until she could breathe again, and then he started all over again.

It didn't take long this time, and she was sobbing against his shoulder, clinging to him. "Please," she was whispering. "Please."

He knew what she wanted. He'd taken everything from her, and now she wanted an equal sacrifice. And he should have pulled away, let the water cool him.

"Please," she said.

And he was lost. He thrust up into her, hard, again and again, and then with a hoarse cry he was lost, filling her, draining himself into her, body and soul.

They would have both gone under if she hadn't reached out and grabbed the railing.

"Oh, hell," he said weakly, pulling away, into the center of the pool, leaving her clinging to the side, staring at him.

No longer stricken. Her mouth was swollen from his, and if he thought about it he'd probably get hard again. So he turned away and swam to the shallow end, climbing out.

She hadn't moved from her place at the deep end. It was almost full daylight now, and she could probably see him quite clearly as he walked over to where she waited. He reached down and pulled her out of the pool, effortlessly, and she stood in front of him, wet, dripping and naked.

He caught her chin in his hand and kissed her, a brief, ruthless kiss that should have told her how lost he was. "You need to sleep," he said, grabbing the sheet she'd dropped and wrapping it around her body. He picked her up — he could feel the start of surprise that ran through her but he ignored it. She was lighter than he'd expected, and he had no trouble carrying her back into the house.

He didn't want to take her back to her bedroom, and he couldn't take her to his. There were too many other choices, so he simply set her down on one of the overstuffed sofas in the living room.

"Go to sleep," he said.

She looked up at him. He was still unabashedly naked, and there was no way she could miss his constant, eternal reaction to her. But she closed her eyes without saying a word, and a moment later she was sound asleep.

She wasn't good enough to fake it. She wasn't good enough to fake anything. She was exhausted, drugged by sex and violent emotion, and he could lean over and kill her now, quickly, painlessly, in an instant.

With distant, bitter amusement he realized his erection had left. She'd be pleased to know he didn't get off at the thought of killing her — quite the opposite.

But then, death had never been a turn-on for him. It was simply a job to be done, which made him far more valuable an operative than those who did it for the thrill. Those like Renaud.

He wasn't going to kill her. He'd known that for a long time, almost since the beginning, whether he'd wanted to admit it or not. He was a cold, amoral bastard but there were some lines he wouldn't cross. And that included killing innocents who got in the way.

And that's all she was, right, he mocked himself. She could have been anyone and his decision still would have been the same.

Sleeping with her, getting this weird attachment thing going had nothing to do with it. He could keep telling himself that, and maybe one day he'd believe it.

Still, he was one of the good guys, and his job was to kill bad guys, not people who stumbled in his way.

And he would do just that, without pleasure or remorse, in a few short hours. As soon as he made arrangements for Genevieve.

He couldn't guarantee her safety — too

much was at stake. But she was a smart woman, and he could leave her a trail of bread crumbs that would lead even a child to safety. And with any luck at all she'd never realize he'd let her go.

If she thought she'd escaped by way of her own talents it would give her back some of what he took from her. He shouldn't care, but he did.

He worked with his customary efficiency, and when he left a note by her sleeping form, he only hesitated a moment. He was ignoring a basic tenet — don't put anything on paper, don't leave anything of yourself behind. He'd done both, but he couldn't worry. The note would be gone in the coming conflagration — there'd be no way to trace him. His tracks were covered.

He squatted beside her as she slept. He wanted to push her wet hair away from her face, kiss her one last time and maybe convince himself that a kiss meant nothing.

But he knew better than to take the chance. The chance of waking her up, the chance of finding out that kissing her meant everything he was afraid of.

And he was supposed to be afraid of nothing. He let his hand hover over her face for a moment, tempted, so tempted.

And then he turned around and walked away. Forever.

It was broad daylight on the last day of her life, and Genevieve lay wrapped like a mummy on the living-room sofa, trapped.

It only took her a moment to fight her way out of the enveloping shroud, and she almost didn't see the note on the marble-top table beside her. It was brief and to the point. "Don't go in my room."

She didn't even know which room was his in this rambling estate, so how could she avoid it? What had he done, booby-trapped it so he wouldn't have to factor her into any more of his plans?

She wrapped the sheet back around her and stood up. The house was surrounded by shrubbery, but from the floor-to-ceiling windows she could see the ocean, and it was just as likely someone could see in. How many people were on the island — three? Peter, Hans and Renaud, the brute force. Whoever else was involved in this operation had taken off with Harry's boat.

And of course, Harry was on the island, dead or alive, as much a victim as she was. Maybe Peter was off having sex with him as well — he'd done as much before when he was on assignment, or so he told her.

But then, he had no reason to sleep with Harry. He had him where he wanted him.

He had no reason to sleep with her either. None at all, and yet he had. Finally, finally she'd felt him tremble in her arms, his heart racing. Because of her.

And was that a triumph or, in the end, a defeat? It didn't matter. Time was running out, and she wasn't about to waste even a minute thinking about Peter Jensen. She couldn't afford to.

Victoria's Secret and microbikinis were out of the question — so were the enveloping caftans that would trip her up if she tried to run. And she suspected that might be a very real possibility.

Her discarded clothes were gone, thanks, no doubt, to Peter. The butcher knife lay on the floor beside the bed, unmarred by his blood, more's the pity.

She hiked the sheet higher around her, trying to dismiss memories of *Animal House* and toga parties. She wasn't in any kind of mood to be thinking about gonzo comedies. *The Great Escape,* maybe.

But she couldn't escape wrapped in a sheet. There must be something else to wear in the place — more of Harry's expensive sportswear. It had fitted her well enough on the boat — she could find something similar here, hopefully without courting death from Peter's traps.

She was half-afraid to touch the doorknob of the adjoining room, expecting a lethal shock, but it opened easily enough beneath her hand. Another bedroom suite, this time with no spare clothes at all.

Three others, all the same. Which left two bedrooms — the master suite and one other small one. Peter would have co-opted Harry's rooms as he'd co-opted everything about him, so she could save that one for a last resort, and she opened the small room off the kitchen, hoping for a maid's uniform at least.

She'd miscalculated. This was Peter's room — smaller than the guest rooms, spare and utilitarian for the servant he'd been pretending to be.

The sliding glass door was open to the outside, and she could see a clear path into the shrubbery, away from her luxurious prison. Surely escape couldn't be that easy?

She turned, and froze. A carefully drawn schematic lay stretched out on the table, drawn with a precise hand by a man who paid attention to details. The house was diagramed, including the security system, and so was the entire island. He provided his own escape plan, probably something he always did, complete with food, radio and flares, on the far side of the island. If she could make it that far she could hide until they were gone, then call for help on the radio, assuming she could figure out how to work it. She had a decent chance at surviving after all, simply because he'd underestimated her resourcefulness.

Or had he? There was a handgun lying on the table, a nine-millimeter Luger with a full clip. Most people wouldn't know how to use it, but it was identical to the gun she'd been trained on, after the attack. She'd never be a terribly accurate shot, but at least she knew how to aim and shoot, and maybe that would be enough.

So, had Peter gotten sloppy all of a sudden? Or did he change his mind about killing her, when he'd told her he didn't have that luxury?

It didn't matter. She couldn't waste her time thinking about it — she had to concentrate on getting out of there as fast as she could. Getting to safety.

She found a heavy white T-shirt and a pair of khakis in his dresser. The khakis were identical to the ones she'd cut up on the boat — she hadn't been wearing Harry's clothes after all, but his. It shouldn't have mattered. It mattered.

She didn't bother with underwear. She dressed, picked up the gun and tucked it into the waistband of the pants, pulling the T-shirt down over it. She'd have to go barefoot; her Manolo Blahniks were long gone and even her size-ten feet would disappear in Peter's shoes. She'd just have to manage.

She stood over the schematic, taking in every detail. He might not realize she'd been in there if the paper was still in place, and she had a semi-photographic memory, even under such stressful conditions. All she needed to remember was the path to the bunker. And where they were keeping Harry.

She was an idiot to even consider trying to save him. What good was she, up against three men who could only be described as terrorists? Just because they thought they worked for the supposed good guys didn't make them any less monstrous. And in the last few years Genevieve was having a hard time even figuring out who were the good guys and who were the bad.

Men who killed in cold blood were bad. Men who followed orders and killed without asking why were evil, no matter how beautiful.

If she hadn't had the gun she might not

have considered it. Without it she was essentially powerless — all she could do was run and hide.

With it she had at least a tiny chance to save him. And she'd never be able to live with herself if she didn't try.

She squared her shoulders, pushing her long, tangled hair behind her back, and started toward the open door. He'd told her every exit, every door and window in this sprawling place was equipped with an electric-shock system that might very well kill her. The schematics outlined the security system, but there was no sign of any electrical addendum, and she didn't dare try to mess with it.

All she could do was step through that door, into freedom, and if she died trying, so be it. She was dead either way.

Just to be on the safe side, she jumped over the threshold, careful not to let any part of her body touch the door frame. She landed in the soft dirt on the other side, unscathed. She took a deep breath, hoping for the pure air of freedom, but the rotting tropical vegetation was heavy and strange. She needed to be away from boats, the ocean and islands. If she made it safely back to her apartment in New York, she wasn't leaving again.

Of course, Manhattan was technically an island. But it didn't feel like one — it felt solid and safe, where you only had to worry about rapists and muggers . . .

And crazy people coming out of the sky, crashing airplanes into buildings. Maybe she'd been living in a fantasy world, thinking anything was safe.

She'd have time to figure that out, God willing. In the meantime she needed to get to the place where they were keeping Harry and see if he was still alive. If he wasn't, then she could run for cover with no guilt.

It was the best she could hope for.

12

Genevieve moved through the jungle, trying to envision herself as a stealthy cat, afraid she was more like a water buffalo in a china shop. First off, the white T-shirt had been a mistake — she should have gone for something darker, less conspicuous, something that would blend in with the background. She just wasn't used to subterfuge outside the courtroom. Never in a thousand years could she have imagined herself on the run for her life, a loaded gun tucked in her waistband, ready for use. What if she actually had to shoot someone?

What if she had to shoot Peter?

She'd do it, no questions asked. She wouldn't hesitate, wouldn't think about it. Not until later.

But that wasn't going to happen, she decided grimly. Life had handed her a series of difficult choices, but having to kill Peter Jensen would be too cruel, even for a patently sadistic universe.

She couldn't waste her time with what-ifs. There wasn't enough time left.

She had the gun drawn as she crept up toward the back of the storage shed where Harry was being held, assuming she could believe the schematic. There was no noise — not the muffled sound of someone breathing a deep, drugged sleep. Was it too late?

She edged around the corner, cautiously. There was a small window in the side of the building, but it was blacked out from the inside, and she could see nothing. She waited, long, breathless moments, and unwillingly the memory returned of hiding on the boat, only to face her nemesis after what should have been sufficient time.

If nemesis was what he was. He'd been her lover — what had gone on between them physically, emotionally, made that fact undeniable. No, scratch that. He had no emotions — it had all been on her side.

But his heart had been pounding, his strong body trembling as he'd held her. It made no sense, he made no sense, but she had no time to figure it out right now. If she survived she'd have more than enough time to dissect the madness that had afflicted her during the last thirty-six hours.

She couldn't wait there forever. The shed was still and quiet, and she took a deep breath and rounded the corner, to find the door open and no one, neither Harry Van Dorn nor his captors, in sight.

There were drag marks in the dirt — someone had hauled Harry's limp body in the direction of the main house. He was either too drugged to walk on his own, or . . .

There was no blood in the tiny shed, and no blood on the ground. But that proved nothing — there were bloodless ways to kill people, and Peter would know all of them.

Genevieve glanced over her shoulder. The path to the far side of the island, the hidden bunker, was still clear enough in her mind.

But Harry was being taken back toward the main house. And that was where she had to go, whether she liked it or not.

She heard the noise first — the grunting, groaning sound of a man struggling with too heavy a load.

Make that two men. Their voices came back to her, and she breathed a small sigh of relief that neither of them was Peter.

They were too busy arguing to even notice anyone was approaching. "You told me my job was done once I set the charges." It had to have been Hans speaking. "I've already done enough shit work on this assignment."

"You're the one who gave him too much of the drugs," Renaud snapped. "And you can't expect his lordship to bother with old Harry, can you? He's the brains of the operations, and if we know what's good for us we'll do what he says without arguing."

"I just don't like the fact that he got to spend the last day in a billionaire's love nest with a decent piece of tail while we were camping in the jungle. I'm half covered with bug bites."

They'd reached the back of the house, and if there was any kind of electric security it had been turned off. They dragged their burden through the gate without incident. "That's why he gets paid the big bucks," Renaud said in a sour voice. "Right now he's sitting on the deck of the ship, drinking gin and tonics and waiting for us to get back before he takes off. Count your blessings. We're both expendable and you know it — no one would ask questions if he just left us here to disappear along with half the island. But Jensen has a reputation of never leaving a man behind, even if he's wounded. At least we've got that much going for us."

"Wouldn't do him any good if he did leave us behind," Hans panted, dragging Harry onto the flagstone patio and dumping him facedown. He didn't move. "I set the charges and I'm the only one who knows how to blow them so that it'll look like a gas leak. He's too careful to mess up a plan like this even if he wanted to."

Renaud grabbed one of the heavy wicker chairs and pulled it forward. "Come on, dickshit. We need to get this done and get out of here. This place gives me the willies."

Between the two of them they hauled Harry's body into the chair. His head lolled back, but he was definitely still alive. He made an unintelligible sound, and Hans laughed.

"Just goes to show money can't buy everything, Froggy," Hans said, tying Harry's limp body to the chair with quick efficiency.

Renaud had stepped back, watching from a distance, his back to the spot where Genevieve cowered in the bushes. "It can buy a lot." He sounded detached, almost philosophical.

"What do you suppose he did with the girl?" Hans asked, glancing inside the house. "Think there's anything left of her for a bit of fun?"

"Not that you'd want. He killed her last night — she was getting too yappy, he said, and there was no reason to put it off."

"Well, I can think of one good reason, but

maybe Peter doesn't swing that way. He should have done her on the boat and dumped her overboard," Hans said, disapproving. "He's supposed to be the best closer there is. If he's so fucking good, why didn't he just off her and get it over with instead of dragging her onto the island?"

"She was going to be Harry's excuse for coming here unannounced and sending the servants away. She got caught up in a love tryst and met a sad end."

"Tryst," Hans said. "It rhymes with pissed, not Christ."

"Fuck off," Renaud said in a genial voice.

Hans turned back to face his cohort, and Genevieve could make out a confused expression on his face. "What the hell are you doing, Froggy?" he demanded.

"Money can't buy everything, my friend, but it can buy a lot. Including me."

She heard the faint popping sound almost at the same time the round hole appeared in the middle of Hans's forehead. For a moment everything moved in slow motion, and then Hans's big body crumpled to the ground.

"Poor stupid Kraut," Renaud muttered as he went to untie Harry. "Never call a Frenchman 'Froggy.'"

Genevieve didn't move, frozen to the

thick, damp earth beneath her. She wanted to throw up. She'd just seen a man killed, as easily as swatting a fly, and her stomach churned in protest against such horror.

She forced herself to breathe, trying to pull her shocked wits together. Hans was dead, Harry was alive, and Renaud had been bought. By Harry. With Hans dead, the place wouldn't be blown up; with Renaud busy saving Harry's life she could run for it with no guilt at all.

Peter was already on the boat, ready to sail away. If he came back and found Hans's body, would he abort the mission or reset the charges and blow the place? Or would he track Harry down and finish it himself? And finish her?

Why had he lied and said he'd already killed her? What did it matter if Renaud knew she was dead or not? For that matter, why did he leave her alive in the first place?

She started to move backward, deeper into the undergrowth, when Renaud's voice shattered her illusion of safety.

"Get your ass out here, lady. I can't carry Harry by myself."

She could run. He wouldn't have a clear shot at her, and Harry was a bigger priority for him at the moment.

Then again, he'd saved Harry. Wasn't that

what she wanted?

"And put the gun down. I don't think you know how to use it, but women with guns are always dangerous. And stop dragging your heels. I have no problem killing you if you aren't going to help me."

She emerged from the bushes, setting the gun down on the flagstone patio. She didn't want to look at Hans's body. When she was growing up, the various family cats had brought in bird and rodent corpses as a token of appreciation, and she'd had to avert her eyes while she covered whatever was left of them with a paper towel while someone with a stronger stomach would remove them.

Hans was a far cry from a decapitated sparrow, and she felt her stomach lurch again. She focused her attention on Renaud, not the most appetizing sight himself.

"I have to get him to the far side of the island — Harry was with it long enough to let me know how to get a seaplane to pick us up. You, too, if you do what I tell you. Are you going to help me?"

"Of course. But won't they come after us when you don't show up at the boat and the place doesn't explode? What if the plane doesn't get here in time?"

"By 'they' do you mean Peter? He won't

wait that long — company policy. Rules of the game. Once the place blows he'll be out of here, thinking everyone's dead and the perfect plan went perfectly. He won't like it that two low-level operatives didn't make it, but he won't lose any sleep over it."

"He doesn't strike me as the kind of man who leaves anything to chance," Genevieve pointed out.

"You know him pretty well for such a short time. I wonder why he lied about killing you."

"I have no idea. I assure you, he planned to."

Renaud shrugged. "It doesn't matter. Yes, Jensen's a thorough, exacting professional at what he does. A bloody artiste, if you ask me — I've seen his work. But he also knows just how good he is and he'd never imagine that a hired gun like me could outsmart him."

"And what if he comes back to check?"

"Then I'll kill him. But he won't get that far, if for some crazy reason he decided to leave the boat. Half the island will be gone in another twenty minutes, and if we don't get rich boy out of here, we'll be gone as well. And I don't intend to let that happen. I'm going to end up with more than enough money so that Peter Jensen and his entire fucking Committee can never find me."

"I thought Hans said he was the only one who could blow it?"

"You were standing there that long? You're better than I thought." He rubbed his unshaven jaw. He still had a bruise from where she'd kicked him, and she devoutly hoped he hadn't noticed it beneath the grime. "Hans isn't the only one here who understands demolitions. They've been set and I'm leaving them. We've got twenty minutes, lady, but that's it."

"Wasn't," she said.

"Pardon?"

"Hans wasn't the only one who knows demolitions. Past tense. He's dead."

"So he is," Renaud said. "I'm getting a little tired of everyone trying to correct my English. Get your ass over here or I'll do what Peter should've done."

She skirted the body sprawled on the ground and began to help haul Harry to his feet. He opened his eyes for a moment, flashed the ghost of his engaging, toothy smile before passing out again.

"Shit," said Renaud, struggling under Harry's weight. "I thought he'd be coming out of it by now. I cut back the dosage with him but I hadn't counted on Hans becoming a problem. It's hard to tell how much to dose him — he's got the constitution of an ox. I can give him twice the amount of drugs that would kill a normal man and it barely slows him down." He shifted Harry's weight. "Put your shoulder under his arm and let's get moving. Unless you'd rather stay out here and end up as pixie dust."

He weighed a ton. They half carried, half dragged him away from the house, moving into the greenery at a snail's pace.

"Where are we going?" she managed to gasp out.

"It wouldn't make any difference if I told you," he wheezed. "A beach on the far side of the island."

She flashed back to the detailed schematic stored in her mind, and after a moment she remembered the stretch of beach on the opposite side of the island from the villa. Far enough to escape any damage from the explosion, she hoped. It all depended on how ambitious Hans had been.

Not enough to damage Harry's boat, which was probably back where they'd been dropped off, close to the main house. If they could just get far enough away in time, they should be fine.

The hidden bunker wasn't too far away from the beach, in case anything went wrong. And she fully expected things to go wrong at this point, the way her luck had been going.

Her bare foot caught on a root, and she went sprawling on the trail, Harry's heavy body landing on top of her as Renaud let go with a curse.

For a moment she couldn't breathe — Harry was heavier than he'd appeared, and it was like lying under a horse.

A second later, the weight was removed and replaced by a gun barrel pressed against her temple. "Do that again," he growled, "and I'm leaving you behind."

She was going to point out that it hadn't exactly been her fault, but she kept quiet. She'd been able to fight back with Peter. If she said anything, anything at all, Renaud might very well pull the trigger.

Leaving lawyer brains all over Harry. His cleaning services were going to have a hard enough time getting rid of the dirt and grass stains on his Versace sportswear. Lawyer brains would be almost impossible to get out.

She scrambled to her feet, ignoring her skinned knee, and helped Renaud haul Harry upright again. Harry was marginally more awake — he looked down at Genevieve out of totally stoned-out eyes and murmured something unintelligible.

"Keep going, Harry," she muttered. "We're trying to save your life."

He didn't seem particularly moved by the notion, but he managed to put a marginal effort into propelling his big, drugged body forward down the narrow path and they moved onward, like a macabre funeral procession with the corpse still alive.

This was always the hardest part, even in the simplest, most straightforward of operations, Peter thought, staring at the island from the deck of the newly refitted SS *Seven Sins* run by Mannion and a crew of the Committee's finest. Now called the SS *Tough Break* — someone's sense of humor at work. It was bad luck to change the name of a boat — Harry would be rolling in his grave very soon.

He'd checked Hans's munitions work, and the man had done his usual stellar job. Now it was a simple matter of Hans and Renaud getting Harry's unconscious body to the house and getting back to the boat before the charges went off.

He wasn't going to think about Genevieve — he couldn't. He gave her everything he could to get her out of harm's way, and he simply had to let go of it. Either she'd make it or she wouldn't. The rest was up to her.

But she was smart, and she didn't give up easily. His instincts told him she'd make it to the bunker safely, and it would be a simple enough matter to send someone to rescue her, all without leaving a trace. She'd never be able to find him — no one knew about the Committee and the work they did. No one even knew where their headquarters were located.

There was a chance he might never know whether she survived or not. He could live with that — he'd lived with far worse. And in the end, who was she? Just a stray female who'd wandered into his path for a few days, then wandered out. Easily forgettable.

She was nothing, nothing to him at all . . . And then all his justifications vanished as the island exploded into flames.

The blast hit with almost atomic force. The ground shook beneath them, and Genevieve went flying through the air, her grip on Harry's arm nonexistent.

It knocked the breath from her, it blocked out consciousness as well. A moment, an hour, later, she opened her eyes to find herself sprawled on the ground in a pool of blood, and Harry and Renaud were nowhere in sight.

The smell of burning chemicals and fire

hung heavy in the air, blocking out the thick tropical vegetation, and smoke was shooting up into the sky, great billowing plumes of it. She sat up, looking down at the white T-shirt. It was now dark with blood. Her own.

She must be in shock, she thought absently, counting her limbs, fingers and toes. Everything seemed connected — she touched her head, and her hand came away bloody. Either she'd suffered some kind of brain injury and was about to die, or she'd simply knocked her head. Head wounds always bled like crazy, she reminded herself, struggling to get to her feet. She might as well assume the best and keep moving. She couldn't just lie here on the path and bleed.

Besides, she could hear the fire now, and the smoke was getting thicker. She didn't think a semitropical forest would burn that easily, but she wasn't about to take the chance.

She'd lost any sense of direction, and for a moment she was afraid she was going to walk back into the fire, but Renaud's path through the heavy growth supporting a burden like Harry was easy enough to make out, and she started after them, wiping the blood away from her eyes with calm determination.

She almost missed them. When she stumbled onto the clearing the seaplane was already there, in Van Dorn Enterprises signature orange-and-black colors. The noise of the engines shut out any other sound, and Harry was already on a stretcher, surrounded by an army of caretakers.

She tried to call out, but the sound was carried away by the wind. She made it halfway across the beach and then her strength failed her, and she sank to her knees in the hot sand.

Renaud was standing to one side, and he was the first to see her. He had his gun out, and she wondered if he was going to kill her.

He said something to one of the men hovering over Harry, and they all turned to look in her direction. And then dismissed her as patently unimportant.

She would've liked to march over to one of them, grab him by the lapels of his fancy suit and smack him. Or at least give them a piece of her mind.

But she had nothing left to give. She couldn't even keep her balance, and she pitched forward onto the sand. It was going to get into her head wound, she thought, and it would be a bitch to clean. But then, maybe that wasn't going to matter . . .

The hands on her were rough, but she didn't, couldn't protest. They were dragging her across the sand, and while she could have wished for a stretcher like Harry's, she wasn't in any condition to complain.

Someone bundled her onto the seaplane, dumping her into a seat and then ignoring her while they tended to their fallen master. She leaned her head against the window, not giving a flying fuck if she bloodied Harry's precious plane, and closed her eyes as she felt it begin to move.

She heard a sound, and she managed to surface from her fog for a moment, to look out the window. The doors of the seaplane were still open, which seemed impractical to her, and she opened her mouth to say something. When she looked down below.

The island was on fire, the inky smoke shooting toward the sky. Harry's yacht was moving slowly away from the conflagration, heading out into the clear greeny blue of the Caribbean, when something dark came hurtling out of the sky as they passed directly overhead. A moment later the boat disintegrated, as if it had never existed. There was nothing left but a shower of smoke and dust.

She must have made some sound. A cry,

torn from her smoke-damaged throat, as Peter Jensen was wiped from existence as if he'd never been there at all.

Her cry was enough to catch the attention of the man who'd been hovering over Harry's limp body. A doctor, she thought, wishing she could feel relief, glad that she could feel nothing at all.

"You're a mess, aren't you?" the old man said in a heavy German accent. "Looks like you might have a concussion. We should've left you behind with a bullet between the eyes like that scumbag, but Mr. Van Dorn said bring you along."

What scumbag? Renaud? They'd killed him? She tried to say something, anything, when she felt the pinprick in her arm.

"This will either kill you or cure you," he said.

And they were the last words she heard.

13

The dreams were horrible, never ending. Genevieve felt as if she was being smothered, trapped in a nightmare world of blood, fire and pain. She drank the smoke and it silenced her. She bled and she couldn't move. The flames licked around her, the pain so sharp it blinded her, and death had moved under her skin and settled there.

She could see Hans, revolving slowly in front of her like a carousel horse, the hole in his forehead a silent scream. She could see Peter, but each time she reached out to touch him he disintegrated into dust that sparkled in the sun.

The carousel kept spinning, and she would see Harry, sprawled on one of the benches that moved sedately around, his huge smile unshadowed by all around him. Renaud would come into view every now and then, and the black hole in his face was lower than Hans's — directly between his dark, staring eyes. And the merry-go-round would turn once more the calliope loud and macabre, and Peter would be there again for a brief moment before dissolving once more into nothingness.

She clung to the darkness and pain, stubborn, even as it began to recede. The light was taking her to a place she didn't want to be, and she fought hard to stay in the hopeless night. But in the end her will wasn't strong enough, and she opened her eyes to a strange room.

She had no idea where she was. Presumably it was late afternoon or evening — the room was deep in shadows. She wasn't alone — someone was moving quietly at the far end, and for a moment she wondered if she was in Harry Van Dorn's villa.

But no, that was gone as well, and she closed her eyes again, seeking the black emptiness that had become her life.

"Awake, miss?" The voice by her side was soft, hesitant, and she wanted desperately to ignore it, but her eyes betrayed her, opening to stare into the plain, reserved face of a middle-aged Asian woman, dressed in some sort of dark traditional clothing.

"I'm awake," she said, but her normally strong voice was little more than a husky whisper. "Where am I?"

The response wasn't encouraging — a rapid-fire explanation in a language Genevieve couldn't identify much less speak.

"Where am I?" she asked again, slower.

The woman shook her head. "You wait," she said.

At that point Genevieve doubted she could have gone anywhere at all on her own strength. "I wait," she said, leaning back against the pillows, exhausted.

She was coming back to life when she wasn't sure she wanted to. The first thing she noticed was the bedding. The sheets were like silk — soft and smooth and of the highest-quality cotton. The same sheets had been on the island. She'd slept, wrapped in one. She lay on top of one, clutching it in her hands while he —

She let out a soft cry, sitting up, then moaning as her head began to pound once more. Harry's sheets, Harry's house. But where? And how, and why? Her memories were jumbled . . . She could see herself kneeling in the sand. But she couldn't remember how she got there.

Then on a small plane that took off in a swoop that almost left her stomach behind. Renaud hadn't been on it, and she should remember what happened to him but she couldn't.

Instead, she remembered what she didn't want to remember. The huge yacht being blown to ashes, with Peter Jensen on board.

And she started to cry.

Once started, she couldn't stop. The sobs racked her body, so heavy that she was shaking, and the more she tried to stop them the more powerful they became. She fell back against the pillows, and the tears ran down her face. She shoved a fist in her mouth to quiet the sobs, but it did little good. She finally she gave in, rolling over on her stomach and burying her face in the pillow.

Wherever the woman had disappeared to, it was taking her a blessedly long time to get back to her. Slowly, slowly her tears began to lessen, her sobs quieted, as reality began to drift back in odd-shaped puzzle pieces.

She wasn't crying over Peter Jensen.

He who lived by the sword died by the sword, didn't they say? A man in his profession would court death on a daily basis. It was only logical that one day the match would be made.

No, she had no reason to cry over Peter. It was only a natural response to the horrific few days she'd spent, a normal release of built-up tension. She would just as likely weep over Hans's murder; she'd been forced to witness that in all its horror. Surely that was having a more powerful impact on her than Peter's antiseptic death.

But she hadn't slept with Hans. She hadn't opened her arms and her body and God knows what else to him, letting him strip everything away.

No man had ever done that to her, leaving her so lost and vulnerable. And no man ever would again. She was delighted he was dead. Triumphant. She had complete revenge for what he'd done to her, how he'd made her feel.

And she burst into tears again.

"Come now, little lady." Harry Van Dorn's bourbon-warm voice slithered through her misery. "No need to cry over spilt milk. You're safe and sound right here — no one's going to hurt you."

It was like a glass of cold water being thrown in her face — strange, when his voice was so warm and smooth. She wiped her face on the expensive sheets, her tears cut off, and looked up at him.

He looked the same — tanned, well dressed, wide, friendly smile. There was no sign of his recent imprisonment, whereas she was covered with bruises and scratches from her trip through the island paths.

Either he was remarkably resilient or he had a good makeup artist.

She swallowed the last lingering shudder. "How are you feeling?" she asked.

"Hell, Genevieve, I'm fine. I'm as strong as a horse. It would take more than a few days knocked out on drugs to get me down. You're the one who's been through the wars. You've got stitches, and the doc says you suffered a concussion."

"Where am I? How long have I been here? What happened?" Her voice sounded anxious, almost hysterical, and she wished she could call back her questions, sound calm and professional.

"Now, now, don't you worry your pretty little head about a thing. We've got you safe here. And there's no way anyone can get to you."

"Get to me? Who would want to?" The concussion explained the pain in her head — was it also responsible for the fact that nothing seemed to make any sense to her?

"The people who are out to get me are a very smart, very powerful group of terrorists. They've been after me for a long time, and you screwed that up. Thanks to you we've now got a pretty good idea who they are and where they come from."

"Thanks to me?"

"They found a crumpled-up note tucked in your shorts, and they were able to trace it to the man who wrote it. The man calling himself Peter Jensen. His real name is Madsen, and he works for a group of terrorists called the Committee. Not very original, right? They've targeted me, though I can't quite figure out why. Maybe my money, maybe because of my humanitarian activities. Whatever the reason, they wanted me dead, and you threw a monkey wrench into their plans. I don't know if I've ever owed so much to one person."

She was having a hard time taking all this in. "Terrorists?" she echoed. She'd thought the same thing, despite Peter's insistence that he was one of the good guys. Didn't villains always think they were heroes?

But Harry's explanation wasn't feeling right to her. Something was off, something was wrong.

"Now, don't you fuss. He's dead, and there's no way he can get to either of us ever again. I just wish I'd had the chance to bring him to the justice he so richly deserved."

The blow to her head must have really scrambled her brains, she thought dizzily. Harry Van Dorn was saying the right words, sounding brave and noble and heroic. And all she could think was that he'd stolen her letter, the one thing she had of Peter Jensen. Madsen. Whoever the hell he was.

Or had been. She could feel her eyes begin to sting and she shook her head, trying to fight the overwhelming grief.

Harry was oblivious. He sat down on the bed beside her, and for some reason she wanted to move away from him. Odd, when he was harmless, a victim as she was. Had been. "Even with Madsen dead I'm afraid you've made some very dangerous enemies, and I aim to make sure you don't suffer for helping to save me."

"Where are we?" she asked again, dismissing his facile reassurances.

"Someplace they'll never find you."

"Where?" she persisted. "Are we somewhere in Asia?" She glanced over his shoulder at the still, dark figure of an Asian man, could see the various servants bustling around.

"Not near any chance of tsunamis," Harry said with an easy laugh.

"I wasn't even thinking about that," she said. "And as far as I can tell, we're right on the ocean. How can that make us impervious to tsunamis?"

"Okay, not impervious," Harry corrected with a lazy grin. "You lawyers are all so literal. Let's just say a tidal wave would be a long shot where this house is situated."

"Where?"

"You don't give up that easy, do you, Genevieve? I hope you don't mind me calling you that — I figure since we shared such an adventure we ought to be on a first-name basis."

She wouldn't have called those days of death and danger any kind of adventure, but then, he didn't know that. He'd spent the entire time in a drugged-out stupor. "Where are we, Harry?" she asked once more, her patience a deception that was about to shred.

"I really can't tell you," he said, and she almost believed the regret in his soft, oozing drawl. "The fewer people who know about the location of this place, the better. You'll be leaving here when things are safe, and it wouldn't be wise to have you out in the open with that kind of knowledge. Too dangerous for you, much too dangerous for me."

"In other words, if you tell me you'll have to kill me?"

His smile was exquisitely charming. "You're better off forgetting all about the time you spend here."

She was beginning to get ever so slightly

pissed off. "And do you have some complicated reason for not telling me how long
that is?"

Her slightly acid tone was lost on him.
"Thirteen days."

"What?" she shrieked, and was rewarded
with a stabbing pain in the head. "That's
impossible. I couldn't have slept for thirteen
days."

"Not exactly. You had a concussion, remember? Doc Schmidt decided to put you
in a drug-induced coma in order to give you
time to heal. And don't look so horrified —
my staff took excellent care of you while
you were out of it."

"You drugged me? And how is that different from what those bastards were doing to
you?" she said, practically vibrating with
fury. She was forgetting all her well-behaved,
lawyerly manners and she didn't give a
damn.

"Because we were trying to help you, not
keep you docile before we killed you," Harry
said patiently. "Besides, you were under the
care of a doctor. You shouldn't be so sensi-
tive."

Personally, Genevieve thought she had
every right to be a little high-strung, given
the circumstances, but she kept silent on
that subject. "And how much longer am I

going to stay in this mystery location?"

"Until you're well enough to leave, and until the danger is gone. That treacherous son of a bitch might have been blown to hell, but there are a dozen others to take his place, and they don't give up lightly."

"But . . ."

"Jack, I want you to see that our guest has everything she could possibly want." Harry overrode her objection, rising to his full height. "This here is Jack O'Brien, one of my executive assistants."

"Like Peter Jensen?"

Harry grimaced. "Jack's been with me too long to question his loyalty. Besides, he would never betray me, would you, pal? After all, I know where the bodies are buried."

The man standing in the shadows stepped forward, bowing slightly. "Anything you wish, Ms. Spenser," he said in a soft, deferential voice.

"See?" Harry said, clearly pleased with himself. "You couldn't be in better hands. Jack's one of the best. I know what you're thinking — what's an Oriental man doing with a name like Jack O'Brien? His father was white, his mother a Jap. His real name is something I can't pronounce, so I just call him Jack."

The man nodded again, seemingly oblivious to Harry's casual racism. "You'll be perfectly safe here, Ms. Spenser."

Now, why did they keep emphasizing her safety? Harry was the one who was making her feel unsafe.

"I'll need to leave you in Jack's capable hands, Genevieve. I have a lot of irons in the fire right now, and I've been away too long. Just know that you can trust Jack as you trust me."

For some reason that wasn't comforting, she thought as the door closed behind him, leaving her alone with another of Harry's ghostlike assistants. Her energy was nonexistent — whether from the drugs they'd used or thirteen days of inactivity, she couldn't be sure. And for some reason she wanted to cry again. All over someone who deserved to die.

The man took in her grief-stricken face with a polite air of acknowledgment. "Is there any way I can be of service, miss? I'm afraid I'm the only one here who speaks English, but I'd be glad to offer any assistance you might need. With Mr. Van Dorn's resources my abilities are almost limitless."

"Can you bring people back from the dead?" she said, then slapped her hand over her mouth, horrified at her inadvertent words. She wasn't going to cry for Peter Jensen, she absolutely wasn't. She hadn't even known his real name — how could she mourn him?

The man didn't look daunted, though there was a slightly odd expression in his dark eyes. "I haven't done so as yet, Ms. Spenser."

"Never mind. I was just being ridiculous." Her brave smile was probably pathetic, but Jack O'Brien politely pretended not to notice. "I just want to . . ." She stared up at his cool, impassive face. "What's your real name?" she asked. "I don't care if Harry's too lazy he can't master it — I'd be more comfortable calling you by your real name."

He hesitated for a moment. "Takashi," he said finally. "Very much like Jack — I'm used to it."

"And your last name is O'Brien?" she persisted.

She might almost have thought he'd smiled. "He's right about that. My father was an Irishman. I take after my mother's side of the family in all ways." He frowned, as if he'd already said too much. "I have things to attend to, Ms. Spenser, if there's nothing else I can do for you."

"You can arrange for me to get out of here."

"That's almost as difficult as raising the dead," he said. "But I'll see what I can do. Anh will be bringing you something to eat in a little while. If you don't feel like drinking the tea, you could just pour it out when no one's looking. That way no one will be offended."

Either that was an incredibly strange thing to say, or the drugs in her system were still confusing her. She looked up at him, but his cool expression gave nothing away. "I certainly wouldn't want to offend anyone," she said finally.

He nodded. "It's always better that way," he said. "If you need anything just say my name to one of the servants and they'll come and find me."

"What name?"

He didn't smile. "Either one, Ms. Spenser. Call, and I'll come. In the meantime, I'll see what I can do about your requested miracles."

She should have asked for Tab while she was at it. It was just as likely as bringing Peter back from the dead.

Except . . .

It hit her with stunning force. He wasn't dead. She didn't know how she knew it, but she just did. He hadn't been on that boat when it exploded into a shower of nothingness. She could feel it, in her bones, in her gut. Peter whoever-he-was wasn't dead.

And she was probably still too hopped up on the meds they'd been giving her to know her own mother.

She didn't care. If it was a fantasy then she was happy enough to live in it. After all, she was never going to see the man again, either way.

She'd just be happier believing he was alive. Still on this earth, tormenting some other poor woman who happened to get in his way.

No more tears. She needed to look forward, to get out of this mink-lined prison and back to America. Right now, all she had to worry about was herself. And that was going to keep her busy enough.

Harry's affable smile vanished the moment Jack-shit left him alone in his study. Even for someone as necessary as his Jap assistant there were certain precautions, certain formalities. He'd given Jack the order to kill in the past, and Jack had followed through with his customary silent efficiency, but still Harry had never let his charming smile fade.

It was gone now, and he prowled the study

like an angry jungle cat. He liked the image — he could picture himself as a sleek, oversize panther, a danger to all who knew him. And he was. He was just smart enough to fool them.

She'd fucked him. The little bitch lawyer had fucked Jensen — he could see it on her, smell it on her. She'd kept her distance from him that first night on the boat and then spread her legs for that lying bastard, and for that she was going to have to pay.

Things would have been so different if she'd just done her duty and slept with him that first night. He'd come to expect it from the women his lawyers sent down to him, and Genevieve Spenser should have been no different.

But she'd kept her distance, and he'd been alone when they came to get him. If she'd been there they might have thought twice. Or he could have used her as a shield, slowing them long enough so they couldn't knock him out.

She was as much to blame as Peter Jensen and his crackpot do-gooder Committee. And he was going to have to do something about it.

As soon as he tried to repair the damage that had been done. Destroying the dam in Mysore was out of the question now — the security had been beefed up, the insurgents he'd put on retainer had disappeared. The sabotage of the oil fields was also questionable — the paperwork had disappeared along with his gorgeous boat, and the wells were still in his name. It might give him an even stronger appearance of innocence if something were to happen to them while he still owned them, but he couldn't quite bring himself to make that sacrifice. He'd drop that one as well, for now.

Harry kicked the walnut desk, angry and frustrated. They were getting in the way of his careful plans, and it was more than annoying. He required a certain symmetry, and the Rule of Seven was inviolate. They'd smashed that, and there was no proper ring to the Rule of Five.

And it was only four days till April nineteenth, the beginning of the end. Four days to come up with two equally effective circumstances to throw the financial world into chaos. At least his enemies were way behind the eight ball. They might have found out two of his targets, but they had no idea about the deadly strain of avian flu that was about to hit mainland China, or the diamond mines in South Africa, or the memorial shrine at Auschwitz being blown to pieces when the visitors' center was full.

Maybe he was being too hard on himself. The Rule of Seven had been simple, working east to west. It would start with the massive outbreak of avian flu, the dam in Mysore, the diamond mine in South Africa, the oil fields in Saudi Arabia. Then came the extermination camp in Poland, the Houses of Parliament in London, ending with a three-pronged assault in America, with hits on Waco, Texas, Oklahoma City and Littleton, Colorado, home of Columbine High School. On the most auspicious days of all, April nineteenth to the twentieth, days made for disruption and terror and reaping what you sow.

Peter Jensen had seemed the perfect assistant, given the birthday he shared with Adolf Hitler. It had seemed a sign, that he would be there, keeping things running smoothly as Harry put the final acts into motion.

They'd played him for a fool, and he really didn't like being played for a fool.

That lying scum-sucker was dead, out of his reach, and Harry's frustration level was making him shake. He'd have to make do with Genevieve Spenser. He'd take out his rage on her, and then Jack-shit could clean up the mess with his customary efficiency.

But somehow the notion was only slightly

soothing. He poured himself a glass of bourbon, noticing his shaking hand. And then he slammed the glass against the dark oak paneling, as the rage took control of him once more.

14

Peter Madsen pulled into the weed-choked driveway, automatically checking for signs of intruders as he parked in the cul-de-sac to the right of the old house. This was the only part of the landscaping that was supposed to be untended and overgrown, to provide him just a bit more camouflage when he came home.

Not that he could call it, or anyplace, home. It was mid-April and by now the gardens should have started blooming. Instead, they were desolate — a fitting reflection of its owner, he thought grimly.

He switched off the elaborate, undetectable security system and stepped inside. Not that there was anything in the sparsely furnished house of particular value. He had little attachment to things, and apart from his grandfather's huge desk he had little of any intrinsic worth.

He never could figure out why he'd bought

his grandfather's desk in the first place. He'd just happened to catch sight of the public auction of Dr. Wilton Wimberley's possessions, and he'd gone on an unlikely impulse, when he was never, ever impulsive.

There would be no stray member of the family around to possibly identify him. His parents were long dead, and his mother had been an only child. The proceeds of the estate were going to endow a chair in his grandfather's name at Oxford. One way to secure his legacy, since his offspring had failed him.

He'd be just as happy if someone broke in and carried the damn thing off, though it weighed a bloody ton. He didn't have the kind of job that required a desk, and he was very careful never to leave a paper trail.

No, he hadn't installed the security to protect the house. He simply wanted to ensure there were no unpleasant surprises waiting for him on the rare occasions he got down to Wiltshire. A really good operative could figure out how to bypass the system, but it would be impossible not to leave very visible proof someone had tampered with the place.

He was almost sorry they hadn't. Avoiding a lethal trap would be a welcome distraction, and if, after all these years, his luck failed him, then so be it.

In fact, things were definitely taking a turn for the worse. Harry Van Dorn was the first mission he'd ever failed to complete, and it was little wonder he was feeling like shit. His professional pride was wounded, nothing more. The wrong person had died.

He'd done his best for her, given her tools and a map and as strong a hint as he dared. If she hadn't gotten away it wasn't his fault, just part of the grand cock-up that the Van Dorn assignment had become.

The house smelled stale and empty and faintly of mice. If he was going to sell the place he'd have to get a massive cleaning crew in to rid it of its neglected air.

Putting it on the market was the smart thing to do. For some sentimental fool it would seem the perfect house — slate roof, diamond-pane windows and the kind of winding floor plan that attested to almost three hundred years of additions and improvements. His wife had always complained that it was too old-fashioned, and she hated to garden. He'd never taken her to the stripped-down, ultramodern flat in London where he spent most of his time. It would have suited her perfectly and she'd never even known it existed.

Funny, he never thought of his ex-wife by

her name, only by her relationship to him. That was part of the problem. He'd chosen the perfect trophy wife and he'd never given a rat's ass about her.

Annabelle. Annabelle Lawson — how could he have forgotten? But then, why should he remember? Women came and went through his shadowy life, some lived, some died. But in the end he forgot them, and he wasn't going to let that change.

He better turn up the heat while he was here — it might improve the damp chill. He took the two steps down into the old kitchen. The Aga sat in solitary splendor at one end, and the stone hearth had been swept clean of ashes. He sat at the scarred old oak table, the one his wife had tried to replace with some upscale form of plastic, and stared out into the gathering darkness.

He heard her coming, of course, but she knew he would. Madame Isobel Lambert, his superior and current head of the Committee, seemed to know just about everything, including the fact that he'd recognize her from a distance and not kill her before he identified her.

"Moping, Peter?" she asked, pausing in the kitchen doorway. If it was anyone but Madame Lambert he would've said she did it for dramatic effect, but that was very small currency in Madame's arsenal.

He leaned back in the wooden chair. "Have you ever known me to mope?" he asked in a steady voice.

"No. But then, I've never known you to fail in a mission before."

"Is that what this is about? I thought I made a complete report while I was in London. I wouldn't have left if I knew you still had questions."

"Your report was crystal clear in every detail, as it always is," Madame Lambert said, stepping down into the kitchen. She was a remarkable woman. She could have been anywhere between thirty-five and sixty, and the perfection of her well-tended appearance was like an impenetrable suit of armor. No one and nothing scared Peter Madsen, but Isobel Lambert came close.

"Then why are you here?"

"I wanted to make certain you were all right. It's the first mission you've ever failed to complete, and I was a bit . . . concerned."

"You think I'm going to blow my brains out because I failed to do the same to Harry Van Dorn? Not likely."

"I was more concerned you might decide to resign."

"I'm touched," he drawled.

"Surely you don't expect my concern to

be personal, do you? We've both been in this business a long time, and we know the mortality rate. My job is to make certain the Committee is well staffed, and since Bastien left you're the best we have."

He raised an eyebrow and she laughed her light, silvery laugh. "I'm sorry," she amended. "Since Bastien left you're the only good operative we have left."

"I'm not resigning," he said after a moment. "I'm not really equipped to do anything else, am I? I can kill. I'm certain there will always be a job opening at the Committee for that."

"Everyone has a failed mission now and then, Peter. You'll be a better operative now, knowing you can fail."

"You make it sound like I lost my erection. 'Don't worry, dear, it happens to everyone,' " he said, mockery hiding his anger.

"Well, metaphorically, isn't that exactly what happened?"

"Metaphorically, I fucked up. I didn't pick up on the fact that Renaud had turned, and I waited too long to go back and make certain Van Dorn was dead." He knew why he had hesitated. He didn't want to run into Genevieve Spenser. He didn't want to find her dead, he didn't want to find her alive and have to decide what to do about it. He left her fate in her own hands, and he hadn't wanted to have to take it back.

Madame Lambert simply shrugged. "Everyone screws up occasionally — I trust you more as a fallible human being than an efficient robot."

"Then I did it all for you," he said lightly.

"Besides, you don't need to worry. Harry Van Dorn is well in hand. This operation has always been too big to have it rest with one plan. We already have someone in situ, and when the time is right, Van Dorn will be taken care of. Chalk it up to a learning experience."

Peter resisted the impulse to snort. One didn't snort at Madame Lambert. "You set my mind at ease. So why don't you tell me why you're really here."

Isobel Lambert smiled her perfect, ageless smile. There wasn't a line, a wrinkle, a mark of character on her exquisite, porcelain face, and he wondered how many face-lifts she'd had to keep her skin like that. Just another tool of the trade. "To tell you to take a couple of months off. You've been working nonstop since the fall of 2001, and you need a break."

"Not particularly."

"Your wife left you."

"I know that. It was more than two years ago, and we were never well suited. She's already remarried."

"And she never had the faintest idea what you really do for a living?"

She might have suspected, but he wasn't about to tell Madame Lambert that. Annabelle had been a fairly unimaginative creature, but she wasn't stupid. She probably got out before she learned what she didn't want to know.

"Not a clue," he said.

"I wasn't going to have her killed, Peter," she said mildly. "I'm not Harry Thomason, you know."

He hadn't been about to take that chance. Thomason had been a ruthless old buzzard, and yet he'd retired with honor after overseeing countless needless deaths. Absolute power corrupts absolutely. He wasn't about to take a chance on it for Annabelle's sake.

"The poor girl," Madame Lambert said. "It would take a hell of a woman to stand up to you."

Involuntarily his mind went back to Genevieve glaring at him, arguing with him, baiting him even though she knew she was doomed.

And what good did it do her in the end? At least it would have given her some fitting sense of revenge to know he couldn't wipe her out of his mind. But she wasn't going to be feeling any triumph, was she?

"She's still alive."

He jerked his head up, to meet Madame Lambert's calm gaze. "Of course she is," he said. "She's married to a dentist in Dorking."

"I'm talking about Genevieve Spenser. She joined forces with Renaud to get Harry Van Dorn off the island and he took her with him. Renaud wasn't so lucky."

"Van Dorn has her?" He didn't bother pretending not to care. "She might be better off dead."

"Perhaps. But there's nothing you can do about it. This is no longer your mission — even I have people to answer to, and personal involvement is the first step toward disaster. You are to keep out of the situation. Which is why I'm putting you on two months' leave, with pay, of course."

"Fuck the money," he said, furious. "Where is she?"

"Are you planning to ride to the rescue like some white knight? That can't be the Peter Madsen I've known for so many years. You don't care about anyone or anything. The Iceman cometh and all that."

It was a needed reminder. "You think that

I suddenly developed a heart, Isobel? Not likely. It's a matter of professional pride and personal responsibility. If she had to die, I should have seen to it, quickly and painlessly."

"Ah, but would you have?"

He ignored the taunt. "You know what kind of man Harry Van Dorn is. We have no right to leave anyone to his tender mercies."

"We have no responsibility either. She was in the wrong place at the wrong time. You know that as well as I do."

"So you're leaving her where she is?"

"We can't afford to compromise the mission by trying to get her out. Our man has too much on his plate already. So I want you to put it out of your mind and spend the next couple of months relaxing. Fix this place up a bit — it looks terrible. It needs a woman's touch."

He'd never been particularly slow to understand even the subtlest of hints, but Isobel Lambert was one of the best. She looked at him out of those calm, expressionless eyes. She'd told him for a reason.

"I keep forgetting you're not Thomason," he said after a moment.

"I try. Enjoy your vacation. You do realize that while you're on leave there's nothing the Committee can do for you? You're entirely on your own."

He almost smiled for the first time in days. "Of course. I'd expect nothing else."

"Enjoy your time off. I expect you back in two months, at the top of your game." She took a parting glance around the room. "Definitely needs a woman's touch."

Genevieve heard voices. She was scarcely Joan of Arc, and it wasn't the voice of God, that rich Texas drawl that oozed warmth and compassion. It was the voice of the devil, some huge, slimy, warty creature who stank of death and bourbon.

She drank that tea. She tried not to, but the patient, implacable Anh had stood over her, her English limited to "You drink."

And Genevieve had drunk, because she'd had no choice, hoping she had misunderstood Takashi O'Brien's implied warning. But it hit her so fast she had only time to whisper, "Oh shit," as Anh caught her falling teacup.

She fought the effects, but it was like wrestling in marshmallow fluff — everything was white and thick and sticky, and when she tried to push it away it clung to her hands. The sheets were wrapped so tightly around her body she couldn't move. She could only lie there, mummified, hoping she was suddenly transported back in time to the couch in Harry's living room on the island, and she could somehow stop the inevitable.

But the voices told her otherwise. It was Harry Van Dorn's familiar voice, but the words were strange.

"She screwed him," he said. "I can see the stink of him on her. Get rid of her. I'm no longer interested."

"As you wish." It was his assistant's soft voice. Takashi — who'd warned her about the tea.

"On second thought," the voice that was and wasn't Harry said, "maybe there's some fun to be had. I don't get to play with a white woman very often — too many people ask questions when they disappear. But she's already been declared dead — I can do anything I want, take as long as I want, and I don't need to worry about repercussions. Why don't you keep her like this until I get back."

"Of course," Takashi O'Brien said, ever the obedient servant. "If you have no problem with Madsen's leavings."

Madsen? Who was Madsen, Genevieve thought uneasily. And then she remembered. She should open her eyes, tell them she could hear them, but someone had sewn her eyelids shut and put one-hundred-pound weights on them.

They were standing over her as she lay on the bed — she could tell that much even without being able to see. Harry made a sound of disgust. "You're right, Jack," he said. "You always are. I certainly don't want sloppy seconds, even if there is no trace of him.

"What would I do without you, Jack? You protect me from my mistakes. If it weren't for you, I imagine I would have stopped having fun long ago."

She didn't have to see to know that Takashi O'Brien was giving an obsequious bow, but Harry's laugh confirmed it. "That's what I like about you Japs," he said. "Always bowing and scraping, and you understand loyalty. You know who's master, and you'll die to protect me."

"Certainly."

"So you take care of the bitch. You can have a bit of fun with her, if you're not picky, but just make sure you get rid of the body so that it's never found. I've got a lot of irons in the fire right now and I can't have anything get in the way. There's a lot of money riding on my current project, and she's endangering it. One false move and the entire thing would come tumbling down, and I'm out billions of dollars. And I like money, Jack."

"Yes, sir."

Genevieve would have given anything to open her eyes and see his face. But the fog was still surrounding her, and she decided she didn't really give a shit. If Jack/Takashi was going to kill her there wasn't a whole lot she could do about it — not at this point. If he waited long enough, maybe she'd be able to roll out of bed and hide underneath it. But at that point she couldn't even manage to summon the energy to open her goddamn eyes.

Someone leaned over her, and gentle hands patted the covers that imprisoned her useless body. "I told you not to drink the tea," he said, his soft voice a welcome change from Harry's drawl.

But then he was gone, and she was alone, and since she wasn't dead yet she might as well go back to sleep. So she did.

15

It was midnight, though she wasn't certain how she knew. There were no clocks in her luxurious bedroom, and her Patek Philippe watch had disappeared along with the clothes she was wearing. And the enigmatic note Peter had left her.

It shouldn't bother her. It was just a hastily scrawled note, with no signature, no tender words. But it was part of him, all she had, and she wanted it.

She sat up in bed, strangely alert. The drugged tea had worn off, leaving her with only a little fuzziness. She slid out of bed and stood, a little weak but steady enough.

She glanced down at her clothing. More of the lacy clothing Harry seemed to provide for all his guests, willing or unwilling. If she went to the drawers she'd probably find the same absurd collection of thongs and demi bras designed to turn an A cup to a C cup. Since she was already a firm C, the idea of such infrastructure was alarming.

She crossed the darkened room slowly, but with each step she felt a little stronger moving toward the bank of windows she hadn't noticed before. The house was on a bluff overlooking the ocean, but which ocean was a mystery. There were boats, but without glasses she couldn't even begin to guess their size, much less their nationality, and she turned away, frustrated. She could feel a burning, knotting feeling in her stomach, and for a moment she was afraid the drugs in her system were reemerging in a particularly unpleasant fashion.

And then she realized she was hungry. Starving, in fact. She couldn't remember how long it'd been since she'd eaten. Harry had said she'd been in an induced coma for some thirteen days, which meant her sole sustenance had been given intravenously. She reached up and touched her hair. It was clean, as was the rest of her body, and she wondered if the impassive Takashi was responsible for that. He'd be as efficient and impersonal as anyone, but she didn't like the idea of any male messing with her while she was naked and unconscious. She was a little picky about such things.

No mirrors, not even in the adjoining marble bathroom. Clearly this was no place for the model-perfect women Harry usually entertained.

It didn't matter — as long as she was clean she could manage just about anything.

She heard someone approaching, and she dived back into bed, pulling the covers up around her again and closing her eyes. She knew instinctively that it wasn't Harry; even without looking she could feel the miasma of evil that emanated from the man she'd been determined to save. The sick creep who'd ordered her death.

Why the hell did everyone want to kill her? First the attack in upstate New York, then Peter Jensen, then Renaud. At least with Peter it had been nothing personal, more a matter of simple expediency, the polite son of a bitch. And in the end he hadn't done it, no matter how practical and simple it was.

And now good old Harry Van Dorn wanted her dead, and his henchman would doubtless be ready to carry out his orders at once because . . .

Why? Was she a victim of bad timing over and over again? Or maybe it was the fact that she never took the smart or easy way out, throwing her lot in with Harry Van Dorn. She knew there was something dodgy about him — her instincts had screamed it while her brain was trying to reason with her. And yet she'd gone blundering ahead.

And no one deserved to be executed by a vigilante Committee, no matter how bad they were. Or so she thought, rescuer that she was.

Big mistake. Was he coming to kill her now? If so, she could, and would, put up a hell of a fight, even though she hadn't even the slightest chance of winning. She'd never been the kind to give up, even when it was the smart thing to do.

She recognized the voices — Takashi O'Brien and Anh conducting a muted conversation in a language she couldn't begin to understand. And then O'Brien spoke to her.

"Ms. Spenser? Are you awake?"

She considered faking it, but he was far too observant. Besides, she didn't want to be there with her eyes closed and suddenly find her throat cut.

But no, he wouldn't do that. Harry had told him not to leave a trace, and cutting her throat while she lay in bed would be a messy business.

How long did someone live after their carotid artery was severed? Could they run around like a decapitated chicken, spraying blood? Or did they slip quietly into Ophelia-like oblivion?

She didn't intend to find out. Her eyes blinked open, and she kept them dazed and deliberately unfocused. She'd been right about her two intruders, but there was no knife, or any other weapon, in sight.

And except for the omnipresent cup of tea. Had she imagined Takashi's warning? God knows how she'd been able to think straight, given what she'd been going through, the drugs she'd taken the past couple of weeks.

"You drink," said Anh in English.

If the tisane wasn't poison it was at least a powerful enough drug to knock her halfway to Sunday. She let her eyelids flutter closed, once more murmuring a very convincing "sleepy."

Anh was small and skinny, but strong, and she slid her arm behind Genevieve's back and pulled her upright, without any particular help from Genevieve. "You drink," Ahn said, insisting.

Rather than have her pour the scalding liquid down her throat and over her chest, Genevieve reached up and took the cup in both hands. Anh stood over her, eagle-eyed, until Takashi said something to her, drawing her away from her post by the bed for a few precious moments.

It was all Genevieve needed. She leaned over the bed, lifted the heavy silk dust ruffle and tossed the contents of the cup under the bed onto the thick carpeting. By the time Anh turned back she was obediently draining the last drop, shuddering delicately in reaction to the faintly acrid smell.

While Anh's back was to her, Takashi had been watching. Now was the moment of truth, Genevieve thought as she handed the cup back to Anh and slid down on the bed.

He said something in that strange language, and Anh nodded, clearly satisfied. Genevieve tried to remember how long it'd taken for the drugs to kick in last time, but it was a blur. She expected it had been pretty fast, so she closed her eyes and forced her body to relax, not moving when Takashi came to stand over her.

"Ms. Spenser?" She made no response. And even though she sensed his hand approach her face, she forced her muscles to remain slack, and she didn't flinch when he touched her face, lifted her eyelids and let them drop again.

"Sound asleep, Ms. Spenser?" he said. "And you'll stay that way for the next twelve hours while I decide how to get rid of you. In the meantime, we won't have to bother you and you'll be left alone."

It was simple enough to glean the warning from his statement, and she remained obediently still.

He turned to Anh, issuing a string of orders, overriding the woman's objections with ruthless determination, and then they were gone.

Her eyes shot open, and she sat up again. It seemed she had an ally in her executioner. Maybe she'd get out of this mess alive after all.

And if she did, Harry Van Dorn was getting his head handed to him, the murderous creep.

She tried the door to the rest of the house with great care, in case Anh was stationed outside, but as she expected it was locked tight. The windows were all sealed, the air artificial, and there was no way out. She had no choice but to put her trust and her life in the hands of Harry Van Dorn's executive assistant. And hope Harry had made as big a mistake in hiring Takashi as he had with Peter.

It seemed unlikely. Harry had said Takashi had been with him for over three years — that was way too long for anyone with a hidden agenda.

But she had no choice but to trust him. She was trapped in this hermetically sealed room, and her only hope lay in Takashi O'Brien's long, elegant hands.

She had a horrible feeling she might be royally screwed.

Peter Madsen wasn't used to being a white knight. There were those in the Committee who specialized in getting important people out of dangerous situations, but that had never been his particular area of expertise. He brought death, not life, to those who deserved it. At least he bloody well hoped so.

And here he was, risking everything for the sake of a stupid girl who kept getting into trouble. If Genevieve Spenser had just followed his implied directions she'd be safely home in New York, her sojourn in the Caribbean a nightmare she'd rather forget. She would suffer a convenient case of short-term amnesia, brought on by the finest drugs money could buy, and she'd never remember a thing. And more than likely, no one would bother to ask.

But he'd fucked that up by letting himself get distracted. Once she'd stepped in harm's way she should have been the least of his concerns. And instead, whether he wanted to admit it or not, she'd overshadowed everything, the mission, Harry Van Dorn, his own safety. And he had ended up com-promising everything.

Thirty-eight was too damn young to be having a midlife crisis. But then, his line of work aged you, he thought. Made you stupid when you needed to have all your wits about you.

Leaving him with the task of cleaning up some of the mess he'd made.

He didn't give a rat's ass about Harry Van Dorn. Someone would see to him, someone who wouldn't get distracted by something as ridiculous as a cantankerous lawyer.

So here he was, halfway across the world, acting on his own with none of the Com-mittee's formidable resources. And he wasn't even going to stop and consider whether this goddamn rescue mission was simply clearing up some of the mistakes he'd made, or something more personal.

The passageway was cold and clammy, the stone walls sweating, the carved steps rough beneath his feet. It would be funny as hell if he took a pratfall and broke his neck. A perfect slapstick ending to a joke of a life.

White knight to the rescue, he thought, moving deeper into the bowels of the earth. The last thing he wanted was to see Gene-vieve Spenser again. The last thing he needed. Yet here he was.

Thomason would have sent him after her with orders to kill. Isobel Lambert had left it up to him. Everything about this whole affair was uncharacteristic — of him, of the Committee, of the people he worked with. Renaud was one of the last people he thought could be turned — he'd had too healthy a fear of what could happen to him if he tried to sell out to a higher bidder.

Peter reached the bottom step, switching off the small flashlight he'd brought. He leaned back against the cold, damp wall, and waited for the damsel in distress.

What the hell was he doing here? Going against every one of his well-honed instincts for the sake of someone he didn't give a damn about. If he wasn't so pissed off he'd laugh. At himself, at the absurd situation.

As it was, he had no choice but to wait. And fume.

She didn't make the mistake of turning on the lights as darkness closed in around her. She was supposed to be comatose once more, why would she need light?

She couldn't make herself lie in that bed a moment longer, but she kept her ear out for any unexpected sound so she could jump back under the covers without being caught.

Her nerves were screaming with anticipation. If she was getting out it would have to be tonight. Somehow she didn't think it was going to be as easy as being put on a plane for the safety of the U.S. Sooner or later Harry was going to want proof that she was dead. Unless this was all an elaborate, sadistic hoax on the part of O'Brien, and he was simply using the easiest way to get her out of here and into a death trap.

She considered laughing at her own paranoia, except that it wasn't paranoia if people were really out to kill you. But at this point she had no choice — it was Takashi O'Brien or nothing.

She ended up back in bed, lying in total darkness, when the door opened and someone slipped inside. Something soft and silky was dropped on her head as she lay still, and for a moment she was afraid he was going to smother her.

"Put those on." O'Brien's voice was barely a whisper, and she sat up, pulling the dark cloth from her face.

"But what . . . ?" she began.

"Be quiet!" He barely made a sound, but the point was made. He took a step away from her, and her eyes, already accustomed to the darkness, could see that he'd turned his back. Obviously he meant her to strip down here and now, and just as obviously she wasn't about to object. He had probably seen more of her when she'd been unconscious, and he was clearly uninterested.

The clothes were a pair of black silk pajamas. An odd choice, presumably to give her some camouflage in the darkness, and she pulled off the lacy confection they had dressed her in with relief. She'd never been a glutton for frills and lace; when she was on her own she usually slept in a ratty T-shirt and panties.

The pajamas must belong to Harry — the silk was so fine she could barely feel it against her skin. The sleeves and legs were too long, but at that point there wasn't much she could do about it. She fastened the buttons up to her neck, and he turned, instinctively knowing she was done.

He reminded her of Peter — that preternatural awareness, that calm, waiting watchfulness. Was he a part of Peter's shadow Committee? And if he was, did that make him a good guy or a bad guy?

As far as she knew he'd decided not to kill her, which clearly made him a good guy.

He pushed her down on the bed and proceeded to tie her wrists together, tight enough to hold, just short of pain. She didn't bother to ask why — even in the hushed darkness she could make a reasonably intelligent guess. It was to provide a good cover in case they ran into Anh or any of Harry's other inquisitive servants.

She held still as he braided her long hair into a thick plait, his hands efficient and impersonal. He put some sort of slippers on her feet, then pulled her to a standing position.

He was going to gag her — she could see the cloth in his hand, and she tried to move away, shaking her head vigorously, but it was too late. A moment later she was silenced before she could say a word.

She half expected him to put a leash on her and make her walk like a dog, she thought impatiently, her mind filled with all the insulting things she wanted to say.

And then they were moving, out of the room where she'd been for so long, down a long, narrow corridor. It was almost as dark as her unlit room.

She lost count of the doors, the flights of stairs. If she had to retrace her steps she'd be totally lost. The last door he opened was different, the air beyond was damp and cold, smelling of the sea.

He said nothing, pulling her inside and closing the door behind them, closing them into darkness.

It felt like a grave — cold and damp and black. Genevieve never like confined spaces, but having a panic attack wouldn't help matters, particularly with the gag covering her mouth. She forced herself to take deep, calming breaths through her nose as he put her bound hands on his shoulder and started to descend into the earth.

She thought she should count the steps, anything rather than think about the darkness and the night closing in around her.

Two hundred and seventy-three steps carved into the side of the rock. She'd long ago stopped thinking of anything, anything but descending those endless steps to what might be her death after all. She'd lost all sense of time, space and reality in the narrow, twisting stairway — all she could do was follow the man who might be her executioner.

She felt dizzy when they finally reached the bottom, and she swayed for a moment. And then a match flared in the darkness, almost blinding her. She looked straight into the ice-cold eyes of Peter Jensen, and as he moved toward her she saw the knife in his hand.

She was going to die after all, at the hands of the man whose job it had been. He was alive, and he was going to finish what he started.

Her knees gave way, and she slumped onto the hard cold floor, finally giving up.

Harry Van Dorn seldom indulged in temper tantrums, but he was about to indulge in a royal one. He took a deep breath, another sip of his fine old bourbon and told himself he was overreacting. Things weren't falling apart everywhere he turned. It just seemed like that, but if he took a step back and viewed the situation objectively he'd realize these were just minor annoyances. It would take a lot more than a few half-assed commandos to think they could get in his way.

They'd shut down the diamond mines in South Africa and sent the workers on a three-week holiday. The word given out was safety inspections, but he knew for a fact that no one gave a shit about safety in those mines. If workers died, there were always hundreds available to take their place, and every penny — every moment — spent on safety precautions meant less profit. There would be no accidental explosion after all.

Three out of seven down, with so short a time to go. He wasn't a man who adjusted his plans when he hit a snag — he blew through the opposition with bullying force.

But he was up against an immutable time frame, which left very little choice.

The Rule of Seven was being threatened, and he couldn't have that. He wasn't going to settle for anything less. Compromise wasn't in his vocabulary, not when money could always buy his own way. Things were not about to change at this late date.

The Rule of Seven had been simple: lethal strain of Avian flu in China, the dam in Mysore, diamond mines in South Africa, oil fields in Saudi Arabia, the Auschwitz shrine in Poland, Houses of Parliament in London and the American terrorist sites.

But there was still hope — he'd lost India, South Africa and Saudi Arabia, but the other four were still undiscovered, and he'd taken steps to ensure that. And, in fact, the American plan was three, not one, which brought him back up to six.

Still, the Rule of Six was not acceptable. He'd have to come up with something, fast, or lose the beautiful elegance of his favorite number. His plans had been simple, exact and unchangeable, and he'd spent a great deal of time setting up a trustworthy network in each of his chosen targets. Making any new moves would entail sloppiness, and he couldn't abide a mess. It was too late to trust anyone new — he'd ensured that in the end he had complete control, and nothing would go down until he gave the order. If those bastards at the Committee had gotten away with destroying his complicated design it would have all been down the toilet, all those careful months of planning.

But fate had been on his side, as it always was, in the form of the late Renaud and the soon-to-be-late Genevieve Spenser. He would have liked to have killed her himself but Jack-shit had a point. He did tend to get aroused when he hurt people, and he wasn't one for self-restraint.

He needed one more glorious event to set the world on its heels and throw the financial community into disarray. He'd chosen the American terrorist sites because of the timing, the anniversary of the previous bloodbaths, and he didn't want to bother with anything connected to 9/11. He couldn't hope to equal the mass destruction wrought by that day, and he certainly didn't want his work to be viewed as an afterthought.

Washington was too well guarded for him to come up with something fast enough. Assassinating the president was a possibility, but not logical. Harry had bought and paid for him, which made access easy but logic fuzzy. His old Texas buddy was more help alive than dead.

He just needed one more inexplicable disaster, accident or terrorist sabotage, something to put the icing on the cake.

A nuclear-power plant in Russia? Latin America had been sadly neglected in his original plans, maybe he should give them a bit of attention.

Or maybe something small and personal and very nasty. The American public was always horrified when something happened to children. Sick children. He could think of a number of disarming possibilities.

And he poured himself another glass of bourbon, giving himself an imaginary toast.

16

Peter Jensen's hands were rough and impatient as he hauled Genevieve upright. She looked awful — shadowed eyes, pale skin, and she'd lost weight.

"She looks like shit," he said, slicing through the bonds on her wrists. "What the hell did you do to her? I thought you were keeping Van Dorn off her?"

"Harry didn't touch her. In case you hadn't noticed, she's a stubborn woman. She's not very good at taking hints."

"That she isn't," he agreed, looking down at her. "Why the gag?" He reached for it, about to cut it free, when Takashi's words stopped him.

"You warned me she was mouthy. I figured it would make life easier if I didn't have to listen to her complaints."

Peter hesitated. She was glaring at him over the encompassing gag, and he tried to ignore his feeling of relief at her first sign of life. "Good point. Maybe I'll leave it on."

She shoved herself away and began clawing at the gag herself. The woebegone waif was already fighting back.

Takashi's knots weren't likely to be undone by a simple New York lawyer. "Put your hands down or I might cut off a finger," he said, slicing through the silken bonds. He cast a knowing glance at Takashi — the restraints must have come from Harry's well-known supply. Silk was soft and sleek but very strong, and there was no escaping a silk binding no matter how much the victim struggled. Blood, sweat and tears only made it stronger.

The gag fell to the floor and Genevieve Spenser's mouth started working. "You son of a bitch!" she began.

"Yeah, I'm glad you're alive, too," he snapped. "Now shut up and let me get us the hell out of here."

"I leave her in your capable hands," Takashi O'Brien murmured.

"You've got things covered? Dumb-ass question, of course you do. Thanks for this."

"If by *this* you mean me —" Genevieve said.

"Shut up," Peter said. "If you want to get out of this alive without screwing me or Takashi over you'll keep your mouth shut."

"Your well-being has never been my particular concern," she said haughtily as she stood at the bottom of a cave dressed in black silk pajamas that were too big for her. "Mr. O'Brien, on the other hand, deserves my complete gratitude."

"God, no!" Takashi O'Brien's expression was pure horror. "Just a favor for a friend."

"We're both going to get our asses handed to us," Peter said, "so if you could just shut up and follow orders we may have a snowball's chance in hell of surviving."

Any trained operative was adept at concealing his expression, and Takashi O'Brien was one of the best, but even Peter couldn't miss the light of amusement in his dark eyes. "Who would have thought it?" he murmured half to himself.

"Who would have thought what?" Peter demanded, incensed.

But Takashi had already vanished the way he'd come, leaving him alone with the extremely angry Ms. Genevieve Spenser.

He wasn't feeling any too happy about the situation either. "Are you going to shut up and come with me, or am I going to have to leave you down here for Harry's goons to find you?"

"I'm not sure who I'd prefer."

"Lady, if you haven't figured that out by

now then you aren't even as marginally intelligent as I thought you were," he said. "I'm leaving. Follow me or not."

She did, of course. He'd never doubted it for one moment, but her damn pride insisted that she put up at least a token resistance. The descent down the rock-carved stairs had been bad enough for him — after days of forced inactivity she'd be having a miserable time getting her body to climb back up. But he couldn't afford to adjust his pace. The only way he was going to get her out of there alive was to move fast, and for some idiotic reason he'd decided to rescue her. He must be out of his mind.

At least it was all she could do to keep up — she had no energy left to harangue him. She hadn't lost her fighting spirit, even if exhaustion was silencing it. He'd found her anger, her refusal to be cowed, one of the most appealing things about her.

Scratch that. One of the least annoying things about her. If she'd been a docile dishrag he probably would have left her to her own devices. After all, she'd gotten herself into this mess by ignoring the escape plan he'd practically delivered to her on a silver platter.

This was a favor for a friend. Takashi

O'Brien could do what needed to be done, but no one deserved to be saddled with the fate of Ms. Genevieve Spenser except the idiot who'd fucked up the mission in the first place.

Yes, he deserved her all right, he thought, slowing his steps imperceptibly as he felt her compromised strength fail her. Just a simple case of paying the price for his screwup. After twenty years he knew you couldn't afford to let your mind wander for even a moment, not until the mission was accomplished.

But then, years of experience and training had never included dealing with someone like Genevieve, clearly the most dangerous female he'd ever met, even without automatic weapons. At least as far as he was concerned. Takashi took pity on her, Bastien would have ignored her. In his case he was royally screwed.

She faltered on the slippery stairs, and his hand shot out to catch her before she could tumble backward down the long, treacherous stairway. In the murky darkness he could only see her eyes, staring up at him, full of pain and confusion. And anger.

It was the last that reassured him. As long as she could fight, she'd survive. With or without him.

They were at the top of the stairs, and he pulled her up to the tiny landing beside him.

"You'll need to keep your face down, your voice low, and pay attention to my signal if you aren't going to kill us both. The place is pretty well camouflaged, but too damn many people live around here to make it completely safe."

"Don't you want to put me in a burka and veil? Maybe gag me again just for good measure?" Even in a whisper her acid tones were familiar.

"I trust you."

That took the wind out of her sails, at least for a moment. And then she was fighting back. "Well, I don't trust you and your vigilante friends. I want you to put me on a plane for New York and then get out of my life."

There was nothing funny about it, but he laughed anyway. "I'd like nothing better than to get out of your life, but you keep screwing things up. And you're not going back to your apartment right now. Takashi's one of the best, but by now Harry won't be trusting anyone, and if Taka doesn't produce your head on a pike he'll always wonder if Takashi followed through. Your return to New York would be impossible to cover up."

"I'd stay in my apartment and hide," she

said, and there was a pleading note in her voice that she must have hated. "I can order in food and no one will know I'm there."

"No one but the doorman and the delivery service and anyone watching the building, which trust me, they will be until Harry's certain you're no longer alive. I'm taking you somewhere safe, and the less you argue the easier it's going to be."

"Easier on whom?"

"Whom?" he echoed, biting back a laugh. Trust Ms. Spenser the lawyer to keep her language precise even in the most dire of situations. "Easier on you," he answered. "If you shut up then I won't be forced to smother you."

"You've been threatening to kill me since the moment you met me," she said. "It's getting tiresome."

"When I met you I was the discreet gray ghost, as you called me. I didn't threaten to kill you, I just wanted to."

"Just get me out of here. As long as you take me someplace safe and then leave me the hell alone I won't say a word."

"That'll be the day," he said under his breath. "Keep your mouth shut and follow me, understand?"

"Yes, my lord and master."

She really was a pain in the ass, he

thought, opening the heavy, reinforced door carefully. The cavern beyond was dark and still, and he didn't think anyone had come in while he was down picking up his albatross. But he needed to be certain before they moved for the car.

"Get down and stay down while I scout the place and make sure no one's left any nasty surprises."

She didn't argue, sliding and leaning against the wall. He squatted beside her, his face close to hers, and she averted her head so as not to look at him. He simply took her chin in his hand and forced her to face him. "I'm leaving the door propped open. If anything goes wrong, if there's shooting, you need to dive back behind the door and slam it shut. No one will be able to get past security for a good long time, and you'll stand a fighting chance. Go back the way you came, carefully. If I know Takashi he'll do a final check to make sure everything went as planned. He'll come up with an alternative if I'm out of commission."

She stared at him. "Out of commission?" she echoed in a whisper. "What the hell does that mean?"

"You know what it means. Your fondest wish. Now stay down and keep quiet." He released her chin and moved away. She probably thought he'd wanted to kiss her. Foolish Ms. Genevieve Spenser. Of course he wanted to kiss her. And that was the last thing he was going to do, ever again.

Harry had always had a weakness for theatrics, and he liked to think of his secret escape route as the Batcave, and Peter couldn't argue. Takashi had given him the code that opened the hidden garage door, and he'd pulled his car into the cavern, parking it beside Harry's Porsche. There'd been a guard, of course, but he'd taken care of him, and his body was resting in the backseat of Harry's car, just to keep things tidy. He hadn't needed Takashi's help to bypass the security system and find his way down to the bottom and the annoying Ms. Spenser. Now he simply had to make sure the coast was clear before he got her into the nondescript Ford he'd brought and took her the hell out of there.

Those black pajamas had been a good choice — she blended well into the shadows except for her pale hair, and that had been pulled back. He supposed some men might find her appealing, but he wasn't one of them. No, the sight of Genny Spenser in black silk pajamas was leaving him absolutely cold . . .

The gun spat fire in the darkness, and he

felt something sting his shoulder. He dropped instantly, his gun in his hand, and rolled between the parked cars. The first guard had definitely been dead — this must be a new one. Or more.

He touched his shoulder and swore silently. He was bleeding, which would make him easier to track in the darkened cavern. His assailant wouldn't know whether he'd winged him or killed him, but he wasn't saying a word, just moving through the huge room with a pitiful attempt at stealth.

Clearly the man was outmatched by Peter's training. He rolled to one side, half under the Ford, and held his breath. He heard the door to the stairs slam shut and breathed a sigh of relief. At least she'd gotten out of harm's way. With luck the shooter would think he was the one who'd gone back down the stairs, and Peter would be able to take him by surprise.

He could see the door from his vantage point, even better when the guard switched on his high-powered flashlight and shone it around the cave. Peter moved under the car a bit more, but he'd left a smear of blood on the concrete floor, and not even the worst amateur would miss something like that. The gun felt cool and deadly in his hand, and the familiar iciness spread through him. He'd have to rise and take his best shot, and know that was good enough. He'd never missed, but then, he'd never fucked up the way he'd been fucking up. If it was his time, so be it. At least Genevieve was out of there, and Takashi would see to her.

The flashlight was switched off, and Peter could hear movement in the cavern, movement designed to be stealthy and failing completely. There were two of them, he realized belatedly. Why hadn't he realized that in the first place? Two of them circling the area, looking for him.

He rolled out from under the car, pulling himself to a sitting position without making a sound. He had excellent night vision and didn't doubt for a moment he could take at least one of them out. A second one was more problematic, but he was still one of the best shots in the world, and the odds were in his favor.

He drew his knees up, waiting in his calm, icy zone, waiting, waiting.

It all happened at once, in the kind of disjointed slow motion that always seemed to take over. The flashlight flashed onto him, full brightness, and beyond it he could see the barrel of a gun, just as someone came hurtling toward him, throwing themselves in front of him. "No!" she screamed, and in a millisecond he realized who the second person was. Genevieve hadn't ducked for cover — she thought she was saving him. If he weren't so annoyed he would have been touched by her naiveté, but at that point he simply swept her aside and put a bullet into the head of the man behind the flashlight a split second before he fired.

The man fell, the flashlight crashing to the floor and rolling to one side. Peter moved toward him and rose, but he already knew the unknown guard was dead. Even blinded by the flashlight Peter's shot had been perfectly centered between his eyes.

He felt her come up behind him, and he could barely keep his temper in check. He moved away, picking up the flashlight and shining it into the dead man's face. He wasn't sure why he did it — maybe to punish her — but her reaction was no more than a choke of horror. It would have served him right if she'd thrown up on him.

"Good shot," she said in a rusty voice, trying to sound casual. "Why do you people always shoot people between the eyes?"

He turned to look at her. She was far from as calm as she sounded — her color was ashen, and he wondered if she was going to pass out. "Because a smaller gun has a smaller bullet and it's neater. If I was carrying something bigger I would have blown his head off, and it would have made a huge mess. Are you going to faint at my feet again?"

That put some color back into her face. "I don't faint."

"You also don't obey orders. What the fuck did you think you were doing back there?"

She didn't answer, but then, he didn't really expect her to. "Get in the car," he said wearily. The ice had drained from his veins, leaving him empty and tired.

"Which one?"

He managed a laugh. "Not the Porsche, babe. That's Harry's and it would attract too much attention. Besides, there's a dead body in the back."

She was about at the end of her limit, as was he. But she said nothing, moving around to the passenger side of the nondescript sedan and climbing inside. By the time he joined her she'd already fastened her seat belt, and for some reason it made him want to laugh.

"You ever disobey my orders again and I'll kill you myself," he said, starting the car.

She didn't say a word. She simply turned

her face away from him, staring out the window, as he made his way out of the subterranean garage that now held a Porsche and two corpses.

You ever disobey my orders again and I'll kill you myself, he'd said, and Genevieve hadn't said a word. Too many threats, too many deaths had left her numb and tired and unwilling to fight. The headlights speared through the dark cavern as the car climbed higher, and Genevieve had the stupid fancy that he was taking her out of hell. Except that he was the devil himself, and wherever he took her would be full of death as well.

"I want to go back to America," she said, finding her voice. She didn't, wouldn't look at him. At the hands that had touched her. At the hands that had killed for her.

His derisive laughter wasn't going to improve her shaken mood. "Oh, yeah?"

"I don't care if this third-world bog is safer, I want to go home. If not New York, then at least somewhere in the States."

She glanced over to see him pull something that looked like an upscale BlackBerry out of his pocket and punch in a few buttons. A moment later the rock wall opened in front of them. "How about California?" he said as the door closed behind them.

She was momentarily silent, feeling disoriented and stupid. "Where are we?"

"Near Santa Barbara. Where did you think we were? What was that . . . some third-world bog? But isn't that exactly where you'd originally planned to go? In another week I can ship you off there and you can wallow to your heart's content."

"What difference will a week make?" she asked.

"It'll be the end of April, Harry Van Dorn will be dead and you won't ever have to see my face again."

"Promises, promises," she whispered, leaning her head back against the seat. She turned to look at him for the first time, and she almost laughed. He looked like a normal, middle-class American male, driving his conservative sedan on the crowded California freeways. Except that he'd just killed two men. And his left shoulder was soaked with blood.

Isobel Lambert was going to have to call in help from unexpected places, and she wasn't happy about it. She was someone who believed in keeping promises, and once someone left the Committee they were free, as long as they showed their usual discretion.

But these weren't ordinary times. Every-one she had was working on breaking the Rule of Seven, and the clock was running out for them. Two more parts were coming together through painstaking hard work — Harry Van Dorn had neo-Nazis working on some kind of mess at the memorial at Aus-chwitz, and he actually thought he might get away with blowing up the British Houses of Parliament despite the watchfulness of English security. He'd overstepped his capabilities on that one — even though foolproof security was practically impos-sible, he hadn't realized that the Committee specialized in the impossible. They'd picked up Harry's chosen suicide bombers in a random sweep, and the transit workers had very kindly decided to call a strike on the nineteenth and twentieth of April meaning no one could get to work. Problem solved.

But that still left Peter Jensen stuck in the middle of America with what sounded like a pain-in-the-ass companion, and no way to use agency resources to get him out.

There was only one person she could turn to. He might not do it for her, but he'd do it for Peter. He'd probably put up a fight, refuse to help her, but in the end she knew he'd do the right thing, as he always did. They'd saved each other's lives countless times. It was time for Bastien Toussaint to do it again.

17

"I'm hungry," Genevieve said.

"I'm happy to hear violence doesn't impair your appetite."

She wanted to slap the snarky son of a bitch, but she was too worn out. Her stomach was twisting, she felt weak and shaky, and she was so hungry she was tempted to sink her teeth into Peter's leg. She wasn't going to say a thing about his shoulder. He could bleed to death for all she cared, and they could go careening off the freeway head-on into a semi and then she wouldn't have to worry about being hungry ever again.

"He shot you," she said grudgingly.

"Kind of you to notice. Don't worry, it's just a graze. Stings like crazy but it's already stopped bleeding. I just need a little first aid."

"Don't expect it from me. And I'm not worried. I just want to make sure you can still drive."

He smiled, the rat bastard, and she remembered his mouth all too vividly. She jerked her head away again and closed her eyes. It was the middle of the night and there were people everywhere. The bright lights of a thousand cars all around her, the noise and color of the freeway were an assault on her deprived senses, and part of her wanted to crawl back into a dark, safe hole and hide.

"What do you want to eat?"

"A cheeseburger," she said dreamily. "The biggest, greasiest cheeseburger in the world, with French fries and Diet Coke."

"No Tab?"

"I think that's beyond you at the moment," she said. "Diet Coke will do in a pinch."

Before she realized what he was doing he'd crossed four lanes and taken the exit, amid screeching tires and honking horns. By the time they'd made it safely off the freeway and she'd caught her breath, she glared at him. "Do you have a death wish?" she demanded.

"I thought we'd already established that."

"Well, don't include me. I'm not ready to die."

Again that small smile. "Glad to hear it.

Otherwise it would be a waste of time and money to feed you."

He was pulling into a drive-through hamburger place, one of the West Coast chains, and she looked at him suspiciously. "What about McDonald's?"

"This is better. Trust me."

"Trust you? You've got to be kidding me."

He said nothing, merely pulled up to the window and gave her order. He got the food, put it in her lap and drove away, into the night.

She was too busy wolfing down her food to pay much attention to where he was going. He hadn't gotten back on the freeway, and the streets were darker, less busy, with only the occasional car passing in the other direction. She shoved the last French fry in her mouth and lifted her head to look around her. He'd managed to find a dirt road somewhere, and even in the midst of such a densely populated area there was no one around.

He pulled to a stop on the side of the road, killed the lights and the engine, and looked at her.

"What's this all about?" she demanded. "Surely you didn't go to all that trouble to get me out of there just for the pleasure of killing me yourself?"

"Tempting as the idea is, no. Unfasten your seat belt."

"You're abandoning me in the woods?"

"No," he said, reaching over and unfastening her seat belt.

She hit at his hands to stop him, but he simply captured her wrists in one hand while he undid the belt. The he leaned over farther so that he was brushing against her, so close she could remember the familiar scent of his skin and soap. She felt dizzy, and she held her breath.

He pushed open the door, then leaned back, releasing her hands. "Goddammit, why are we here?" she demanded. The dizziness should have faded once he moved away, but in fact it was growing stronger, and her stomach, momentarily appeased, suddenly decided to move into overdrive.

"You'll know in just a minute."

It didn't take that long. She had just enough time to get herself out of the car, on her knees by the side of the road, throwing up everything she'd just wolfed down.

And him! Damn him, he'd gotten out of the car, come around beside her and was holding her, holding her braided hair away from her face, supporting her as she puked her guts out. She couldn't push him away, she couldn't do anything but let him hold her until everything was gone, and she was racked by dry heaves. She wanted to die, both from misery and humiliation, and all she could do was let him hold her.

"Finished?" he asked in a kind, business-like voice. He had a handkerchief with him — of course he did — and he wiped her face with it. His cold blue eyes were dispassionate as he looked down at her. "You'll do. Get back in the car and we'll find someplace to spend the rest of the night. I could have told you that death and fast food don't mix but I didn't think you'd listen."

She wanted to protest, but she was too weak to do anything but let him bundle her back into the car and fasten the seat belt around her trembling body. She leaned her head back and closed her eyes, stifling her instinctive moan of pure misery, and it wasn't until he was driving again, back toward a more populated area, when his words sank in.

"Where did you say we were going?"

"We're going to the cheapest, sleaziest motel I can. We both need to sleep."

"I'm not sleeping with you!"

"I know this will come as a shock to you, but I don't find someone spewing their guts out to be a particular turn-on. I certainly didn't rescue you for the sex, which, while pleasant enough, was nothing special. I assure you I can do better without half trying."

The words stung. Why did they hurt, and why had he said them? "Then why did you?"

"I told you, a favor for a friend."

"That's what Takashi said. You couldn't both think you're just helping each other."

"He told you his real name? That surprises me. He's usually a better judge of who to trust."

"Whom to trust," she said automatically. "Why did you come halfway across the world to get me?"

"Unfinished business."

"Who? Me or Harry? Or both of us?"

He closed down on her, his face that cool, enigmatic mask once more, and he didn't answer. They were moving away from the city, into the massive suburban sprawl, and she didn't want to think anymore. About her stomach, about her future, about him. She just wanted everything to go dark and stop moving for a while.

She opened her eyes with a start. He'd finally found a motel that suited him — the *M* in the sign had burned out, one of the streetlights was broken, the building looked as if it wouldn't withstand the next minor earthquake. The paint was cracked and peeling, but they'd have beds, and that was all she cared about.

"This'll do," he said, getting out of the car.

"Get two rooms. I'm not spending the night in the same room as you."

"Yeah, right," he drawled. "Stay put, or next time I'll use handcuffs."

How did he know she'd considered running the moment he went into the motel office? Without a purse, decent clothes, money or identification, her one instinct had been to get away.

But then, he had a wretched tendency to know what she was thinking. "I don't have the energy to move," she said. It was a lie.

She waited until he'd gone into the motel office, and she opened the car door slowly, carefully, rolling out and onto the cracked pavement as she closed the door again. The light in the car would have only been on for a second, and his back was to the parking lot. He wouldn't know she was gone until he came out.

She didn't make it very far. He caught up with her two streets over, in the darkness, coming up over her like a dark, silent bat, knocking her to the ground. He hauled her up, and even in the darkness she could feel the fury vibrating from him. "If you make one sound I'll strangle you," he said in a cold, deadly voice. "It won't kill you — it will shut you up and knock you out long enough for me to get my 'drunken wife' back to the motel room. The problem is, it's a technique that's hard to master, and sometimes you cut off the oxygen to the brain for too long and there's some permanent damage. Though you'd be a lot easier to take in a semivegetative state."

He'd do just that, and not give a damn if he killed her, she believed it with all her heart. He pulled his arm around hers in a show of husbandly concern that concealed the iron-hard grip of his hand on hers, and marched her back to the Sleepy Time 'otel.

It was a corner room on the second floor — she had a pretty good idea it hadn't been a random assignment, but she was too tired to ask why. The room was small and dingy, with two double beds taking up most of the space. He closed and locked the door behind them, then jerked his head toward the back of the small room. "Bathroom's over there — you might want it."

She went in, slammed and locked the door. At least this was one place where he hadn't been able to tamper with the locks — she'd have at least a modicum of privacy. The second thing she did was look for a way of escape. There was a window, but it was small and high, and even if she was able to get through it there was no telling where it led except straight down. She washed her face and did her best to wash her mouth out, then looked up at her reflection.

She wasn't sure whether she wanted to laugh or cry. She looked like a ghost — pale, frightened, lost. Like someone just released from a mental hospital, she thought, in her black silk pajamas.

And suddenly she needed to be clean, washed free of anything left from Harry Van Dorn. "I'm taking a shower," she called through the door.

The only response was a grunt.

The tub was small and stained, the flimsy shower curtain had mildew along the bottom, the bar of soap was not much bigger than a book of matches and the shampoo was mostly water. She didn't care. She stood under the hot water, letting it scald her, and she soaped herself, over and over again until the bar was not much more than a sliver. She used up the tiny bottle of shampoo — too damn bad if Peter Jensen had the sudden desire to get clean.

No, his name wasn't Jensen, was it? She couldn't remember what it was, and she didn't care. In a short time it would never matter again.

The hot water finally ran out. She didn't think that was possible, even in the cheapest of motels, but she must have overburdened the system. She turned the water off and stepped out of the tub. Her skin was red from the scalding water and her scrubbing, her hair was a mass of tangles, and the entire room was filled with fog. The Sleepy Time 'otel didn't come equipped with an exhaust fan, so she opened the tiny window a crack and wiped the mirror with the edge of her towel. She'd left the black silk pajamas on the floor of the bathroom and they were now crumpled and wet, and she picked them up with all the enthusiasm of someone picking up a dead rat, then dropped them again.

A sheet had worked before, it would work again, and too damn bad if it made Peter think of the night they'd spent together. He'd already informed her it was nothing special; he would hardly be swept away by uncontrollable lust at the sight of a tangle-haired ghost in a bedsheet.

She opened the bathroom door a crack. "Could you hand me a sheet?"

No answer, the son of a bitch. He probably wanted to force her to come out in a towel, not for any prurient reason but just to humiliate her. Well, she wasn't going to let that happen. Humiliation was a state of mind, and she'd already reached the pinnacle, or was it the nadir, an hour ago when she lost the entire contents of her stomach while he held her. Traipsing around in a towel was nothing compared to that.

Except that in such a cheap motel the towels were incredibly skimpy, and she was a tall woman. She'd been knocked out for God knows how long — weeks if what Harry said was true — long enough to lose the extra weight? She looked down at her body and it still looked the same — smooth and curvy. Clearly running for her life and almost dying hadn't gotten rid of those fifteen pounds. The universe must want her that way.

Besides, it was the least of her worries. She wrapped the towel around her as best she could, opened the door again and announced, "I'm coming out."

There was no snotty rejoinder. Because he wasn't there. The room was empty.

She yanked the top sheet off one of the beds and wrapped it around her, refusing to think about Harry's island, and went straight to the door. Locked, of course. He'd somehow managed to secure it from the outside, and no matter how she fiddled with the door it wouldn't budge.

The room had one small window next to the door, and she pulled back the curtains, ready to pick up a chair and crash it through the glass. Unfortunately the Sleepy Time 'otel didn't believe in chairs — apparently people came there to use the bed and not much else. The bedside table was fastened to the wall, and the TV was bolted in place. There was nothing to break the window with.

Except her fist. She'd seen it done in movies and on television, and it was simple enough. Just wrap your hand in a towel and punch it through the glass. She picked up one of her discarded towels, wrapped it around her fist and slammed it against the glass.

Unfortunately even the thin terry cloth absorbed the blow, and the windowpane didn't even shake. She cursed beneath her breath, dropped the towel on the floor and stripped one of the pillowcases off, wrapping that around her hand. She made a fist, and tried to channel Jet Li or Sonny Chiba, punching straight into the center of the glass.

There was no way she could silence her screech of pain as the force of the blow jarred her entire body. Her hand and fingers were numb, her wrist aching, and the window remained solid.

The glass had to be reinforced, which only made sense, given the neighborhood and the obvious clientele. Her entire hand was throbbing, and shaking it only made it worse, so she cradled it against her stomach with a quiet little moan. But she wasn't giving up.

She loved martial arts movies, even though she knew just how far-fetched most of them were from her training with Master Tenchi. She'd never been terribly good at kicks, and she was out of practice, but if Jet could take out a car window with his foot then she could certainly manage a reinforced household window.

She stuck her foot in the pillowcase, using her one good hand, but she couldn't figure out how to keep it on. She certainly didn't need her ankle going through shards of glass.

She finally gave up, dropping down on the bed in defeat. What if Peter wasn't coming back? What if he'd dumped her there, locking her in so she'd starve to death? She looked around for a telephone to call for help, something she should have thought of sooner, but of course there wasn't one. She had no idea whether the rooms were soundproofed or not, but she suspected that was one area where the owners might have put some money. This was clearly a motel designed for an hourly rate — hence the lack of phones and chairs. People would also want to be able to make as much noise as they wanted without being heard.

Maybe he'd just left her for a little while, long enough to make sure they'd gotten away, and he'd be back. Or maybe he was simply calling in reinforcements, handing her off to someone who didn't want to strangle her every other minute.

That would be the best possible scenario, she told herself. That Peter Whoever-He-Was had gone, and some sober bureaucrat was about to show up to take her to a nice cozy safe house until someone figured out how to stop Harry. A place with high thread-count sheets and lovely food and . . .

She was out of her mind. Harry's sheets had been the best money could buy — she was better off with the scratchy white crap she'd wrapped herself in.

She wanted to go home. Back to her beautiful, sterile apartment, back to her designer clothes and her Chanel makeup and shoes that cost too much and hurt her feet. She may not have been happy there, but she'd been safe.

She lay back on the bed, wrapping her sheeted body in the quilted bedspread as well, curling up into a pathetic little ball of misery. She was tired, she was frightened, and yes, damn it, she was hungry again.

And she was alone.

She closed her eyes so she wouldn't cry. Crying only made it worse, and it served no earthly purpose. There was nothing to cry for — she was away from Harry Van Dorn, who'd casually ordered her torture and death, and she was abandoned by Peter . . . Madsen, that was the name! Abandoned when he probably would have rather killed her as well.

Sooner or later someone would come and get her, someone safe and solid. All she had to do was wait. And not feel so bereft.

It would have been better if she hadn't fallen asleep. It lowered her defenses, made her emotional and vulnerable. The sound of a key turning jarred her into wakefulness, and the moment Peter walked in the door she flung herself at him in relief.

Unfortunately, he didn't know relief when it hit him upside the head, and he slammed her face down on the carpet, her arm twisted behind her back, his hand like a manacle on her twisted wrist.

Hong Kong was quarantined. Harry's ship, filled with infected pigeons, had been detained twenty miles out at sea, with a Hazmat team covering every inch of it. His captain had just time enough to warn him before they burst into the engine room. But not time enough to free the pigeons.

Harry threw the phone across the room so that it crashed into a glass-fronted cabinet, and there was broken glass all around. He began to pick up and throw anything he could reach — a lamp, a pile of books, a heavy bronze award attesting to his humanitarian efforts in the third world, a cat.

The cat managed to land on four feet and scamper away to safety. Harry liked cats. He liked their "fuck you" attitude, their haughty style. The only drawback was they ran too fast when he wanted to get his frustration out on something. He hadn't yet been able to kill a cat, and he'd been trying for years.

Everything else crashed with what should have been a satisfying violence. But Harry was beyond satisfaction.

The phone rang. Unfortunately the handset lay smashed against the marble floor, but he knew the number by heart. He pushed the speakerphone, barking his name.

It was his second in command in London. Somehow hearing the words spoken out loud instead of in the privacy of his ear made it even worse. He pulled the base of the telephone from the wall and threw it, and it shattered in a pile of plastic and wiring, with a disembodied voice still apologizing for fucking him over.

Harry walked across the room and kicked the phone into silence. It was all falling apart, everything he'd planned and dreamed and worked so hard for. The Rule of Seven lay shattered — there was still a faint hope he could carry off the nuclear accident in Russia but he suspected that had been aborted as well — the place was just too remote for him to have heard as yet. Or maybe Vlad had been terminated as well.

And there was no name, no face he could put on his deadly rage. All his resources could track down only the vaguest of information about the Committee, and it wasn't enough. Peter Jensen aka Madsen was dead — there'd be no satisfaction from gutting him. And Takashi had already taken care of the girl, her body long gone, in so many pieces no one would ever be able to put

Humpty back together again. He giggled softly, and then his rage returned.

There had to be some way to get to the Committee, to exact his revenge. The Rule of Seven was smashed, but there was always another day. As long as he found a way to show his enemies just how dangerous he could be. As long as the so-called Committee existed, they would try to stop him. Therefore the Committee must be dealt with.

He needed to do something, anything, to show he wasn't the patsy they took him for. Something bloody and brutal and undetectable enough that they wouldn't be able to stop it. Something that would make them think twice before they tried to get in his way again.

He needed a sign. He firmly believed in divine guidance. After all, wasn't he one of the chosen ones, to whom all things are given? He could do any number of things to find a clue — but that would require having someone come and read the signs. And he couldn't afford to waste the time.

He closed his eyes and focused his entire body, tight and angry, like a child desperate for a toy train at Christmastime. "Give me a sign," he said out loud. "Show me what to do."

This time it was his cell phone, and he pulled it from his pocket and snapped it open eagerly. Ask and ye shall receive.

It was Donahue. He'd done his usual sweep of the garage, and found two of his men in the back of his Porsche, dead. There'd been blood on the ground as well, not belonging to the two men. And a couple of strands of long, blond hair clinging to the damp wall.

Takashi had told him he'd disposed of her body through the underwater entrance, piece by piece, and Harry had been so taken with the notion that he'd wished he'd asked for pictures.

Now he knew he should have. Because Takashi O'Brien, his right-hand man for the last three years, had betrayed him.

And Genevieve Spenser was still alive.

18

"Let me up," Genevieve gasped into the carpet fibers that held God knows what. "You're hurting me."

Peter released her, stepping back and slamming the door behind him, locking them in. "Serves you right. When are you going to learn to trust me?"

She sat up, pulling the sheet more snugly around her, leaning back against the foot of the bed and cradling her hand. "Never," she said flatly. "But the fact is, I wasn't trying to attack you. I was afraid you weren't coming back, and I was relieved."

He stared down at her. "Never jump a man, no matter how relieved you are, unless you're certain he's not dangerous. And you know that I am."

Yes, she knew. She'd seen him kill a man not many hours ago, and knew he would do so, again and again, without a second thought. The idea should have horrified her.

But she was way past that point. She was just grateful that he could kill to keep her safe. "Sorry," she muttered.

He'd been carrying a bunch of plastic bags and he'd dropped them on the floor when she'd jumped on him. He proceeded to pick them up again, not looking at her. " 'Sorry?' " he echoed. "You're actually apologizing? What kind of drugs did Takashi feed you?"

She should have known he'd mock her. "What's in the bags?" she asked, changing the subject.

He turned. She was sitting at his feet, not a good position, psychologically, and she tugged the sheet up higher.

"Supplies. Including some clothes for you. There was an all-night Wal-Mart down the road. I know their clothes are not your usual style, but they're more secure than that sheet. And what have you got on your foot?"

She glanced down, having forgotten. "A pillowcase," she said sheepishly, pulling it off.

"Your feet were cold?"

She shook her head. "I was trying to break the window."

He said nothing for a moment. "I assume that's how you hurt your hand?"

He was an observant bastard, she thought.

"Just bruised it a bit," she said, reaching her hand up and flexing her fingers. Or trying to. They felt stiff and swollen.

"Get on the bed," he said.

There was a sudden uncomfortable silence in the room as both of them remembered the last time he'd said those words to her. And then he broke the spell. "Don't get your hopes up," he added. "I just want to look at your hand."

She did get to her feet, but not on the bed. "You don't need to look at my hand — it'll be just fine. Where are the clothes?"

He tossed one of the larger bags to her, and she made the mistake of trying to catch it with her bad hand. It dropped on the bed, but at least she'd managed to swallow her cry of pain.

"I assume you're going to take over the bathroom for another hour and a half," he said, dropping the rest of the stuff on the other bed. His bed, presumably. She was nothing special, he'd said.

"Just long enough to get dressed. I'm sure you're just dying to primp."

"What I'm dying to do is get these clothes off me and clean my wound. It's a lucky thing I managed to steal a jacket from the front office — I could hardly walk around Wal-Mart with a bullet wound. Though if I could anywhere, L.A. would be the place."

She'd forgotten all about his wound, and she felt conscience-stricken. "Do you need any help?"

"No, thank you," he said, sounding horrified. "I can manage a field dressing as well as anyone, and if the bullet hit anything vital the wound would be hurting a lot more and I'd be doing a lot less. Just go in the bathroom and change into your clothes so I can get on with it."

She wanted to call his bluff, strip off the sheet and take her time putting the new clothes on, but there were some things even she was afraid of. Whether she was afraid of what he'd do, or what he wouldn't do, she couldn't be certain.

She grabbed the bag, holding the sheet around her, and marched to the bathroom, doing her best to ignore him as he sat on his own bed and began to peel off the stolen jacket gingerly.

He'd shown a decided lack of imagination when he'd been at the discount store, and she could only be glad. Plain cotton underpants and bra, two sets, a pair of jeans, a couple of plain T-shirts and a zippered sweatshirt. Socks and sneakers as well. She hadn't worn clothes like these since she'd lived in upstate New York. She'd forgotten how comfortable they could be, even starchy and brand new. For the first time in years she felt like herself.

He'd even brought her a toothbrush, toothpaste and a comb and brush. She could almost be grateful, if she weren't so busy being annoyed at how exact he'd been on guessing her measurements, including her size ten feet. She managed to get the comb through her tangles, and simply braided her hair once more. Long hair was great when you had a stylist on Park Avenue and time enough to fuss with it. Not so good when you were on the run for your life.

She stepped back into the bedroom and stopped, frozen.

He was sitting on his bed, shirtless, dabbing at the raw, bloody streak on his shoulder with cool efficiency, and Genevieve couldn't move. It wasn't as if she hadn't seen him without his clothes on — he'd stripped down when they'd had sex on the island, and he'd had no particular modesty walking around when he'd dragged her from the swimming pool.

Ah, but then she'd been distracted by what was below his waist.

He had broad, slightly bony shoulders, with the kind of lean, muscled body that radiated health and strength. He was tanned from the tropical sun and undeniably gorgeous, and she was sorry as hell she had to see that.

"Do you need help?" she asked. The last thing she wanted to do was touch him, touch that tanned, golden skin.

"I can manage. I brought you some food. Saltines and ginger ale. I've heard it's excellent for morning sickness."

"I'm not pregnant," she snapped.

"I'm delighted to hear that. I certainly didn't think you were. However, it's the cure for an upset stomach either way. And I got you a bucket of ice. Stick your hand in it and it'll bring down the swelling."

"Then can I touch you?"

He laughed. Her request seemed to surprise him, it certainly shocked her. "Don't try it unless you have something extremely kinky in mind," he said.

That shut her up. She went back to her bed, plumping the limp pillows behind her, and sat down, shoving her hand into the plastic ice bucket. There were few things she hated more than putting ice on an injury, but she had more sense than to argue.

"Serves you right," he said, carefully applying a disinfectant to the furrow on his shoulder. He was having a hard time bandaging it, and her own fingers were icy, but she sat back and said nothing. When he was finished he stood up, and examined his handiwork in the mirror. She could see the trace of faint scratch marks along his beautiful back.

"What happened to your back?" she asked. "An old wound? Scars from being tortured?"

"You did," he said.

And she remembered. Holding on to him, digging her fingers into his skin as she arched into a frenzied, uncontrollable response, and she felt the color flood her face.

"Oh, God," she muttered weakly.

"Don't worry about it," he said in his cool voice. "My fault. I was the one who made you come."

He wasn't making the situation any better. She was nothing special, she reminded herself. Maybe he was used to having women claw his back, the marks still showing countless days later. The very idea made her sick with a kind of primitive rage that couldn't have anything to do with jealousy.

"How long do we have to stay here?" She could be proud of how unaffected her voice sounded, even though she could feel the heat on her cheeks.

It wasn't getting any easier. He stood up, unfastened his jeans and stepped out of them, totally oblivious to her reaction. At least he was wearing some kind of underwear — pale blue, a cross between boxers and briefs. His cock was also pushing against the fabric. He glanced down at his obvious erection, then back at her.

"Does getting shot turn you on?" she said, struggling for a way to defuse the situation.

"Not particularly," he said, flipping the covers back on his bed and stretching out. He was just as pretty lying down as he was standing up, and Genevieve was not happy.

"Can we turn out the light?" Her voice was caustic. "Now that you've finished parading your assets around I'd like to get some sleep."

Again that smile. "You really are the most annoying female I've ever met," he murmured, switching off the light.

"Same goes double for you," she muttered.

"In case you hadn't been looking that closely, I'm not a female."

"It was hard to avoid," she said, her voice muffled.

The room was dark, only a faint light from outside coming through a crack in the heavy curtains. She didn't like lying here in the dark with him; it felt too intimate. Then again, she had no place else to go.

"I'm going to sleep," she announced.

"So you said." He stretched out, putting his hands behind his head, perfectly at peace.

She turned her back on him, flouncing over in the bed, and closed her eyes. Five minutes later she flipped back, only to find he was still awake, staring at the ceiling. Still aroused.

"I know what it is," she said in the quiet, shadowed room. "It's the danger that excites you. You're an adrenaline junkie, and running for your life gives you a hard-on."

"Such talk, Ms. Spenser," he mockingly chided her. "Why are you so obsessed with my erection?"

She considered dumping the melting bucket of ice on him, then wisely reconsidered the notion. "Just curious. Since I was 'nothing special' it seems odd that you'd be . . . er . . ."

"Hard? You said it before — you're brave enough about other things."

"I don't feel particularly brave. Too many people trying to kill me, I guess. I just want to go home."

"So you said. And I'm here to see to just

that. Get you tucked safely back in that elegant apartment on Seventy-second Street where you can curl up on your white leather furniture and forget all about this."

She wasn't likely to forget about anything, but she had the sense not to say so. They had ways of making people forget, he'd told her, and she wasn't in the mood to be a guinea pig. "How do you know what my apartment looks like?"

"I was just there. It's been searched at least once, by Harry's people, and they're watching it pretty closely, just to make certain you don't show up. Harry trusts Takashi as much as he trusts anyone, which means not at all, and he doesn't leave things to chance. Which is why you're not going back there until Harry is dead."

"Why you? Why did they send you to rescue me?"

"I'm the one who botched the initial mission. It was my responsibility."

"Punishment for screwing up?"

"You could say so." He rolled on his side to look at her through the shadows. "You know, this isn't a girls' sleepover where we can gossip all night. I need to get some sleep."

"Just figure it's part of your penance. I know if you had any choice in the matter you'd be half a world away. Tell them to send someone to relieve you. Tell them I hate you and I can't stand being around you and they need to send someone else to babysit me."

"They don't care what you want or don't want, Genevieve," he said wearily. "And there's no one to send."

"What do you mean?"

"I mean they didn't send me. As far as the Committee is concerned, you're collateral damage, just part of the fortunes of war, and they don't waste manpower on unimportant details like you."

She swallowed. "If you're not manpower then what are you?"

"On vacation. My time is my own, and I can do what I want with it. Even killers get time off. We get excellent benefits as well, if you ever think you might want to change careers."

She felt as if the ground had shifted beneath her feet and everything she believed was suddenly in question. "The only person I've ever wanted to kill was you," she said.

"Was? You no longer want to kill me? Things are progressing."

"You came after me on your own? Why? Don't tell me true love — you already said I was nothing special."

He lay back on the bed, and she could see the faint smile at his mouth. "That rankled, didn't it? It was meant to. Where have you spent the last three years — in a convent? You have the sexual inventiveness of a nun."

"I didn't want to sleep with you."

"Sure you did. You just wanted to be talked into it."

"I really hate you," she said fiercely. "I know why you decided to come after me. You weren't through making my life a living hell and you wanted to add to my misery."

"That's it," he agreed in a pleasant voice. "Now, either shut up and go to sleep or I'll find something to use as a gag. For some stupid-ass reason, I've decided to save your life, and I'll do a better job of it if I get some sleep."

"I didn't ask —"

"Shut up, Genny. Or I'll shut you up."

It wasn't the threat that silenced her, a threat she knew he'd carry out. It was his calling her "Genny." It shook her, it always shook her. After all these years he was the only one alive who called her that, a name she associated with tenderness and safety. He probably wouldn't be alive that much longer, given his profession.

And neither would she, if she didn't let him sleep. So what if she was wide awake, obsessed by every little thing, including the man in the next bed? She wasn't going to make sense of it, or him, no matter how hard she tried. All she could do was lie there, her eyes staring up at the stained ceiling and wait. . . .

She was asleep. Peter had been wondering whether she was going to stay awake, prattling at him, for the entire night. The woman could talk — probably part of the curse of her being a lawyer — and he was a man who didn't want to talk. At least to her, right now.

He didn't know why the hell he told her it had been his choice to come after her. She was better off thinking he was there under duress. Which was, in fact, the truth. Something was forcing him to be there, to come after her, to pluck her from the jaws of danger. He just didn't know what it was.

He could rule out conscience. That was a luxury he couldn't afford. And it wasn't her sexual prowess, though he'd deliberately insulted her on that one. She was afraid of him, not that he'd hurt her, but that he'd have sex with her. Make her want him again, make her vulnerable. The only way to alleviate that nervousness was to assure her he had no interest in her curvy body, her long legs.

He'd barely had her and he had to let go of her. It was one of those unpleasant facts of life, part of his penance. And he'd told her nothing more than the truth. The sex had been nothing special, just body parts behaving as they ought to. But she was something else.

He glanced over at her in the darkness. She'd lost a little bit of weight in the two weeks, he could see it in her hips and breasts. It was a shame — he loved her unfashionable curves — but in the end it made it easier on him. She bothered him enough already, as in hot and bothered. He'd chosen plain, baggy clothes to make her look less appealing, and they'd had the opposite effect. He probably could have put her in a burka, as she'd sarcastically suggested, and he still would have wanted her.

You can't have her, he reminded himself. *She's off limits. You messed with her once and screwed things up. You made her life miserable — you have to leave her alone. You owe her that much.*

Unfortunately his conscience wasn't listening. And he had no interest in sleeping — despite what he'd told her, he tended to work at peak efficiency with very little rest. He could make it till the end of the week, well past the twentieth of April, without more than a quick nap. He'd just wanted her to go to sleep and leave him alone.

But even asleep she didn't leave him alone. He could hear her breathing, sense her every movement, and he had to turn away so he wouldn't watch the rise and fall of her breasts as she slept.

He was getting her out tomorrow, to Canada, to a safe house he knew of. He'd considered taking her to his old friend's place in North Carolina, but at the last minute he thought better of it. No one could protect Genevieve better than Bastien Toussaint, but he had a pregnant wife and in-laws surrounding him, and it wouldn't be fair to put them in the danger that would come with Genevieve Spenser. Nor did he necessarily want Bastien to have to put up with the annoyance.

No, he'd turn to people still in the life, who'd keep an eye on her and wouldn't let anything get to her. While he kept his promise to Madame Lambert and stayed as far away from Harry Van Dorn as possible.

At least Van Dorn was convinced he was dead. If he had any notion Peter had been off the boat before it had exploded, he would be moving heaven and earth to find him. Harry Van Dorn was an implacable enemy. Peter knew far too well some of the things he was capable of when his ire was aroused. For the kind of betrayal he'd perpetrated, Harry would be wanting a very special kind of revenge.

But he'd had to look elsewhere, and it had only been Takashi's quick thinking that had kept Genevieve safe. He'd read the reports on what Harry sometimes did to women, and it had turned even his cast-iron stomach.

But they'd gotten her safely away, and the only way Harry would get to her now was over his dead body, as foolish and sentimental as that was. It didn't matter if the fate of the world rested in his hands — he wasn't going to let Genevieve Spenser be hurt.

And he had absolutely no intention of examining why he felt that way. He didn't have to answer to anyone, including himself. It was just the way it was.

She was making sounds in her sleep, anxious little crying noises, like a lost kitten. She was moving restlessly, kicking out, but he could tell she was far from awake. He shouldn't be surprised — given the drugs and the things she'd witnessed, it would be a miracle if she had a decent night's sleep for months.

He sat up and looked at her, putting his

legs over the side of the bed, wondering if he should wake her from her nightmare. But then she'd start yapping at him again, and he'd say something else that he shouldn't, something that would get him tangled in deeper than he already was, and he didn't dare.

He looked over at her. She was crying. He'd never seen anyone cry in their sleep, and he watched with complete fascination.

He'd only seen her cry once, despite all the stuff he'd thrown at her. She'd cried in the pool, right before he'd had her again. The sex had stopped her tears, but it had been the most dangerous thing he could remember doing in years. Because it had almost started his.

He should lie back down and ignore her, ignore the anxious sounds she was making, the restless way her body was moving. She was just having a nightmare, and it would pass. No one ever died of a nightmare, for God's sake.

But he knew he wasn't going to follow his own advice. If he woke her up and she hit him, then so much the better. If she didn't, he'd deal with what happened as it happened. And he got out of bed and slid in beside her, pulling her trembling body into his arms.

19

He was hoping she'd wake up instantly, order him to get out of her bed, and he would leave, grateful. But instead she reached out for him, her hands cool on his heated skin, and she buried herself against him, her wet face pushed up against his shoulder, and she clung to him, still crying.

He held her — what else had he expected? he mocked himself. He pulled her into his arms, wrapping his larger body around hers. She was wearing just about every stitch of clothing he'd bought her, thank God, because even so, her body against his bare skin was agonizing in its ability to arouse. What the hell was wrong with him? You'd think he was the one who'd gone three years without a lover. She was just one of a hundred women, a drive-by fuck, nothing special. And she was everything.

He tried to pull away, but she clung tightly, whimpering in her sleep. Since he didn't really want to let her go he stayed where he was, gently brushing the tears away from her face as she slept on. He was an idiot; he wasn't the answer to her nightmares, he was the cause of them. If she opened her eyes and saw him she'd start screaming, and that's what he needed to do, wake her before it was too late, before he was in too deep.

It was even easier to wake a woman than to knock her out, and he used the same trick, just a different pressure point, and a second later her tear-drenched eyes flew open, staring into his.

She didn't scream, didn't even speak, her silence more disturbing than any protest as she simply looked at him in the darkened room, so close. Finally, she spoke.

"Nothing special?"

"Nothing at all," he said, and kissed her, as he'd always known he would. She rolled onto her back, taking him with her, and kissed him back, her arms around his neck, her mouth full and sweet and generous, and he knew he was doomed.

And it didn't matter. She didn't say a word as he stripped off her clothes — he kept her mouth busy with his, and even when he wasn't kissing her they were silent. It was in the dark, a dream, they weren't doing this. But if they spoke it would suddenly make it real, and the price they would have to pay was enormous.

She didn't resist when he pulled the last piece of clothing, the plain white underwear that he'd foolishly thought wouldn't be sexy, down her endless legs. He remembered everything he knew about her, including her sexual history and the things she didn't like, and he knew she was going to do every one of them and like it. She was going to be on top, and she was going to go down on him, and she was going to tell him she loved him. And he didn't know what would cost her more.

Her skin was cool against his warm flesh, and it tasted like soap. He kissed the side of her neck, feeling her pulse jump beneath his tongue. He knew his own pulses were racing and he didn't give a shit. Her breasts were full and taut, the nipples hard against his fingers, and she arched up when he touched them, making a whimpering sound of need in the back of her throat, a sound that changed to a cry when he put his mouth over one, drawing the nipple deep into his mouth, and sucked at her.

He could make her come this way, he realized. He could make her come any way he wanted — she was trembling with need and ready to fall. But the longer he waited the more powerful it would be for her, so he reluctantly lifted his mouth, blowing softly on the wet, distended peak of her breast.

She gasped, and when he tried to move away she put her hands on his face and drew him back to her other breast, insistent, silent, jerking slightly when he suckled her, her hands sliding down to his shoulders, fingers digging in.

He could have stayed there for hours, his tongue exploring the taste and texture of her nipples, and for a brief, dark moment he considering doing just that. Making her come without being inside her, even touching her, making her come with his mouth on her breasts, all the while holding himself away from her, to prove that he could, to prove that she didn't matter, that he was inviolate. He would be safe again in the ways that mattered most. Not from guns and knives and the uncertainty of a violent life. But safe from the strangling tendrils that had wrapped around him and wouldn't let him go, apron strings, an umbilical cord, something that tied him to her and wouldn't let him break away.

He could do it. And once she realized what he'd done, what he'd proved to her, she'd retreat in on herself in silence. Leaving her in Canada would be fast and uncomplicated and they'd never have to think about each other again.

But that wasn't what he'd come halfway across the world for, and he knew it. He'd come for her, in every sense of the word, and he was going to take her. In every sense of the word.

He bit the underside of her breast, lightly, just a tender nip that made her jump, and soothed the bite mark with his tongue. She had such a lush, rich body he could get lost in it, and he nuzzled against her skin, awash in the taste and the scent of her.

He needed to slow things down. She was trembling, ready to explode, and he wasn't ready to have her. She really knew so damn little about sex and pleasure — he wondered how she'd managed to live so long without someone taking her in hand and showing her. He could only be selfishly glad the men she'd met were so stupid; he could be the first to taste the fullness of her response, to show her just how limitless love could be.

Sex could be. He pulled away from her for a moment, lying back on the bed to catch his breath. He wasn't worried that she'd change her mind, kick him out of the bed, run away. She had already gone too far down that road to draw back — he could practically feel the need thrumming through her body.

And then there were words from her. Anxious little words in her slumberous, aroused voice. "Why did you stop?" she asked. "Did you change your mind?"

God knew how such a maddening woman could have such a capacity to make him smile. And he knew what he was going to ask, had to ask, even if she gave him the wrong answer and tore him apart.

"Do you want it?" He'd started this when she was half-asleep, vulnerable, and brought her almost too far to draw back. But she brought out the decent idiot inside him, the man he'd tried to bury long ago, and he had to ask her.

She didn't answer. Not with words. She put her cool, soft hands on him, and she kissed him. Kissed his mouth, full and sweet, kissed his throat and his chest and his nipples, her tongue swirling against them with agonizing, arousing delicacy. She put her hands on his stomach, and slid them beneath his briefs, and she managed to pull them off him despite the unflagging stiffness of his cock getting in the way.

He knew what she wouldn't do. What he needed her to do. He didn't say anything as she put her cool, soft fingers on him, learning the shape of him, the size of him. And then she leaned forward and learned the taste of him, her loose wet hair falling around her face as she drew him into her mouth.

He made a sound of pleasure and despair, reaching down and pushing the hair away from her face so he could watch her as she took him deeply, her lips and tongue closing around him, pulling at him so that the pleasure was almost unbearable.

She was shaking, trembling, her hands holding his hips, and he knew he'd reached his limit. He pulled her up, away, and she clutched at his hips, fighting him, as he pulled her up. "No!" she protested. "I don't want to stop. I liked it, I want —" He filled her mouth with his tongue as he pulled her over him, her knees straddling his hips, so that she was just above him, ready for him. She could feel him, and all she had to do was sink down and take him deep inside her. If she would.

She was shivering, and he brushed the hair away from her face and broke the kiss, pulling her back enough to look at him, to meet his steady gaze. "Do it," he whispered to her. "If you want it, do it."

She closed her eyes and touched him, placing him against her, and she sank down, taking him inside her, slowly, where he needed to be, where he belonged. When she stopped, just short of completion, he caught her hips and pulled her the rest of the way down, so that he was deep inside, and he owned her, belonged to her, and there was nothing else but his cock inside her, her fingers digging into his arms, her eyes closed and her head thrown back as she began to move.

He'd gotten her this far, he couldn't disgrace himself by coming too quickly, ending before she had even begun, but the feel of her body, wet and tight around him, was a pleasure almost too powerful to bear. She was moving faster now, and he caught her hips, helping her find the rhythm, pushing up to meet her, the thick slide of flesh against flesh, and she was gasping now, clutching at him, reaching for a release that she didn't know how to take.

But he knew how to give. He took her hand from his shoulder, put it between their bodies and made her touch herself. The effect was instant, electric. She cried out, and he could feel her body clenching, milking him, and he wanted nothing more than to let go.

But she wasn't finished. He knew women's bodies, loved women's bodies, and he knew that even with the power of her orgasm she needed more. He put her hands back on his shoulders, put an arm around her butt and turned her underneath him without breaking the connection, still lodged deep inside her.

She hadn't come down from her first powerful climax when the second hit her body. She held on to him, head thrown back, eyes closed, holding on to him as wave after wave of pleasure ripped through her body, and he knew he wouldn't be able to hold out much longer, but the sight of her, the feel of her caught up in her climax was almost better than his own.

He pulled her legs up higher around his hips, pushing in deeper still, and she made a quiet noise, one of both pain and pleasure, and he knew she was finally ready, he was finally ready, as her fingers curled onto his shoulders . . .

And then she started to pull her hands away, and he knew she was thinking about the scratch marks on his back, and he could feel her begin to retreat.

He caught her hands, curled them and pulled them onto his back, raking down his skin.

And she was lost. He could feel her shattering in his arms, and then he was with her, torn in a thousand pieces, holding on to her as he spilled deep inside her, an endless release that took everything, *everything* from him.

He was too heavy for her, but he knew he had no strength left to support himself, so with his last bit of power he pulled free, rolling to his side and taking her with him, keeping her tight within the circle of his arms as he held her.

They were both shaking. It was small solace, he thought as his mind slowly returned from that bright, treacherous place. He already knew he was lost. He'd hoped to keep some part of himself safe, but the moment he'd kissed her, the moment he'd come for her, the first moment he'd seen her standing in Harry's salon with a stick up her ass, he knew it was going to be like this.

He'd be better off dead.

He wasn't the kind of man who could love a woman, live with one, not one he cared about. He was made to be alone, with no connections and no strings. It was the only safe way to be, even if in the end it killed you.

Bastien was the only one he knew who'd been able to escape. But he was the rare exception — people who'd been chosen by the Committee were made for a different kind of life. No home and hearth and babies. Just cold solitude and deadly efficiency.

And while he was lying there angsting, she'd fallen asleep, her body totally relaxed for the first time he'd known her. There were no stray signs of worry in her peaceful face, no unconscious clenching of her fists. She lay sprawled in glorious, naked sleep in the circle of his arms, as if she belonged there.

Maybe she did, but he doubted it. It could kill her. But that wasn't anything he could think about, not now. Right now he was going to spend exactly one hour thinking about absolutely nothing at all except the utter peace that had spread through his body, the kind of peace he might never have again.

And he closed his eyes, pressed his lips against her unlined forehead and fell asleep.

Isobel Lambert leaned back in her chair, staring at the tiny screen in her communications device. She could still imagine Harry Van Dorn's smug, smirking image, and if she had the choice she would have smashed it. She had no choice.

The ultimatum was clear. Genevieve

Spenser was to be handed over thirty six hours from now, on April 19th, put into Harry Van Dorn's hands. He hadn't bothered to spell out the alternative — he didn't need to. Van Dorn was too powerful to circumvent in such a short period of time, and he didn't bluff. They had no choice but to be prepared to make some kind of exchange. Unfortunately it was too late for Takashi.

Van Dorn had found the Committee when their very existence was under such deep cover that no one had broken it in years. If he could get a message directly to Isobel, he could do almost anything, and they needed to be prepared. It was the best chance to stop him for good.

Madame Lambert set the communications device back in its holder. Her hand was shaking, and she could only be glad no one was around to see it. She worked very hard on her image of unruffled strength, and she didn't want anyone to have an inkling that beneath her perfect exterior she was human after all.

The answer from Peter Madsen hadn't come in yet, perhaps he hadn't even gotten the message yet, but she knew what that answer would be. Brief, to the point. One word, yes, to the awful, necessary thing she was asking. Not that she expected any other answer. They both knew there was no alternative, or she wouldn't be asking. They both knew it had to be done.

She kept a pack of cigarettes in the top drawer of her desk as a reminder of her iron will. She'd given up smoking seven years ago, but each month she replaced that untouched pack of cigarettes with a fresh one, to remind herself that she could go back at any time.

She opened the drawer, pulled out the cigarettes and lit one, drawing the tobacco deep into her lungs with remembered pleasure. It never did leave you, she thought, that need for a cigarette. And it was always waiting for a moment of vulnerability, and then you were hooked again.

Too damn bad.

She moved back to the computer screen, punched in a few buttons and brought up Genevieve Spenser's file. It wouldn't be the first time she'd sent someone to their death, but it had always been someone who'd signed on for it, who knew the dangers and risks and chosen to accept them.

She'd never forced it on an unwilling participant.

She had no doubt that the woman would agree. She had no chance of ever being safe, being free, if she didn't. And besides, she would do anything Peter asked of her, she knew it with the instincts that had brought her to the very pinnacle of her dangerous profession. Genevieve Spenser was madly, hopelessly in love with Peter Madsen, and if he asked her to walk unarmed into a pitched battle, she'd do it. And if she balked, he'd talk her into it.

She wasn't as sure about Peter. She'd known him for many years, and never seen him connect to anyone outside the Committee. He kept himself on ice, away from entanglements — even his short marriage had been cold and sterile, according to the operative they'd sent in as a marriage counselor. Peter didn't know about that, and if he did he probably wouldn't care. He knew how things were done. Which is why he would let Genevieve Spenser go straight into danger. Because it had to be done.

Isobel Lambert refused to consider what might happen if the woman didn't survive. She'd already lost one of her best operatives — at least Bastien had somehow managed to carve himself a good life. If this latest venture fell apart, Peter Madsen wouldn't be so lucky.

The plan had to work. There was no other choice. Genevieve Spenser had to put herself in Harry Van Dorn's sadistic hands.

If Isobel Lambert believed in God, she would have offered up a little prayer. As it was, she simply lit another cigarette and stared out the window.

And then she picked up the phone once more.

20

Genevieve woke slowly, deliciously, her entire body feeling relaxed and sated, like a pampered house cat. It was a slow awakening, and she wasn't in any hurry to rush it, letting the sensations drift back bit by bit, the taste, the texture, the myriad delights that were both gentle and not gentle at all. Her body glowed with a power that was foreign and irresistible, and her soul was equally enthralled.

She didn't want to think about her heart. She knew where that was — the most dangerous place in the world. She was too smart, too careful to have done such a stupid thing, and once she got back to the safety of her apartment in New York she'd have no trouble reasoning with herself, convincing herself she'd just let a temporary dependence feel like something else.

Because in truth she couldn't be in love with Peter Madsen. He was hard and cold and dangerous, and he'd already told her sex was one of his best weapons. He knew how to use his body, how to use hers, for maximum effect, and if she had any sense she'd be furious at the way he'd broken past her defenses again, made her vulnerable.

But she had no sense. She was bone weary, in the best possible way, she was starving, she was on the run for her life. But she was safe with Peter — he wouldn't let anything bad happen to her — and she was in love with him. Just for now, she promised herself. Just for a few, short, indulgent days, she'd accept it and even enjoy it. Enjoy the heady rush of feelings, the way her body tightened when she thought of him. She was much too smart to let it last, but for the time being she'd enjoy the illusion, just because she wanted to.

She was alone in the bed, and there was no sign of Peter anywhere, but this time she wasn't worried. He was coming back. He was going to take care of her. He'd gotten her away from Harry Van Dorn, charming, monstrous, good ol' Harry, and there was no way he'd let her be in harm's way again.

She didn't even want to consider his feelings for her. He'd told her he had no emotions, and she had no reason to doubt him. He'd come halfway across the world for her, and he still hadn't told her why, but she could guess. He was a man who didn't like to accept failure. If he'd completed his assignment she never would have ended up locked in Harry's oceanside fortress.

Then again, if he'd followed orders she'd be dead. He must have some kind of logical reason for coming to get her. But if she couldn't even figure out her own feelings, she could hardly get a handle on his. She'd simply have to accept things as they were and go from there.

Normally that would have been anathema to her. She protected herself with the world of ideas and thoughts and arguments. Not with raw emotion and simple trust.

But the bottom line was, she trusted him. Completely. And maybe that was even more powerful than thinking she was in love with him.

There was no clock in the room, the television didn't work, but she guessed it was sometime in the early afternoon. She'd fallen into a deep, heavy sleep in his arms, and she realized with shock that she still wanted him. Again. And again. And he'd gone somewhere and left her alone, and the more she remembered about last night the hotter, the needier she grew. She was going to take a shower, and the moment he walked through the door she was going to jump him.

No, cancel that. He'd probably slam her down on the floor again, and while she appreciated his tensile strength, she didn't like it being used against her. She'd wait for him to come to her. Which he would. Because he wanted her as much as she wanted him. It made no sense, but she knew it to be true, and she sang as she used up the last of the little sliver of soap.

She considered wearing nothing but the sheet, but then she'd really enjoyed the way he'd taken off her clothes, and she was perfectly willing to experience that again. She pulled her damp hair back and looked at her reflection in the mirror, and laughed. Last night she'd looked like a pale, drowned rat. Today she looked vibrant, alive. And happy.

How could a man like Peter Madsen make her happy? It made no sense. But it was true.

She strolled out of the steamy bathroom and stopped short. Peter had returned — there were two cardboard mugs of coffee on top of the television. Starbucks. She knew she loved that man.

Except that she didn't know what to say. He didn't even glance at her — he was busy with something that looked like a space age BlackBerry, and she knew his gorgeous body well enough to see the tension radiating through him. Wasn't she the one who was supposed to have postcoital regrets?

"Which of these is mine?" she asked when he still didn't lift his head.

"The one on the left. It has soy milk instead of cream in it," he said, staring down at the machine.

"Soy milk?"

He looked up at that. "You're lactose intolerant," he said. "I figured you couldn't handle real milk but you needed some extra sustenance."

How could he have remembered such a tiny detail? "Thank you," she said, reaching for the cup. In fact, she hated soy milk — she preferred her coffee black if she couldn't find lactose-free milk — but she drank it anyway, testing the taste against her tongue. There were all sorts of new things she was getting used to, she thought.

She wanted to sit down on the bed next to him. Hell, she wanted to take the Black-Berry out of his hand, fling it across the room and push him down on the bed. She'd been thinking about that ever since she got in the shower. It no longer seemed like such a good idea.

She sat down on her own rumpled bed, trying to shove the images out of her mind of the two of them, moving, entwined, breathing, kissing . . .

"So when do we leave for Canada?" she asked brightly.

He didn't answer for a moment. Then he closed the machine and turned to look at her, his ice-blue eyes hooded and unreadable. "There's been a change in plans."

"What do you mean?" Genevieve said. She'd finished the coffee, choking on the soy milk, and it was hitting her stomach like a bomb. "We aren't going to Canada?"

He rose. "Harry knows you're alive."

She'd already thrown up in front of him once, she wasn't about to do it again. Besides, except for a few crackers there wasn't anything in her stomach to throw up. By the time she made it home those fifteen pounds would be well and truly gone. If she made it home.

And then the ramifications hit. "What about Takashi?"

She'd managed to surprise him by her question, enough so that he looked at her. The mask was in place, last night might never have happened. She let go of it, because she had no other choice.

"We assume he's dead. No one's found a

body yet, but Harry's good at covering his tracks." His voice was totally without expression.

Another man dead, this time one of the good guys. All for her sake. "Are you sure?" Her voice was rough with grief and guilt.

"We're not sure of anything. Except that Harry has got us over a barrel. He wants something bad enough and he knows how to put the screws to us. Problem is, the Committee doesn't negotiate."

"And?"

"We'll give him what he wants, but there'll be backup. He won't get away with it."

She knew what was coming. The ice-cold veil settled down around her, freezing the blood in her veins, freezing her heart and soul. Ice everywhere.

But she had to hear the words. "What are you going to give him?"

She thought he wouldn't meet her gaze, that he'd be too ashamed. But his cold blue eyes met hers, totally devoid of any feeling at all.

"You," he said.

21

He expected her to fight back. To tell him to go fuck himself, that she wasn't walking back into Harry's sick world no matter what the cost — they could find some other way to get him. Wasn't that what their job was? Saving the good guys, killing the bad?

But she didn't. "And what did you tell them?" she asked, her voice deathly calm.

"I told them you'd do it. We'll have a sniper there, and the moment he gets a shot he'll take it. All you have to do is stay calm."

"I'm very calm," she said. "Just answer one question. Why were you so sure I'd do it? Because I'm in love with you?"

He flinched, the first real blow she'd ever managed to inflict on him, and she told herself at least she had that much.

"You aren't in love with me," he said flatly. "You're much too smart for that. You know the difference between great sex and true love. Though maybe I'm wrong — you didn't even know where your clitoris was."

He was fighting back, but he couldn't embarrass her. She was beyond that point. "Then why did you think I'd do it?"

"Because you're a foolish, sentimental woman who thinks she can make a difference in the world. In fact, it's for the same reason you made the mistake of thinking you might be in love with me — because you're emotional and romantic and you think you need to be in love to have great sex."

"At least we've graduated from 'nothing special,' " she said coolly.

He ignored the comment. "You'll do the right thing. Whether it kills you or not. That's why you didn't take the out I gave you back on the island and make for the bunker, but went back to try to save Harry Van Dorn's sorry hide. And look at what it got you. The man wants to kill you, to get back his lost pride because we scuttled every plan he had."

"And you're going to let him." It was a statement not a question.

It wasn't enough to get a rise out of him. "No. There'll be people all around you, even though you won't see them. Someone will take Harry out before he gets within ten feet of you, and then you can live happily ever after in your fancy New York apartment."

"Don't you think Harry will have thought of that? Won't he have snipers as well?"

He didn't deny it. "We're professionals. We do this for a living and we know what we're up against. If I didn't think we had a very good chance of getting you out alive I wouldn't have told them you'd do it."

" 'A very good chance?' " she echoed. "How touching. And when is this all going to happen?"

He shrugged. She was taking this about as well as he'd expected — maybe even better. She wasn't crying, she wasn't begging. She was accepting the inevitable. With the bonus that she now hated him for betraying her. "Tomorrow sometime. He's made the initial contact, set the terms. He'll let us know when and where it'll go down."

She looked smaller, sitting on the rumpled bed in the plain clothes he'd bought her. Smaller, more vulnerable, and he wanted to shout at her, tell her to say no. They couldn't make her do it, they couldn't make her do anything. It didn't matter what he told them, in the end it was up to her and she knew it. All she had to do was say no.

"All right," she said. "On one condition."

"There are no conditions. Either you do it

or you refuse."

She went on, undeterred. "You said there'll be backup?"

"A whole team of operatives focused on keeping you alive."

"Lovely," she said. "Just so long as you aren't one of them."

He shouldn't have been surprised, but he was. "Why?"

"Because I want you to walk out of this room and I never want to see you again." Her voice was steel, hard and unbendable, a voice he'd never heard before.

"I'd be happy to but I can't. Not until backup arrives. Harry won't have stopped looking for you, even though he's hatched this plan, and I'm not leaving you alone until someone comes."

"You can sit outside the door and keep watch. Or you can get back in the car and watch from there. I don't care what you do," she said in a cool, impersonal voice. "I just don't want to have to see you."

"I can do that," he said. "If you keep the door locked."

She nodded, as if she didn't trust her voice. He picked up his cold coffee and headed for the door, but her voice stopped him as he opened it.

"Just one question," she said. "Did you

know about this last night? Did you decide to fuck me into compliance so I'll do what you want?"

He could see her beginning to unravel, and he couldn't have that. They couldn't. She had to be strong, and angry, or she'd never survive. She needed rage, not pain. So he did the best thing he could for her. He lied.

"Yes," he said.

She nodded, and he closed the door behind him, waiting long enough to hear her lock and latch it. He couldn't sit outside the door — it would be too obvious, but he had a perfect vantage point from the car. No one could even approach that room without risking death.

He needed to toss the cold cup of coffee. He looked down, and the damn thing was shaking in his hand. He stilled it instantly, letting the icy wall form again. And he headed down the stairs to the car.

The television was unplugged, and someone had yanked the cable wire out of the back. Genevieve plugged it back in anyway, and was rewarded with one very grainy channel with nothing but infomercials. She lay on her stomach on the bed, his bed. Because he'd claimed hers, taken her on hers, and she wasn't going near it. She lay on the rumpled sheets and watched people tell her how to make a fortune in real estate, how to whiten her teeth, how to use kitchen appliances that were strange and incomprehensible. She could clear her nonexistent acne, take ten years off her face, learn to apply makeup, cut her own hair, remove unwanted hair and make scrapbooks.

They just didn't tell her how to go on when she was twisted and broken inside.

If she got out of this alive she'd make her own infomercial, something along the lines of Fifty Ways to Kill Your Lover. She started coming up with some, but with violence looming over her head the exercise lacked a certain pleasure. Pushing him in front of a train, feeding him to the sharks were both nice ideas, but once it came to guns and explosions she shied away. She'd be facing that soon enough.

She slept off and on, not because she was tired but because she didn't want to be awake. Maybe she was depressed, she thought wryly. Didn't people sleep too much when they were depressed? And she sure as hell had a good reason. The man she loved was sending her to her death.

At least she'd learned that much. He was wrong about her being too smart to fall in love with him. She was dumb as a brick, because even after his betrayal she still loved him. She wanted to kill him, but she didn't want him dead. She wanted him out of there, safe, and that had been half the reason she'd sent him away.

The other half was that as long as he was around she ran the risk of bursting into tears and begging him. And she had much too much dignity for that.

Harry Van Dorn was resplendent in crisp white slacks, a navy blazer and blue oxford shirt made of the finest Egyptian cotton, which he ordered by the dozen from Paris. He always liked to look his best when he was being filmed. His tousled blond hair fell in perfect waves — he had gone through half a dozen stylists before someone got it right, and his warm, lazy grin flashed whitely in his tanned face. He shoved his feet into soft leather loafers — no socks, of course — checked his reflection one more time and walked out into the huge hallway.

The lights and camera were all set up, and the children had already arrived. They were a pathetic-looking bunch, but then, he'd chosen this group for their abject misery. They were the useless and unwanted of this world — sick and dying, and a large amount of his donated money was spent on prolonging their wretched little lives. They were ugly, all of them, and he didn't like ugliness. They were a variety of colors — every dark race in this convoluted country. There was one pale-skinned blonde, but she had the thin, hollow-eyed look of an AIDS victim, and he wouldn't touch her, or any of them, with a ten-foot pole.

But he would kill them. If he didn't get what he wanted.

"This is so very kind of you, Mr. Van Dorn," the woman who'd accompanied them gushed. She was in her twenties, a little plump, and she had a crush on him. She was always fluttering around him when he made his mandatory visits to bestow gifts and smiles on the revolting little patients to further ensure the world knew Harry Van Dorn was a kindhearted philanthropist. She even had the temerity to suggest he might like to have a cup of coffee with her, to discuss the patients, of course. She was some kind of social worker, he remembered, though her name escaped him.

She was still nattering on. "These children get so few treats — I know they'll love a visit to your estate at Lake Arrowhead for the carnival you've arranged. They don't get out of the hospital, much less out of the city, and I know a day in the mountains will be wonderful for them."

"The pleasure is mine, Miss . . ." He deliberately let the sentence hang, just so she'd know how little he'd noticed her. She was expendable goods. But then, in the end, so was everybody.

Her bright smile faltered a bit. "Miss White. Jennifer White."

He didn't like the name. Jennifer was too much like Genevieve, and it was hard to keep his charming smile in place when he thought about her.

"I consider it an honor to escort these little tykes around for the day. If things run too late I'll have my staff see that they're well taken care of and they'll be back in the morning."

Jennifer White's face creased in sudden worry. "But I thought we were talking about the afternoon only, Mr. Van Dorn?"

"Hell, it takes an hour to get up into the San Bernardino Mountains from here. You needn't worry about them, Miss White. I have a fully qualified staff to look after them."

"But I'm coming with —" she said.

"I'm afraid not. You've got orders to report back to the hospital — some kind of crisis." It hadn't taken much to ensure that.

St. Catherine's Children's Hospital received a very large sum of money from him, and in the past couple of years they weren't even forced to turn a blind eye to the damaged children he'd eventually given up to them. His tastes had changed, but one could never tell when he'd want to enjoy a bit of childhood innocence, and he always kept his resources in place.

"Then perhaps I should take the children back and we could do this another day," she suggested nervously.

"Miss White, do you seriously believe these poor little munchkins aren't completely safe with me and my fully trained staff?" He used his best aw-shucks grin, and she melted, the silly cow.

"Oh, of course not. I just thought . . . I mean, it's too much of an imposition . . ."

"Not an imposition at all," he said grandly. "One of my drivers will get you right back to the hospital so you can take care of things, as I know you're so capable of doing. In the meantime, these poor kids will have the treat of their life up at my place by the lake."

She was still protesting as one of his men hustled her out the door, and he waited until the sound of her voice died away before turning to the children.

He clicked his fingers to his film crew, and they began rolling. In Los Angeles you could find anything for a price, and the one for having a live-in film crew who could record anything he wanted to preserve and relive, no matter how nasty, was surprisingly cheap. Drugs and whores and elegant surroundings kept them pretty well satisfied, and when that began to pall it was easy enough to dispose of one and replace him. It tended to keep the others more compliant.

"It's a beautiful spring day here in L.A.," he said, addressing the camera. "April nineteenth, in fact. You people know I had a lot of plans for today, but for some reason those have all fallen through. I'm not particularly worried about any fallout — suspicions are one thing, proving a damn thing would be just about impossible. Not with my resources backing me up.

"So I accept defeat gracefully." He bared his teeth in an affable grin. "You managed to put a spoke in my wheels, all without understanding what I was trying to accomplish. It may have seemed harsh, but in the end the new order would have been better all around."

He looked at the unpleasant children. Not that he tended to like children in general, except the very pretty ones who didn't cry too much when he touched them. They never seemed to respond to his famous Van Dorn charm. It was almost as if they could see through him, past the smiles and the jokes.

Dogs didn't like him either. Maybe dogs and kids were smarter than the rest. Or maybe he just didn't care enough to try to fool them. Either way, the handful of scrawny, ugly kids were looking at him with deep distrust.

"I'm a man of many charities," he continued. "This here is an important one to me — looking after dying kids, trying to make their last few months on earth a little brighter."

The camera moved, panning the children's faces. He didn't know children well enough to guess how old they were — probably all under twelve — which made them even more pathetic. Heart-wrenching, to the right people.

"Now, we'd hate to have anything happen to these kids, but the roads up in the mountains can be very treacherous, and there aren't even guardrails in some places. The van they're driving in could go over the edge if someone isn't careful, and I like to think of myself as a very careful man."

He half expected the kids to start weeping and wailing at that veiled threat, but none of them even blinked, the stoic little bastards.

"I have to admit my pride is wounded. And it really burns my hide to think I have to let go of everything I've worked for. But I will, no fuss, no ugly publicity, I'll just slink back and keep giving my money away to hopeless causes and you won't need to worry. But I need one thing, and if I don't get it, these children aren't going to be happy. Accidents are bad enough. Burning to death's a sight worse — real painful, I've heard. And if a van goes over a cliff somewhere up in the mountains there's a good chance it'll catch fire just in case there are survivors. I always carry extra fuel in my vans, just in case I need it." He smiled at the camera, feeling very benevolent.

"So I'm taking these children up to my place in Lake Arrowhead, and don't make the mistake of thinking you can get there first. It's an armed fortress, and anyone who tries to get in will blow themselves to kingdom come. Oh, and you may not know which place I'm talking about — I own a number of properties around Lake Arrowhead and Big Bear, most of them so tied up in dummy corporations that it'll take you too long to guess which one.

"So here are the details you've been waiting for, Ms. Lambert. We'll have a little trade. You bring Ms. Genevieve Spenser, Esquire, back to me and I'll hand off the children, clean and neat. Now, why would I want Ms. Spenser, you ask yourself? Because I've already killed every motherfucker who tried to mess with me on this, and she's the only one still walking around. And I don't like that. It's kinda salt in the wound, you know what I mean?

"I will kill her — don't try to fool yourself into thinking otherwise. The Rule of Seven is just going to have to be the pissant Rule of One, and I don't like it, I can tell you that. So you have your choice. Half a dozen little brats who are going to die anyway, or one less lawyer in the world. You know that old joke — 'What do you call a hundred lawyers at the bottom of the ocean?' — 'a good start'? I know what your choice is going to be, because you really don't have any choice at all. I'll let you know where the trade-off is going to be."

His cameraman was well trained — he knew a closing line when he heard it and he shut off the camera, the bright klieg lights going out.

"You'll get that where it needs to go? Find

out where the she-wolf that runs them has gotten to, and get an answer. You understand?" he said. It was a foolish question — they all knew what would happen if they failed him, and Takashi's unfortunate death had been a recent reminder.

There was an absolute jumble of hurried reassurances, and Harry flashed them all his brilliant smile before turning to the ugly little children. "Come on, little ones," he said. "We're going on a journey."

The one he liked least, a tall, skinny black girl, had clearly appointed herself leader. "We don't want to go with you," she said, stubborn.

"Well, now, ain't that too damn bad?" he said, actually amused. "Because you're just a bunch of sick little kids and I've got twenty big strong men who live just to see that everything I want happens. So do as I tell you and get in the fucking limo."

A smaller child spoke up, the feisty little shit. "You're not supposed to swear," he said sternly.

"Well, hot damn, you're right. I do beg your pardon. Follow my men and you'll get a nice ride in a big white limousine up a big tall mountain."

"And if we don't?" the leader demanded.

It would be so easy to snap her scrawny

little neck, he thought dreamily. Maybe, when the deal went through, as he had no doubt it would, he'd return five kids instead of six.

"What's your name, little girl?" he asked.

"Tiffany Leticia Ambrose."

Tiffany. That was the funniest damn name he'd ever heard for a ridiculous little piece of trash. "Well, Tiffany, if you don't shut your mouth, your little friends are going to pay the price for it. Understand?"

Any other child would have dissolved into tears. She simply nodded, and stepped back, and Harry flashed his benevolent grin over all of them. "So, we're all agreed? Off to the mountains?"

And without waiting for an answer he took off, leaving them to trail behind him, like sheep to the slaughter.

When Genevieve woke, it was mid-morning — she could tell that much because the infomercials had switched to mindless cartoons. Not even decent Americanized anime, she thought foggily. And then she heard the sharp, staccato footsteps, the firm knock on the door, and she knew it was time to wake up. A good day to die?

She certainly wasn't expecting what waited patiently at her motel-room door. The security hole had been blocked by some previous inhabitant, but she figured Peter wouldn't let anyone dangerous up to her door. Or if he did, then she was screwed anyway.

She opened the door, staring at the creature in front of her. Elegant, ageless, with a cool, serene beauty that was almost eerie, the woman met her shocked stare with a smile. "I'm Madame Isobel Lambert," she said, pronouncing her last name the French way, even though her accent sounded British. "I'm Peter's boss, the current de facto head of the Committee. May I come in?"

Without a word Genevieve opened the door wider, resisting the impulse to peer over the walkway and see if Peter's car was still there, with Peter in it. Madame Lambert was about five foot four, though her stiletto heels brought her up higher, but even in bare feet Genevieve felt as if she was looming over her.

"Sorry I can't offer you a chair or some coffee," she said, her voice brittle. "But I'm not equipped for entertaining."

Isobel Lambert looked at the bed, the one she'd shared with Peter, and Genevieve wanted to scream. Did all these people have some kind of sixth sense? Why didn't she look at the other bed where people had slept alone?

Genevieve sat, claiming the other bed, and let the woman think what she wanted. Hell, it was probably simpler than that — Peter had doubtless given her a full report. Or even worse, he'd been following her instructions in the first place.

She couldn't go there. Not if she wanted to make it through the day, though that was already not a sure thing. She'd slept in her clothes — stupid, when she only had one change — and she was feeling rumpled and grungy. Then again, she might only need one change of clothes.

Madame Lambert had taken a seat on the other bed, crossing her elegant legs at the ankles and taking out a cigarette. "Do you mind? I've just started again."

The room already smelled of stale smoke, and Genevieve didn't care. "I don't know that I'm going to have to worry about dying from secondhand smoke," she said. "Go ahead."

"You aren't going to die, Ms. Spenser."

"Call me Genevieve. No need to stand on formalities when you're turning me over to a murderer."

Madame Lambert smiled. "Peter told me you were a fighter. That's very good. If you were a useless crybaby I wouldn't have even considered this option."

"I could cry," Genevieve offered instantly. "Give me a minute and I'll be a useless, sobbing wreck." In fact, it was true. For the past twenty-four hours, for the past God knows how many days, she'd been on the edge of it, ready to start crying and never stop, but she was far too pragmatic to give in.

"I thought Peter said you agreed to this." Her perfect, unlined face managed to express concern. How many face-lifts, how many Botox injections had gone into making that perfect, ageless mask?

"Do I have a choice?"

"You always have a choice. I'm not sure the same could be said for the six children Harry's planning to kill if we don't deliver you."

She felt sick inside. Could things get any worse? "No choice at all," she said.

Madame Lambert nodded. "The trade-off is going to be at his place up in Lake Arrowhead. I don't know why he's chosen it — there are only two main roads down out of the mountains."

"Maybe he thinks you'll just let him just walk away."

"It's happened in the past. We have to

make some uncomfortable moral decisions in this business, Genevieve. Sometimes evil gets to walk away untouched. But he's not walking away with you or the children, I promise you."

"Have you found Takashi yet?"

Again that faint, imperceptible shadow. "No," she said. "But he's a hard man to kill. If anyone could make it then O'Brien could. I haven't given up hope."

"He saved my life."

"So did Peter," Madame Lambert pointed out. "Several times, in fact."

"He was also going to kill me. Your orders?"

The woman didn't even have the grace to look embarrassed. "Yes. Trust me, it was a difficult order, and I'm glad he chose to ignore it."

"And now I get a brand-new way to die."

Madame Lambert rose and stubbed her half-smoked cigarette out in the ashtray. "You aren't going to die," she said again. "Not if I can help it. We've got a Kevlar vest for you, just as an extra precaution, there'll be snipers all around, and the moment someone gets a clear shot they'll take it. You won't get anywhere near him."

"How about having a few paramedics around, just in case."

Madame Lambert looked at her coolly. "We always do."

"Did he tell you my conditions?"

" 'He' meaning Peter? Yes. He said you didn't want him anywhere around. You shouldn't let adolescent emotions interfere with something that could make the difference between life and death. Peter's a crack shot — you couldn't have anyone better watching out for you."

"Thanks, but I'll pass," she said. "And I don't have adolescent emotions. I just don't like being used."

"Who says the adolescent emotions are yours?" Madame Lambert said with a faint smile. "The trade-off time is three o'clock this afternoon. They're expecting some fog up in the mountains, and it can be quite treacherous. In the meantime, you must be famished. Why don't you freshen up and I'll take you out for a late breakfast?"

"I'm not really hungry," she lied, still smarting from the "freshen up" comment. She did look rumpled, particularly compared to Madame Isobel Lambert's perfection, but then, a few weeks ago that perfection had been hers as well. Designer clothes and shoes, perfect hair and makeup, the quintessential corporate goddess.

Now she was rumpled, barefoot, tangled

hair and no makeup. No defenses. "Food sounds great," she said wearily when the woman made no comment. "As long as I don't have to run into anyone who'd ruin my appetite."

"Peter's already on his way back to England," Madame Lambert said. "I'm afraid he didn't leave a message."

Genevieve knew her expression didn't change. She was already prepared for it — desertion was just one more thing to be expected. It didn't matter that she'd told him to go, he was still feeding her to the wolves and abandoning her so he wouldn't have to watch. Bastard.

She rose. "Give me half an hour and I'll be ready," she said in an even voice.

"That's fine. We're in no particular hurry." Madame Lambert made no attempt to move.

"Could I have a little privacy?"

"Don't be silly, child. You Americans are all so prudish. I promise not to look. But we're not letting you out of our sight for the next few hours."

"In case I change my mind?"

"You can always change your mind. Harry Van Dorn has just suffered a series of disappointments, and he's not about to leave anything to chance at this point. He'll be working on any number of ways to grab you. He'd much prefer not to have to barter — we've already screwed the pooch for him with his grand and glorious scheme, and he wants revenge. Killing Takashi and Peter isn't enough."

"What?" Panic swept through her, and she didn't even try to hide it.

Madame Lambert's smile was smug and reassuring. "He thinks Peter died on the island. If he knew he was alive he'd much rather have him than you."

"Then why don't you just let him go in my place?" It wasn't what she wanted, but surely Peter would have a better chance with Harry than she did.

"Because he's much more valuable when Harry thinks he's long gone."

"And I'm dispensable."

"I didn't say that. You can change your mind."

"Stop saying that! You know I won't. You might be able to live with the deaths of six children on your conscience, but I can't."

"Trust me, child, I live with far worse on my conscience," she said, reaching for her cigarettes again.

"On second thought, you can't smoke," Genevieve said. "I don't want to die smelling like an ashtray."

Peter would have come back with some cynical crack about cremation. But Peter wasn't there, and Madame Lambert wasn't Peter. She put the cigarettes back in her Hermès handbag — an item so expensive even Genevieve had denied herself — and snapped it shut. "As you wish," she said. "But I'm still not leaving you alone."

"Suit yourself," Genevieve said, and stomped into the tiny bathroom.

It wasn't until she'd finished with the longest shower she could manage that she realized she hadn't brought her clean clothes in with her. She grabbed the skimpy towel and walked into the room, throwing modesty to the winds. Madame Lambert wasn't going to have any prurient interest in her body. In fact, Peter probably hadn't either. It had all been part of his job.

Madame Lambert had made the bed and was lying on it, the pillows tucked behind her, her expensive shoes lying neatly on the floor beside her, and she looked at Genevieve with casual interest. The new clothes were folded neatly at the foot of the other bed, and Genevieve thought, fuck it, and tossed the towel.

"You're probably wondering what Peter saw in me," she said in a conversational voice as she pulled on the plain white panties and bra. "And the answer, of course, is nothing at all. He was doing his job."

Genevieve had marks on her, and she knew it. Not just the love bite on her neck, the whisker burns on her breast. Her whole body was covered with him, and no matter how often she washed she couldn't wash him away. He was inside her still, breathing through her skin, his heart making hers race.

"How very young you are," Madame Lambert said in an obnoxiously cheerful voice. "Like a teenager who's first discovered sex."

Genevieve paused in the act of zipping up her jeans. "Look, I'm putting my life on the line for you guys. I don't have to listen to condescending remarks while I do it."

"You're right. I'd just forgotten what it was like to be young and in love."

"You'll have to ask someone else. I've never been there."

Madame Lambert said nothing. But her catlike smile said it all.

God, but Harry hated children. Healthy, pretty ones were one thing, but these were pallid, sickly and obnoxious. They didn't know when to shut up, and during the twists and turns up Route 330 one of them threw up on the leather upholstery of his white limo.

It was the final straw. He hadn't been riding in the back with them, of course. He'd been up front with his driver, in a far less comfortable seat than he should have been enjoying, and the brats behind him never shut up.

"Can't you turn off the noise back there?" he demanded of the driver.

"Sorry, sir. This particular limo isn't soundproofed."

"Well, at least can you do something about the smell?"

The driver shrugged, not having the good sense to be afraid of Harry's temper. Not enough people were afraid of him, he decided, particularly not those people who'd managed to mess with his glorious Rule of Seven.

He'd gotten past that initial disappointment, priding himself on his resiliency. He had a new goal now — destroying the Committee and everyone in it, and he'd already gathered powerful reinforcements. The shadow group was a threat to everything he held dear — free enterprise, the right to enjoy himself however he pleased, democracy. He was going to bring them down, every one of them, and then he could turn to rebuilding a new Rule of Seven, something even grander and more glorious.

Because this was personal. Not just the destruction of his carefully laid plans. The infiltration of his private life, with Jack-shit O'Brien and Peter Jensen. There was something so . . . underhanded about that. But then, what could you expect from people who didn't have the advantages he'd had. Weren't as gifted as he was.

He was going to enjoy himself with Genevieve Spenser. First, because Jack-shit/Takashi had tried so hard to have him keep his hands off her. Second, because it would make Peter Jensen turn in his grave. Hurting the woman would be the next best thing to hurting the man who'd betrayed him. Hell, it might be even better; this way he could get his revenge twice over.

But first he had to get rid of these noisy, puking, disgusting children before he grabbed a gun and shot them.

"Stop the car," he ordered.

And the driver slammed on the brakes.

22

The Kevlar vest was too small, and Genevieve had the sudden, distressing thought that if Peter were there, if he'd been in charge of outfitting her, it would have been the right size. Of course, he'd known what size she was before he'd gotten her naked. Now he'd know even better.

She managed to fasten it anyway, then pulled her T-shirt and sweatshirt over it. Her boobs were squashed and she was having a hard time breathing, but none of it mattered. She sat in the back of the nondescript car, uncomfortably similar to the sedan Peter had showed up with, and let them drive her up the winding road into the mountains, twisting and turning.

She wondered if she was going to throw up again all over her Kevlar vest. It would serve the elegant Madame Lambert right if she puked on her designer shoes, but then some might get down into the vest and that would be very unpleasant. Not that she figured the vest was going to do a bit of good. If Harry's plan was to have someone shoot her, he'd have them go for a head shot. Lawyer's brains, she thought again, with a little shiver.

"Are you cold?" Madame Lambert asked. "It gets a bit chilly and damp up here, and there's supposed to be fog tonight. I can get you a blanket."

"I'm fine," Genevieve said in a tight voice.

"What about medication? Peter said you were fond of tranquilizers."

"Fuck Peter," she snapped. As a matter of fact, she hadn't thought of her blessed little yellow pills in a long time. *I guess when things get really bad I don't need them,* she thought. *They're just for minor annoyances, not life and death.*

"I believe you already did," Madame Lambert murmured. "I can get you whatever you need. It will just take a phone call and it'll be waiting for us."

She almost asked for Tab. She'd been careful with her last meal — her experience at Carl's Junior had taught her not to shove food into her face — but she'd had to make do with Diet Coke. Surely she deserved a can of Tab before walking into the valley of death.

"I'm fine," she said. They were climbing higher and higher into the mountains, and a light fog was rolling in. There must have been some kind of massive forest fire in the last few years. Twisted black stalks of dead trees covered the hillsides, making it look like a strange sort of cemetery. She kept her eyes away from the road; the driver was going way too fast for the conditions, and she was nervous enough. Was she ready to die on this strange, barren hillside? Was she going to have any choice?

The fog was getting thicker the higher they climbed. Madame Lambert was busy with her BlackBerry-like device — a duplicate of the one Peter had used. Modern technology and the spy world, Genevieve thought. Except they weren't spies, were they? She didn't know what the hell they were, and she didn't care.

"Supposing you manage to kill Harry?" she said. "What then?"

"Then it all gets covered up very neatly. We have the full cooperation of certain branches of the U.S. government, and no one will ever know he didn't die in an unfortunate car wreck on one of these twisty roads. They have rock slides all the time — sometimes boulders the size of a Volkswagen bug come down on the road. One could squash Harry, and even his good friend the president will have no idea what really happened."

"Squash a bug with a bug. Sounds fitting," she said. "And what about me with all my unfortunate knowledge? Aren't you going to have to squash me, too?"

"You read too many thrillers, Genevieve," Madame Lambert said. "You aren't going to say a word to anyone. For one thing, no one would believe you. For another, you'll want to forget these past few weeks, put them completely behind you. And there's one more thing."

"And that is?"

"You won't want to endanger Peter. You wouldn't blow his cover, no matter how wounded you are."

"Are you talking potential physical wounds? Because I promise you I have no emotional scars at all."

"Of course you don't," Madame Lambert agreed in her cool voice. "And there'll be no physical wounds. You're well protected."

There wasn't enough Kevlar in the world to protect her from the damage Peter Madsen had already done to her. "Bring it on," she said wearily. "I'm ready."

"That's good," her companion said. "Because we're here."

Peter was cursing the fog with steady, pungent curses. He'd staked out a small spot overlooking the wide circular driveway by Harry's lavish mansion, and Mannion, who'd been part of the original team to take Harry hostage, was with him, squinting at the text message while Peter tried to see through the gathering fog.

"You suppose Van Dorn can even control the weather?" Mannion said after a moment. "I wouldn't put it past him."

"He's got enough money," Peter said grimly. The billowing fog moved and writhed like a living thing, giving him a tantalizing glimpse of his target and then covering it again. He set the rifle down and leaned back against the tree, closing his eyes for a moment.

"There's no movement down there," Mannion said. "Aren't they supposed to be here by now? Maybe they're hoping the fog will clear."

"It could just as likely get worse, and Madame Lambert knows it," Peter said. "They'll be here soon."

Mannion punched a series of buttons, then smiled. Smiles sat strangely on Mannion's rough, battered face, but they were never without good cause.

"What's up?"

"They found Takashi. In one piece. He's pretty messed up, and they're not sure he'll make it, but you know our boy. No panty-waist billionaire is any match for a born-and-bred Yakuza."

"That's something," Peter said, returning to his post. The dark black sedan was sitting there, and he was pretty sure the engine was running. Sound carried strangely in the fog, but every now and then he heard the rumble of an engine. Did Harry have the children in the car? Or had he betrayed them and already killed them?

They'd gone into this knowing there was a good possibility that Harry would renege on his end of the bargain. A thwarted billionaire was a dangerous thing, particularly one of Harry's twisted temperament, and he'd like nothing better than to fuck them over. He thought he was inviolate — he could get away with anything, no matter how heinous. His grip on reality was slipping, which made him even more dangerous.

The fog shifted, and he could get a clear view of the car. No sign of any children, no sign of anything. And then he heard another car approach, and he didn't need Mannion to inform him that Genny had arrived.

He didn't want her to do this. He should have told her that, but something had stopped him, and now she might die because he'd been too fatheaded to say anything. The car pulled up to the heavy iron gate and waited. Waited. Peter's mouth was dry.

Mannion had enough sense to keep quiet. He kept his attention riveted on the scene below, not glancing at the machine in his hand.

There were other snipers around, but no one with as clear a vantage point, and Peter knew in the end it would be up to him. He'd never missed a shot, no matter how difficult it was. He could see through fog and a moonless night, he could see through anything to keep her safe. He couldn't waste his time making excuses or telling himself lies — they were down to the bare bones now. All that mattered was that she lived. Because he'd done the unthinkable. For only the second time in his life he'd fallen in love, when he didn't even believe it existed.

It wasn't the sex. It wasn't some crazy protective notion motivating him either; there were plenty of other people who could do as good a job of keeping her safe.

And it certainly wasn't that he wanted to spend the rest of his life with her. He might be in love with her, but he devoutly hoped he'd never have to see her again after this afternoon. He wanted his old, calm, cold life back. He didn't like the heat melting the ice around his heart.

The iron gates swung open, slowly, and the back door of the car opened as well. He saw her blond hair first, and he held his breath. As far as he could tell, Harry had no comparable snipers overlooking the site, but he couldn't risk her life on that belief.

She stood very still, and he looked at her down on the driveway with the thick white fog blanketing her. She stood tall and straight, probably because of the armor they'd given her, and she didn't look around, or look back. Harry would know she wasn't alone. She took a step forward, and then another, and the door to the waiting limousine opened and Harry stepped out.

He had him in his sites, a perfect target, and then he was obscured again, fog rolling down in thick, wet waves.

"Peter!" Mannion's voice was urgent.

"Shut up," Peter hissed. "I can't see."

"Take your shot, man. He doesn't have

the kids. They were found wandering down in the woods just off 330. She doesn't need to go."

Peter rose, but everything had disappeared. It wasn't a thick blanket of fog, it was a deep, poisonous shroud, and he couldn't see anything anymore, not the cars below him, not Genny's stalwart figure as she walked toward death.

He didn't hesitate. "Run, Genny! Get the hell out of there! Run!" he shouted. And then he started scrambling down the hillside, trying to make it to the driveway in the impenetrable mist, and it clung to his skin like tiny particles of ice, as he felt the first burst of fear crack inside him.

He slipped, rolling down the hillside, landing on the wide driveway just as the headlights of a car zoomed down on him. He rolled out of the way, into the bushes, and it moved on, clipping the waiting car as it went. And then all was silence in the cottony darkness.

He scrambled to his feet, the sniper rifle still with him, when Madame Lambert loomed out of the mist. "He's got her," she said, and he almost thought he heard emotion in her cool, controlled voice. "He shoved her in the limo and got away. I'm so sorry, Peter. At least he won't be able to take her off the mountain — we've got all the roads blocked. If it weren't for this goddamn fog . . ."

He'd never heard her swear before. It didn't matter. "I'm taking the car," he said.

"You should wait for backup . . ."

"I'm taking the car."

And a moment later he vanished into the mist, letting the darkness close behind him.

Harry Van Dorn was in the best mood he'd been in since he could remember. After weeks of having each of his careful plans dismantled, finding his most trusted servants betraying him, things had finally turned his way. Genevieve Spenser was sitting beside him in the back of the limo, looking pale and frightened, and he'd just been given a gift by the universe. He should have known his position as one of the chosen ones wouldn't have faltered.

"So Peter's alive after all," he said, reaching for the minibar and pouring himself a drink. "Can I get you something, sweet cakes? Afraid I don't have any of that bellywash soda pop you seem to like, but I've got just about everything else. Might make things a bit easier on you."

"No, thank you," she said. "I'm fine."

Harry chuckled happily. "I doubt that.

Now, why didn't you think to tell me that Peter was alive after all?"

"What makes you think he's alive?"

"Don't try that shit on me. I heard his voice, clear as day, telling you to run for it. Too little too late, but then, you've always been his worst nightmare, haven't you? If it weren't for you, I'd already be dead as a doornail."

"Then I'd think you'd be a little grateful," she said.

He backhanded her across the face, a casual blow that still snapped her head back. "I don't like mouthy women, did I ever tell you that? Your bosses should have known better than to send me a mouthy broad."

"Lawyers tend to be mouthy."

He slapped her again, and this time her lip started bleeding. He liked that, but he didn't want to let her leave any trace behind in the car. He would already have to get rid of the car the kids puked in. He'd set them down in the middle of the burned-out landscape — they'd never find their way out through those dead trees, and it got right cold on an April night up here in the mountains. The fog would just be icing on the cake.

He hadn't decided on a cover story for

that one yet — he was still concentrating on the delicious package of revenge sitting beside him. If the kids were found alive no one would believe anything they said, not when charming Harry Van Dorn came up with a plausible explanation. He didn't know what that was, but it would come to him, spur of the moment. He was blessed that way. Everyone loved Harry Van Dorn — he could do no wrong.

"Watch yourself, missy. I plan to take my time with you, and I don't want you annoying me. Having Peter still alive changes everything. He's going to come after you."

"Don't be ridiculous. If he's really alive and cared the slightest bit about me, he wouldn't have let me walk into a trap like that."

"Good point," Harry conceded. "But I'm not giving up hope. Look at it this way, I'm keeping you in one piece until I'm certain Peter Jensen isn't going to ride to the rescue."

"His name is Madsen."

He contemplated hitting her again, then decided it wasn't worth it. "You see, it would be twice the fun making him watch. Double the pleasure, double the pain."

"I'm sure he's seen a lot of people die, Harry," she said, too calm for his liking.

"He's not going to give much of a shit whether you kill me or not — he's not that sentimental. You could always kill him first and make me watch, but I'm afraid I'd simply enjoy that, and you wouldn't get your rocks off . . ."

"Don't you ever shut up?" he demanded.

"Not if I can help it," she shot back.

Oh, he was really going to enjoy killing her, maybe more than he'd ever enjoyed killing anyone. She was rapidly becoming even more infuriating than Peter Jensen . . . Madsen himself.

"Guess what?" he said cheerfully, slapping some duct tape over her mouth. "You can't help it."

He could barely see the road, but he tore up it like a bat out of hell anyway, trying to catch up with the taillights that must be somewhere ahead of him. Where the hell could he be taking her in this impenetrable fog? He could just as easily run off the road as Peter could, and they'd have to be careful.

They were in a limo. Presumably with a driver, since Harry never did a thing for himself when he didn't have to, and he'd have a hard time controlling Genevieve while trying to drive in this shit.

Which meant he had her to himself in the back of the car. Peter stepped harder on the gas pedal, guessing where the winding road led. They were heading in the direction of Big Bear, the tackier of the lake resorts, and if Harry got that far he'd be even harder to find.

Peter wasn't giving up. His rifle was beside him in the rental car, which had all the pickup of a donkey, but he didn't expect it to do him much good when he could barely see three feet in front of him. He was going to have to get a lot closer to kill Harry Van Dorn, and that suited him just fine. If he could just find him.

He was just past Running Springs when he saw the taillights, barely visible in the thick fog. They were moving up the road at a steady clip. He slammed on the accelerator and the car fishtailed on the wet road surface. It took him a moment to regain control, and by then the car ahead of him was out of sight, and he punched the steering wheel, cursing.

The road was straightening out a bit, and he sped up. He had no idea what time it was — with the fog that thick it could be daylight or midnight. His headlights bounced back at him, and he tried turning off the brights, hoping he'd be able to see a little bit better, when a vehicle came out of the darkness, slamming into his, knocking the car sideways off the road into a ditch.

He scrambled out of the car, ready to kill, when a voice he thought he'd never hear again broke the swirling clouds of night.

"He ditched the car and took her off into the woods, Peter." Bastien Toussaint's calm voice came out of the darkness. "You're heading in the wrong direction."

Peter froze. He didn't waste his time asking stupid questions, like why was Bastien there and how did he know. What mattered was that Bastien would have the answers.

"Where's he taken her?"

"There's an old abandoned school up this way — used to be some movie star's mountain home, and then it was a school. It's been closed down for years now, but Harry managed to buy up the rights under a dummy corporation. He'll have taken her there. And he'll be wanting you to come get her, now that he knows you're alive."

"That's exactly what I plan to do. What the hell are you doing here? Shouldn't you be in North Carolina having a baby?"

"My wife's got that under control right now. Madame Lambert asked for help, and she wouldn't ask lightly. I owe you, and I pay my debts. Come on. I'll show you the way to the school. We're better off going through the woods. I'm pretty sure Harry's on his own now with your girlfriend, but it doesn't hurt to be careful."

"She not my —"

"Save your breath, Peter. Once we get her out of there and put an end to Harry, you can deny it all you want. It makes no difference to me. But in the meantime we'd better get to her before Harry gets tired of the game. He knows it won't take you long to find him, even without my help, and he'll be waiting. But he never was a patient man, and he'll have a toy to play with while he waits for you to show up."

Peter stopped arguing. Bastien didn't need to come with him, put his own life in danger after he'd walked away from all this, but he would do it, and nothing Peter said would stop him. He'd watch his back, as Peter had done for him, and between the two of them Genevieve Spenser would be safe.

If they could just get there in time.

23

It really was a beautiful old building, despite the years it had lain empty. Genevieve had more than enough chance to admire it — after Harry had bound and gagged her, he'd walked her what seemed like miles through the thick fog, past abandoned buildings and torn-up parking lots. "Watch out for the swimming pool," Harry had said jovially as he'd marched her up a stone staircase. "Most of the water is long gone but there's enough in there to drown you, if the stink doesn't kill you." He pushed open a heavy door and shoved her inside, out of the fog, flicking on dim lights that still managed to hurt her eyes. They were in the middle of a huge room, built like an old hunting lodge, with a massive fireplace, a row of built-in seats around it and balconies crisscrossing overhead. Dead animals were stuffed and mounted on the walls, and across the top of the fireplace was the sign The Truth Shall

Set You Free. If she hadn't been gagged Genevieve would have laughed.

"Great place, isn't this?" Harry said with the enthusiasm of a young boy showing off his newest toy. "It used to belong to John Huston or someone like that, and then it was turned into a school for drugged-out rich kids. They shut it down years ago and I bought it up on a whim. Always liked the place, even if it's seen a lot of hard use. Let me show you around a bit. You'll like it."

She had no choice, of course, trailing along after him, her hands bound behind her back with duct tape that was too tight, while Harry acted like a tour guide straight out of the Travel Channel, pointing out extraneous details like the dining room with its broken furniture, the wide row of decks overlooking the valley. "Too bad they let those little shits get their hands on this place," Harry said briskly, tying her to a chair near the fireplace. "There's nothing you can do with bad kids — hell, there's nothing you can do with good kids either. Might as well get rid of the whole lot."

He was using thick yellow nylon rope, tight around her already bound wrists and ankles, pulling it around her neck, and then flinging it over one of the thick logs that made up the exposed rafters. It took him a couple of tries to get it, but he laughed anyway, clearly in an excellent mood. "Wish you could appreciate those knots I tied, Ms. Spenser. I'm proud to say I was an Eagle Scout. You know how hard that is, what kind of commitment it takes? The years of hard work? I know what you're thinking —" He looped the rope back under her arms, then tossed it back over the rafter. "You're thinking the rich kid's father bribed them. But you can't bribe the Boy Scouts of America, Ms. Spenser. I know, because I tried. The only way I could get to Eagle Scout was to earn it the hard way, and I pretty much did. I think my old scoutmaster would be pleased as punch to see how good I still am with my knots. Of course, he might not be so happy to see how I'm using my expertise." Harry chuckled to himself.

He was kneeling down behind her, and she could no longer see what he was doing, and she wasn't certain she cared. The yellow nylon was scratchy against her throat, and when Harry tipped the chair back she could feel it tighten against her.

She tried to cry out, but the sound was forced down by the gag. Harry took a step back, surveying his handiwork with pride. "Now, that looks just fine," he said, "if I do say so myself. You gotta be careful not to move, not to squirm. That chair is balanced very precariously, and if it slips then that rope is going to tighten around your neck and strangle you. I wish I could promise you that I'd done such a good job that it would be instant, that your neck would break and it would all be over, but I don't think I'm that good anymore. I've done it in the past, but I've lost the touch over the years, and I'm afraid if that chair falls over you'll choke to death, and it's going to be slow and nasty. Just the way I like it," he added with a happy smirk.

"Now, I know what you're thinking. You're thinking Peter will rush in here and cut you loose before you can choke to death, but I'm afraid that's not the case. I did a real good job with those knots, and the more he tries to free you the tighter they're gonna get. You'll be dead, Ms. Spenser, and then he'll get to play with me." He let out a gusty sigh of deep satisfaction. "This is almost better than a paltry dam break in India or a few bombings. Nothing feels better than doing it hands on, doing it yourself, don't you think? But then, you can't answer, can you? Must be murder for a mouthy woman. That's pretty funny, isn't it? Murder? Though I tend to think of it as simple justice. You get in my way, I get in yours."

She stared up at him, trying to put all her contempt and hatred in her eyes, but he was past noticing. "I'm just going to go get myself a little drink. 'Fraid I can't offer you one — your mouth is otherwise occupied. And then we can sit here and wait for Peter to show up. I don't expect it'll take too long — he's smart, I'll give him that. But don't bother trying to escape while I'm out of sight. You'll just wind up killing yourself before Peter even gets a chance to save you, and then how would you feel?" His laugh was getting creepier by the moment. "You just wait for me, y'hear? I'll be right back."

Leaving her alone in the cavernous room, hog-tied and ready for a lynching, staring at the sign over the fireplace: The Truth Shall Set You Free.

It wasn't much of a noise overhead — it might have been the scurrying of mice left behind to clean up after the troubled teenagers, or maybe the faint flutter of bats outside. The wind in the trees, except there was no wind — the damp fog had closed down around everything.

She was afraid to move her head, to look up. Her balance was so precarious, the rope around her neck so tight, that she was afraid any movement at all might send her tumbling to a slow, agonizing death. But she heard the sound again, barely more than a breath of noise, as something moved in the balconies overhead.

It wasn't Peter. She would know if Peter had come, she would feel it in her bones and she wouldn't want to die. It was someone, something else. Maybe the ghost of one of those poor kids, maybe the old movie star haunting the place. No, anything human would have made more noise.

Harry breezed back into the room, a glass of what was doubtless bourbon in one hand, another hank of yellow rope in the other.

"Keeping busy?" he inquired cheerfully. "I bet you're thinking of all the terrible things you'd like to do to me if you had the chance. I'm afraid you won't, but I encourage you to fantasize. The giving and taking of pain is one of life's most intimate acts, and I doubt you've had much time to explore them. I considered instructing you, but in the end, poor old Jack-shit . . . oh, excuse me, I think you knew him as Takashi . . . had it right. I don't want Peter Whatsisname's leavings."

He took the new section of rope and tied it around one leg of the chair he'd bound her to, then moved back to the built-in couches surrounding the fireplace. "Wish I could start a fire — make it right cozy.

Wouldn't want you to get a chill, but then, you've got that extra vest on underneath, don't you? You didn't think I wouldn't notice, did you? I hate it when people underestimate me."

He glanced at the huge, empty hearth. "No firewood though," he said. "I could go get some of the broken furniture from the dining room but I still wouldn't have any kindling. No, I'm afraid you're just going to have to sit very still and freeze, Ms. Spenser. But I promise you, it won't be long." He took another sip of his bourbon and leaned back on the mouse-eaten cushions, perfectly at ease.

She moved her head just a fraction of an inch, and her balance held. She didn't know whether she imagined the shadow or not, flitting across the dusty pine floors. She didn't look up, and Harry seemed unaware that things might not be quite as he hoped.

If it was a ghost she hoped it was a ghastly one who scared Harry to death in a particularly unpleasant manner. Anything that happened to appear out of the dark would be no problem for her — Harry was more terrifying than any supernatural creature could ever be.

But then, ghosts wouldn't leave even the trace of a shadow. Or was she thinking of vampires?

One moment she was thinking of vampires, in the next everything changed. Someone had walked in the door behind her, with a slow, lazy stroll that could only be Peter's, and she tried to call out, to warn him.

"Just in time," Harry said gaily, yanking the yellow rope so that Genevieve fell backward, and the rope tightened, cutting off her breath. The last thing she saw was Harry taking off, and Peter following him, leaving her to die . . .

The pressure lifted, and the chair she was tied to went over backward. The ropes went slack, and she could see up into the rafters, into the face of a man she'd never seen before.

Maybe he was the ghost of the old movie actor; he leaped over the side of the balcony and landed on the floor, as light as a cat. "Hold still," he said, his voice just faintly tinged with French. "I'm a friend of Peter's. I cut the main rope but the others are still a little tricky." He picked something up from the floor and began cutting through the ropes. He must have thrown it from the balcony, slicing through the main rope that held her. What if he'd missed?

She didn't want to think about it, she

wanted to get to Peter. Harry had a gun somewhere — she'd seen it, though he hadn't brought it back into the main hall of the old lodge. The man was cutting swiftly, but he hadn't touched the duct tape across her mouth, and she wondered if that goddamn Peter had told him too that she was yappy.

She kicked at him, to try to get his attention, only to have the rope around her neck tighten again.

"Don't do that," he said. "You'll only make it worse. If you're worried about Peter I promise you he can take care of himself."

He finally cut the last rope, then yanked the duct tape from her mouth.

"He's got a gun," she tried to say, but her throat had closed up and she could barely manage a choked whisper. She tried to get to her feet, to go after them, but the man grabbed her, held her back.

"Leave them alone. You'll only get in the way."

She had no pencils or keys to stick in the man's eyes, nor did she want to hit him across the throat and kill him, since in fact he'd saved her life. But there was one other lesson she'd learned.

She went for his face, and when he immediately responded, to fend her off, she went for her true target, using the sweep that Peter said wouldn't work, knocking him flat on the floor before he knew what was happening.

Harry and Peter had gone through the deserted dining room, and she raced after them. There were two ways out — the kitchen and the deck, and she knew which one Harry would choose, with his sense of the melodramatic. She slammed out the door onto the deck at just the wrong moment, drawing Peter's attention away from Harry, who chose that moment to fire the pistol he held, emptying it into Peter's body as he fell to the deck and lay twitching in a pool of blood.

"No!" she screamed, rushing over to him and falling to her knees on the deck beside him.

"So touching," Harry said, perching on the top of the railing, still holding the bourbon in his other hand. "And convenient. We were at a standstill when you distracted him."

He was still breathing, but the blood was everywhere, and she buried her face against his chest, sobbing. Barely hearing the faint whisper that came from his white, unmoving lips.

"Gun," he said. "Get it."

She could feel it as she wept over his body — a hard, metallic presence just beneath his belt. She didn't dare hesitate — she moved back and reached into his pants.

"Copping a feel on a dying man, Counselor? You surprise me," Harry chuckled. His smile didn't fade when she pulled out the gun.

"I'm afraid I used all my bullets on your dead boyfriend there. None left for you. But I'm not concerned — you won't shoot me. You're too decent a human being to kill an unarmed man, no matter how much he deserves it."

"Maybe not," she said in barely a rasp. "But Peter didn't come alone."

"Does your throat hurt?" he asked with feigned concern. "Oh, I am so sorry. And I'm afraid I didn't quite hear what you had to say. Are you trying to convince me that someone else is here who can sneak up on me and end my wicked ways? I don't believe you. I'm astonished that you managed to get free, but I must have been distracted, and you've proven to be annoyingly resourceful. But the only thing behind me is the hillside — I'll be able to see anyone the moment they try to approach."

There was no sound from the lodge behind her, and she wondered whether she'd made the incredibly stupid mistake of killing her rescuer. She wasn't sure she cared — Peter was lying utterly still now, and she couldn't tell if he was breathing or not.

"You killed Peter," she said. "I'll kill you."

"Don't be ridiculous. Go ahead, try and pull the trigger. You haven't got it in you."

She knew how to aim the gun, how to cock it. She pointed it straight at him, but it was all over the place in her shaking hands.

"You won't hit the broadside of a barn like that, Ms. Spenser," Harry said.

She started to pull the trigger, trying to keep it aimed at Harry's face. She could see Hans, Renaud, the man in the garage, the neat little holes of death in their heads. She could do this, she could blow his fucking head off, she could kill him . . .

She released the trigger, letting the gun drop in her lap. There was blood on her hands, blood on her jeans, draining out of Peter's body by the second.

"You see, you can't do it," Harry said smugly, standing up on the seat, preparing to get down off the railing.

She picked up the gun and threw it at him, and it smacked him in the face, full force. A second later he was gone, tumbling over the side of the railing into the darkness below, and his scream echoed eerily in the fog, accompanied by the sound of crashing trees and then a merciful silence.

She couldn't move — she just knelt in the blood at Peter's side, disbelieving. He couldn't have just disappeared like that — it was too easy.

And then Peter's friend was pushing her out of the way, hovering over Peter's body. "Hang in there, old friend. Ambulance on the way . . . just hang in there." He looked up at Genevieve, who had risen to her feet, standing in shock.

"Remind me not to tangle with you again," he said. "You're as bad as Peter said you were," he muttered.

"Harry . . ." Her voice barely made a sound, but he could hear her a moment before the sound of an ambulance cut through the night.

"Over the side. If he survived we'll catch him. At least you did that right," he said uncharitably.

She moved to the railing. With infuriating timing the fog was just beginning to lift, and she could see partway down the steep hillside the black skeletons of burned trees spiking into the sky.

And then she saw Harry, lying against a stand of crushed tree trunks. But he hadn't crushed them all — one thick pine tree had gone straight through the center of his chest, and it was poking up into the sky, black and red with blood.

She took a step back. She could see the flashing lights of the ambulance, and she wondered if she should go and lead the way, but she didn't know where she was going, so she simply sat down on the deck and stared at Peter's unmoving body and the blood that soaked into her jeans.

She heard one word . . . "dead" in the man's voice, and she let out a sob. "He can't be," she said.

"Peter's hanging in there. I'm talking about Harry. Is he dead?"

She thought back to the body impaled on the burned tree. "Oh, yes," she whispered in her ruined voice. "Most definitely."

"Well, that's something," the man said. "Your first kill."

He looked calm, controlled, and not the slightest bit concerned that his friend lay dying at his side. Genevieve didn't know whether to scream, to laugh or to cry.

She settled for drawing her knees up, putting her head down on her bloody knees and praying.

24

Genevieve couldn't quite decide whether she liked Bastien Toussaint or not. He reminded her of Peter in all the worst ways, combined with a certain French "fuck you" attitude that was particularly annoying. But he'd saved Peter's life, so she could forgive just about anything, do just about anything she had to.

If she hadn't gone charging out onto the deck, desperate to save Peter, she wouldn't have distracted him long enough to get shot. She knew it, Bastien knew it, and she'd have to live with that knowledge for the rest of her life. At least Peter would, too.

The last time she'd seen him he'd been on a gurney, unconscious, taken out of her life. She only had Bastien's word for it that he survived, that he was recovering, slowly, but recovering. Madame Lambert was gone as well, a good thing, Genevieve thought. She didn't want to have anything to do with anyone from the goddamn "Committee," if she could help it. At least Bastien had walked away from it.

She did like Bastien's hugely pregnant wife, Chloe. She was never quite sure how she ended up in North Carolina, staying with them — probably some high-handed decision by Madame Lambert, but at that time she was too rattled to argue. And it was very peaceful up there in the woods in the house that Bastien was in the midst of building for his wife, far enough away from his in-laws to keep his sanity, Chloe had told her.

His wife had not been pleased with her husband's disappearance, and in retaliation had refused to speak to him for the first three days after his return with Genevieve in tow. And then she went into labor, screaming imprecations in languages Genevieve couldn't even begin to recognize, and hadn't stopped until little Sylvia arrived, small and perfect and taking over in the screaming department where Chloe had left off.

It seemed a good time to vacate, but Chloe wouldn't hear of it, and Genevieve had always had a weakness for babies. "Wait until we know Peter is on the mend," she'd said. "Wait until the baby stops crying all the time. Wait until Sylvia sleeps through the night." And "Wait until Bastien tells us what's going on."

It would be a cold day in hell for the last, Genevieve thought. When she finally announced she was going back to New York, no more delays, Bastien simply told her that her apartment had been sold and her belongings packed up and put in storage, by order of Madame Lambert. The only thing sent on to her in North Carolina was her passport.

It was that simple.

He would probably always walk with a slight limp. He no longer needed a cane, and it had only been three months since Harry Van Dorn had riddled him with bullets. He'd come a long way in a short time, but there was nerve damage in his thigh, and all the hard work and therapy in the world wasn't going to change that.

He wouldn't work in the field again. From now on he'd be behind a desk, gathering intel. The Iceman would exist no longer, the best closer in the business would work no more. He'd retired from the field, his last mission a spectacular failure on his part, at least. For some reason it didn't bother him. He'd paid for his screwup, Genevieve was alive and happy and back at work, he expected, having recovered from her brief sojourn in the world of death and intrigue. She would have recovered from her infatuation quite quickly, he expected, the moment she got back into her Armani and Blahniks.

He'd been in London three months — a month in hospital, another month in rehab and a month stuck in his empty, sterile apartment — until he finally got leave to go out of town. He'd put it off too long; he had to put the Wiltshire house on the market. It was part of a world that he'd never live in. Fires in the hearth, babies on the rug, gardens with the scent of wild roses filling the air. Not for him. He'd become another Thomason — cold and efficient, but not quite so ruthless. Madame Lambert wouldn't work forever, even though she looked far younger than she had to be. There was always room for advancement in the bloody Committee.

He couldn't drive his car. It was a standard, and working the clutch was a little more than he was up to, so he rented an automatic and headed out into the country on a bright, warm summer day that seemed to mock his bleak mood.

He stopped for lunch on the way, for some reason putting off getting to the house.

Once he arrived he'd need to call the real estate agent, go through the place and see what needed work, see if someone could come in and do something about the overgrown gardens. He'd meant to do that earlier in the spring, but things had taken a strange turn. But life was back to normal, his icy control was back in place, and he could move forward as he'd meant to all along, before things had gotten sidetracked.

He turned into the winding driveway, frowning. The weeds that had choked the paving stones were gone, the hedges neatly trimmed. Had he hired a gardening firm and not remembered? It was always possible, considering it had been a rough few months.

The back door was unlocked, another unnerving occurrence. He wasn't worried about unpleasant surprises and he was no longer worthy of being terminated. Not worth the trouble of setting up a hit — he could live out the rest of his life any way he wanted it.

He stopped dead in the hallway. The place was spotless — sunlight sparkling through the tiny windowpanes on either side of the door, fresh flowers on the table. There were car keys lying there, but he hadn't seen another car. Then again, he hadn't looked in the garage.

Good God, had Madame Lambert sold the place behind his back? He wouldn't put it past her since she'd already told him he didn't belong here. The table in front of him looked familiar, but it could belong to someone else. He walked through into the study, to see that his grandfather's huge desk was still there. With a sewing machine on top of it.

Left turn and down two steps to the kitchen. He could see new dishes in the glass-door cupboards, and someone had installed a dishwasher. He stared at it in amazement, then looked out the kitchen door to the gardens beyond.

They were beautiful. The flowers were a riot of color, waving in the soft summer breeze, and he could smell the scent of wild roses. He'd been dreaming about that, but he couldn't remember there being any wild roses nearby.

He turned the corner and saw them both at once. The newly planted rosebush that somehow, miraculously, was blooming, the flowers giving off a heady scent.

And the woman kneeling in the garden, her back to him, a straw hat covering her head, shielding her face from the bright sunlight.

He didn't move, didn't say a word, but she must have sensed his presence, because she turned around, pushing the hat off her head so that her blond hair tumbled down around her shoulders. And she actually blushed.

"Oh," Genevieve said. "I didn't realize you were here." She got up hurriedly, stripping off her gloves and brushing the dirt off the flowery dress she was wearing. "I know I probably look ridiculous, but I couldn't figure out what English women wore when they gardened, and Laura Ashley seemed oddly appropriate, except that I think I've ruined three different dresses . . ." Her nervous babble trailed off.

He took a couple of steps toward her, so she could see his limp, and stopped.

She didn't know what to say. For the first time in his memory words had finally failed her, and it was all he could do not to smile. He just stood there, watching her, waiting.

"Well," she said in a brisk voice after a moment, "I'm glad you finally decided to come home. I'm not sure if I've got enough for dinner, but I can always head out to the grocers. What are you in the mood for?"

He didn't answer, simply because his answer would have shocked her.

She came closer. "Aren't you going to say

something?" she said. "Ask me why I'm here? Tell me to go away?"

"No," he said.

"Why not?"

"Because this is where you belong." And he reached for her, in the bright summer sunshine, and she came into his arms, into his heart, into his life. Forever.

ABOUT THE AUTHOR

Anne Stuart loves Japanese rock and roll, wearable art, Spike, her two kids, Clairefontaine paper, her springer spaniel Rosie, her delicious husband of thirty-one years, fellow writers, her two cats, telling stories and living in Vermont. She's not too crazy about politics and diets and a winter that never ends, but then, life's always a trade-off.

The employees of Thorndike Press hope you have enjoyed this Large Print book. All our Thorndike and Wheeler Large Print titles are designed for easy reading, and all our books are made to last. Other Thorndike Press Large Print books are available at your library, through selected bookstores, or directly from us.

For information about titles, please call:
(800) 223-1244

or visit our Web site at:
www.gale.com/thorndike
www.gale.com/wheeler

To share your comments, please write:
Publisher
Thorndike Press
295 Kennedy Memorial Drive
Waterville, ME 04901